# Th MIRROR SOULS

### BOOK ONE OF
### THE MIRROR SOULS TRILOGY

## JULIA SCOTT

EVENSTAR

First published by Evenstar Books

Essex, UK

evenstarbooks.com

Second paperback edition September 2019

Book cover design by moorbooksdesign.com

Interior Formatting by evenstarbooks.com

Edited by btleditorial.com

ISBN 978-1-9160900-1-9 (paperback)

ISBN 978-1-9160900-0-2 (eBook)

Visit the author's website at

juliascottwrites.com

*To everyone who has found, lost*
*or has yet to find their Mirror Soul in this life.*
*Love is always the answer.*

# ONE

"THE EARTH WAS NOT YOURS TO KEEP."

M Y MIND WANDERED FROM THE MOVIE PLAYING on the classroom's screen wall in front of me, and I stared out the round window at the sky. This was the twenty-seventh time I'd had to watch the 'Avalon Reclaim' movie in my seventeen Gaia-cycles. Twice a cycle since I turned four and started my education. Always on this day, the day before Shift Day, and it didn't get any more thrilling than the previous twenty-six times I'd been forced to watch it.

"We are the Avalon, the custodians and creators of Gaia, the planet you once called 'Earth.' For millions of cycles, Gaians—humans—have been responsible for this planet, much to her detriment. In the Gaia–cycle 2084, your species pushed her to the brink and thus, the Cataclysm occurred, destroying billions of people, scarring the land, and disrupting the seas. Because of this, Gaia survived."

I rolled my eyes as the movie's narrator droned on. They've never even updated the damn thing. You'd think they would have since it had been well over a hundred cycles since our planet fell apart, and something like eighty cycles since they took it back. The Avalon wanted us to remember why they were here. We'd gotten the point by now; I doubted any of us could forget it. Mom called it 'never-ending propaganda.'

I looked around the room at the twelve other students in the edu-dome. I wondered what the rest of them thought about the Reclaim. Did they have a thousand questions like I did? Questions that were never answered. Somehow, I doubted it. Most people didn't dare to talk about it, especially if they were new to the Region. The others were sitting upright in their seats, attentive and keen, almost as though they wanted to be here. When I realized I was the only one slumped forward with my elbows on the desk and my head resting on my hands, I straightened myself up.

"War and famine raged, consuming the planet and destroying your cities. Twenty-one cycles later, the Council of the Seven Races, who oversee all, made the decision that the Avalon should step in and take back Gaia. It was our duty to restore her.

To let Gaia recover from the damage done to her, the remaining population has been adapted to be nomadic. The Avalon will be here to guide you..."

I rolled my eyes. Adapted wasn't what I'd call forced relocation every Shift Day. The lucky few didn't have to worry about Shift Day at all. The Avalon, most of the Midorians and a select few Gaians known as the 'Originators' got to stay in one place. They were often allowed to choose which Region to belong to. Most people seemed to be okay with potential relocation every half-cycle to one of the 750,000 Regions on Gaia. It wasn't a problem for other people to never have a place to call home. But it was a problem for me. This was not my home.

I glanced across the room at Genevieve. She sat as attentive as the rest, but she questioned the Reclaim just as much as I did. We'd spent so many hours talking about it. She was just lucky that she got to leave here sooner than I did, or at least she got the choice to leave. Things were different for Gen since she was half Avalon.

At least neither of us had to be students much longer. As soon as we both turned eighteen, our Professions would be assigned, and we would take them with us wherever we ended up. She would turn eighteen a few months before I did, so they'd assign hers before mine. I still didn't know if she planned to stay or leave, and a familiar wave of envy washed over me.

There was a lot to envy about Gen. She didn't have to worry about days like today, days when the rest of us found out if our family had been chosen to leave this Region and be transported to a new one. Gen had the opportunity to decide when and where she went.

I shoved the bitterness down. She'd been my longest friend, which wasn't difficult considering you couldn't make a friend around here without the Avalon moving them or you somewhere else in a short time. Being jealous of her wouldn't change anything.

I'd been staring at my hands for too long, not listening to what Ms. Haims had been saying. I looked up. Most of the other students had left the dome and were heading down the hill outside. Ms. Haims gave me a familiar disapproving glare, and I followed the rest of the students outside.

Gen often waited for me on the stone steps outside the dome where we would walk down the hill together and go our separate ways at the bottom. Today, I had to look for her among the people leaving the edu-dome. She was easy to spot, being so much taller than most people and with her long blonde hair flowing in the breeze like a Greek goddess. She was already halfway down the hill, and I ran to catch up to her.

"Hey!" As I called out, she stopped and looked back at me in surprise as though I'd broken her out of a trance.

"Oh, sorry. I'd gone off into my own little world." She flashed me a half-hearted smile and carried on walking. I had to jog to keep up with her.

"Are you all right?" I asked.

"Yes, I'm fine. It's just today, well… tomorrow." She shrugged. "You know?"

I knew. Everyone knew. It certainly wasn't fun waiting to see if you'd have to move on Shift Day. Except Gen was guaranteed that it wouldn't be her, so she had nothing to worry about except losing some friends.

"Meet me at my place tonight?" she asked. "I've got something I need to talk to you about."

"I wouldn't miss it for the world," I said, and her next smile was a genuine one.

As we reached the bottom of the hill, she turned east to cross the river towards the Village, and I went north towards the Hub.

"Alana!" I turned as she shouted. "Don't get caught this time!"

As I slowly trudged home, I tried my best to stay positive. Rowhill was a nice enough place, probably the nicest Region we'd been in so far. We'd lived in Region 82-1056, the official Avalon name for Rowhill, for three and a half cycles, a record for this Region. I guess since Dad died, they had given us a free pass. I'd even put pictures up on my bedroom walls, as though it were 'home.' Our home to keep. But we all knew it wasn't. Gen and I had been friends since just before I turned fourteen. We had talked about how my time might be up and that we might have to say goodbye. I tensed at the thought. When you were chosen to leave, you pretty much left straight away, with little time for goodbyes. If it was my family's time to go, there weren't many people I needed to say goodbye to. But Gen had lived here as long as I had, longer in fact. Maybe she'd be able to find a way to see me before I left.

My stomach turned as I wondered if 'goodbye' was what she wanted to talk about tonight.

Just after curfew, I told Mom that I'd finish my assignments and get to sleep early because of tomorrow. She acknowledged me with a wave of her hand, hardly looking up from the screen she held as I closed the door to my room. A momentary flash of guilt twisted in my gut. Mom seemed to have no idea that I never did what I said I'd do, and that most nights I was out roaming the Region. Sometimes to see Gen, but most of the time just to be out in the fresh air with no one telling me what to do or where to go.

The Regionnaires had only caught me once, and it had been by pure chance. Or maybe I hadn't been careful enough, I don't know. Perhaps Mom thought it was just a one off. I'd managed to maintain an angelic 'butter-wouldn't-melt' persona in the day time. If you do what you're told by whoever is in charge when you're in sight, they don't expect you to be doing otherwise when you're not. That was my theory anyway, and I hoped it was why the Region law-keepers hadn't caught me again.

The large round windows in the dome had smooth edges that wouldn't snag your clothes, and they were perfect for climbing out of. With all the rooms being on the ground floor, it was like the domes had been purposefully designed to aid escape. I supposed the threat of the Regionnaires and the punishment I'd so far managed to avoid was enough to put people off breaking curfew. But not me.

I pulled my coat around myself, drew the dark hood over my head, and squeezed myself through the gap in the window. Once I had lowered myself down to the ground as silently as I could manage, I pressed my body against the side of the dome in a crouch. The Hub was quiet enough to hear the breeze lifting the leaves scattered across the ground, and so I took a deep breath and set off towards the river, the sense of freedom washing over me.

There was a definite chill in the air tonight. Clear skies brought the coolness this time during the Gaia-cycle, but they also brought a blanket of stars and a bright moon to light the way. Perfect roaming conditions.

The Rowhill river separated where Gen and I lived, but there was a crossing not too far from my home-dome, so it was easy to get to her place. The Hub, where us lowly Gaians had been placed, was on the river's flood plain. In the middle of the Hub stood the Info Center and surrounding it in concentric rings were purpose-built domes that blended into the landscape and served as houses and service buildings. Our dome was on one of the outside rings of the home-domes, and the surrounding flat land was thick with trees at this end of the river which were ideal for sneaking around unnoticed.

Despite its name, the Hub wasn't really the center of things around here. The Regions mostly focused around old Gaian housing areas, with the historical buildings used by the Avalon, Midorians, or the Originators. In Rowhill, we called it the Village. Beautiful houses and cobbled streets climbed up the slope of the hill on the other side of the river, with the Region Councilors homes right at the top. That was where Gen and her family lived.

I hadn't walked far when I caught a glance of the Village ahead of me through the trees and across the water. It was lit up more than usual, especially for this time of night. With Shift Day coming up tomorrow, security would be higher than normal. Damn. But there was no turning back; this might have been my last chance to see Gen.

After taking a much longer route south to avoid the patrolled bridges into the Village, and thankful that she lived on the outskirts rather than right in the center, I was on the cobbled streets heading to Gen's; a place more like home than my own. Even though this part of the Village was much quieter and there weren't any Regionnaires in view, I didn't dare stroll right up to her front door. Instead, I took the back alleyways and climbed over the wall at the rear of the house. It was easy enough to get over, being such an old building, the wall full of notches that gave good hand and footholds.

Gen's dad was out of town, most likely on High Council business, and her mom didn't seem to mind me breaking the rules, so I knocked on the back door, trying to make as little sound as possible.

"Alana! Come on in, quickly now." Gen's mom looked around behind me as she pulled me into the kitchen. Gen had probably told her I was coming.

"The day before the Shift isn't the best time for this," she half-scolded as she pulled me in for a hug.

It wasn't the first time she'd told me that. I was here this time a half-cycle ago, just before the last Shift Day. Gen's mom had been like a second mom to me since we were moved to Rowhill.

She shook her head with an almost mock-disapproval and

smiled. "Go on upstairs, Genevieve is in her room."

As I walked through the wood paneled hallway and up the staircase, I was glad Gen's mom didn't want to get into conversation, just in case she had heard anything about who was leaving tomorrow. I'd rather hear it from Gen. I ran my hands along the beautiful decorative banisters as I bounced up the stairs. This was the only house in the Village that I had ever been in, so I only had our plain home-domes to compare it to. But it was a palace in comparison.

"Thanks Mrs. Portbury!" I called over my shoulder, and she yelled back something about not being so formal and to call her Audelia instead. It wasn't the first time she'd told me that, either.

Gen perched on the wide windowsill in her room, her back against the wall and feet tucked under her. The windows were wide open, and the fresh evening air crept into the room.

"Hey, Gen," I said as I closed her door.

Her face lit up into a gentle grin, and she placed her book down before standing to give me a hug. She moved to lay on her front on the bed instead of going back to the windowsill.

"Sit," she commanded, motioning to the windowsill.

I obliged. She knew how much I loved to look out across the Village. It was a view I didn't get to see often, and it was so much more interesting than the Hub with its identical dome-shaped, grass-covered buildings. Gen's house was near the crest of the hill, so from up here I could see most of the Village and even the edge of the Hub on a clear day. The streets sloped down the hill towards the river, with no straight lines and with nothing looking the same. The moonlight danced across the water, with the jetty that pushed out into it looking like a little road to nowhere and everywhere all at the same time.

I'd changed my mind a hundred times which house I'd pick

for myself if I were ever to live here. But I probably wouldn't. Ever.

"I didn't think you'd make it, I forgot that there would be so many Regionnaires around tonight," Gen said.

I turned back to look at her and laughed. "Who came up with calling them that? Regionnaires. It makes them sound like a disease."

"They *are* a disease, if Ableman is anything to go by!"

Archimus Ableman. The Regionnaire who caught me, the *only* time they had caught me. He was just doing his job I guess, patrolling the Region to make sure the Avalon laws were being upheld. I was sure I was the only person around here who wasn't interested in following the rules though. The one rule I had broken was the one I hated the most; to not leave our home cluster after dusk, after curfew had begun. I'd certainly broken that more than once! Another rule was that we couldn't travel out of the Region without Council permission but, I wasn't sure how I'd even have the opportunity. And we must be at our Profession location at the specified times, without fail. Time would tell if I'd be able to follow that one.

No one had given us a decent enough reason for the inflicted curfew on our Region except for something about it being a 'healthy societal construct,' which wasn't a good enough excuse for me. I got let off with a warning the one time I'd been caught, much to Ableman's disappointment. I saw it in his face every time he saw me.

"Ugh, Ableman. That man gives me the creeps. He's the first in line to be coupled with my mom if she decides to re-couple," I said, shuddering at the thought.

"Seriously?" Gen asked, surprised. "How come you've never told me that?"

"I thought you already knew, you seem to know everything

about everyone! You know things before they even happen."

She sighed, smiled and put on her 'professional' voice. "That's what you get for being the granddaughter of one of the top High Council members of the Avalon. It is my birth right!" She turned her nose up in the air and then giggled as she sat up. "I may have more access to the Info Center than most people, but I wouldn't feel right invading the privacy of your family."

"I wouldn't be able to resist if I had the access you did," I confessed. "Anyway, Mom would never choose Ableman. God, could you imagine? No, I don't think she'll ever couple again. Dad was the only one for her."

An awkwardness hung in the air when talking about my family with Gen. She had the perfect family unit. Her hard-working Avalon dad and her quirky Gaian mom had lived in this Region since just before Gen had been born. Never having to be uprooted, their home was a treasure trove of memories and history. That was one of the reasons I preferred it here compared to my bland dome in the Hub. Memories made a home, well… homely.

"So, I wanted to talk to you about something Alana. It's kind of a big thing," She paused and frowned at me. "Wait, why do you look so worried?"

"Do I?" The tension that had been building up since this morning must have been showing. This day was always full of such unknowing and dread. "I wondered if you had found out anything about Shift Day, whether we were staying or going. That's all."

"I have no idea if you're staying or going. I would have told you if I'd found out!"

"You mean you're not the fountain of knowledge after all?" I gave a weak smile and sighed. It would have been easier if she had known. Now I still had to wait. "So, what did you want to talk about?"

"I saw my grandmother yesterday." I made a mock grimace, and she laughed. She knew what I thought about her terrifying but ridiculous Avalon grandmother even though I hadn't met her yet. "Don't make that face at me, Alana. She's family!"

"Sorry," I laughed, trying to keep a straight face. "Go on."

"She told me they wouldn't assign me a Profession like the rest of the students. I'll be able to choose because of my… position."

"What? Lucky!" If only I had Avalon blood running through my veins.

"I wouldn't say it's lucky. It would be far easier to have someone choose for me. Grandmother has made it quite clear the path she wants me to take."

"She wants you at the top of the High Council," I stated.

"Yes. Well, not straight away. I'd have to start at the bottom and work my way up to that point. Gah, I don't know Alana. I doubt I'd be much good in that kind of Profession. It's so formal. There'd be a lot of sitting in an office. And then there's all the traveling…"

"You don't want to travel?" Sometimes I wondered how much we had in common. As much as I didn't want to be chosen to leave, I was desperate to escape this place. No… I was desperate to not be *kept* in this place.

"Well yeah, I mean, I guess. I like it here in Rowhill. To be honest, I was hoping to go for the farming Profession."

I gawped at her. "Farming?" She had to be joking.

"Well, yeah, it sounds a little basic I suppose. But I'd get to be outside, which you know I love. And it would help the Region which is important. Right?" She gazed back out of the window. Rowhill had extensive farmlands for growing food, and so it was a common Profession to be given around here.

"Seriously? You'd really choose farming over the High Council?" I asked. "Imagine the difference you could make being part of the organization who make all the decisions for the entire planet!"

Gen shrugged. "Yeah, I guess so."

"You guess so?" I shook my head at her, frustrated at her lack of excitement over the opportunity that was being presented to her on a damn silver platter. An opportunity that she didn't seem to be even remotely bothered by. "You'd get to travel the whole of Gaia. You'd get to go to Dracoa, Gen, just imagine it! I'd kill for a Profession like that! God knows where I'll end up. I swear, it better not be the educational Profession. I'll have to watch 'The Reclaim' movie every half-cycle... forever!"

"You'd make a terrible teacher," Gen said, giggling. "But Dracoa? Ugh no, that place is so strange. Why would anyone want to live in a fake planet inside a spaceship a mile above the ground? No thank you!" She gave a small shudder. "It's not very 'Avalon' of me to think that though." Gen swung her legs off the side of the bed in one swift and graceful move. "You really think I should go for the High Council? I'm surprised Alana, you seem to hate the Avalon!"

"Woah, woah." I held my hands up in front of me. "I never said I *hate* the Avalon. Not all of them. I mean... you. I mean... I just think the High Council could make changes that would help us all out. Don't you?"

"I guess so." She sighed, got up from the bed, and came over to the window. I pulled my legs up to make space for her to sit opposite me on the windowsill. "I've always considered myself to be more Gaian than Avalon. It'd be strange working for them," she said, and then hesitated. "I've got a few months to decide but perhaps you're right. Maybe I can make a difference someday."

"More of a difference than I'll ever be able to make that's for sure." We fell into a comfortable silence as we sat watching the flashlights bounce around the Village; the Regionnaires making final preparations for Shift Day tomorrow.

Over the distant sound of the activity outside we heard Gen's mom, her voice carrying up the stairs to the top floor of the house. It wasn't like Mrs. Portbury to raise her voice.

"I'd appreciate you not teleporting into my living room, Keren!"

A rich but sharp voice replied, "Calm yourself, Audelia, I'm here to see my granddaughter."

Gen looked at me, her eyes wide with panic. Gen's grandmother was here? I swallowed hard, my eyes darting around the room for an escape route. I shouldn't be here and getting caught would mean… I tried not to think about what they might do. The Regionnaires wouldn't let me off a second time.

"Your grandmother is here?" I gulped. "Doesn't she tell you when she'll be dropping in?"

"She doesn't ever just drop in. We meet elsewhere. Her and Mom don't exactly get along."

Before we could say anything else, Gen's grandmother was already at the top of the stairs and striding through the bedroom door. Her long, deep purple cloak flowed from her shoulders, partially covering her floor length, ochre dress. Even on first glance, I noticed how much Gen looked like her, though her style was a little more polished than Gen's. Her platinum white hair was pulled up tight into a perfect bun at the back of her head, pulling the skin on her face taut.

Gen and I both scrambled to our feet, moving away from the window.

Councilor Keren was taller than I thought she'd be, even for an Avalon. Seeing an Avalon could be jarring. Every non-Gaian had to wear shape-shifting tech while on Earth, to fit in with the Gaians. In history class, they told us it was to do with the psychological implications of integrating alien species on a planet who thought they were alone in the universe, or something like that. Although they were forbidden to show their original form, every race had an 'identifier.' For the Avalon, their identifier was a glowing aura. It was almost as though the entire surface of their skin was one big lightbulb. And Gen's grandmother was glowing fiercely this evening.

"Genevieve. I didn't expect you to have company." She eyed me with a piercing interest and glowed a little more. "You're not *supposed* to have company. It's past curfew."

"Sorry, Grandmother, I—"

"No excuses! If you are ever to make it to the head of the High Council of Avalon, I require you to understand that the rules are in place for a reason," Councilor Keren snapped and gave Gen a look of dissatisfaction as she turned to face me, her hands clasped together.

"Alana." She knew who I was? She made my name sound other-worldly somehow. "I've heard so much about you. You belong in the Hub, not here. Especially tonight."

I looked down at the ground, not daring to look her in the eye. "I'm sorry," I murmured, waiting for the punishment to arrive. Would she take me to the Processing lab herself or call the Regionnaires to do it instead?

"Well, Genevieve, I had come to discuss your future with the High Council before the busy season of Shift Day. However, it seems that I will have to deal with *this* instead."

"Alana was just leaving, Grandmother. Please don't punish her, it's my fault!"

"If you are found to be involved in illegal happenings, it will ruin your future chances on the Council," she scolded, narrowing her eyes at Gen. Councilor Keren stepped back out of the room. "Alana, follow me. I will return you to the Hub myself."

I knew better than to speak out of turn in front of the Councilor. In fact, it was probably best to say as little as possible. She may be family to Gen, but to me she was only to be obeyed.

"Yes, Councilor," I answered quietly, in shock that punishment didn't seem to be coming my way. I grabbed my coat and muttered a hasty goodbye to Gen, the opposite of what I wanted. If Shift Day turned out for the worse, this was all we had. I followed Gen's grandmother down the stairs and into the living room where Mrs. Portbury, Audelia, gave me an apologetic look but also didn't dare say anything else.

"We will have to transport by alternative means. I do not have the time to walk you back to where you belong. Am I correct in assuming you have not had a prior translocation experience?"

I shook my head, and she held out a small device in the palm of her hand.

Although I had seen them before, the 'Cellular Translocators' or 'CTLs' were the teleportation devices that were only used by those going out of the Region on Profession business which rarely happened, for Gaians at least. The CTLs were Avalon technology, well-regulated and tracked. The smooth silver surface of the almost-ball shaped device gave nothing away to its actual use until split open, hinged on its flat side, to reveal buttons and screens I'm sure only Avalon would know how to use.

"Hold on to my arm, please." I must have given her a nervous, quizzical glance for her to roll her eyes and continue to explain. "The translocation process will work for two people if they connect cellularly. Skin contact is enough." She spoke as though trying to educate a small child, but I knew her patronizing tone wasn't because of our age difference. She sighed and held her arm out again. "Now please, you're wasting precious time."

I should have been more panicked about the fact that I was about to teleport for the first time, but I was mostly relieved that Councilor Keren wasn't handing me over to the Regionnaires. They'd let me off with a warning before, but the next time I got caught stepping out of line, I was sure there would be consequences. Being Gen's friend had saved me this time.

I placed my hand on Keren's forearm, which felt oddly cold considering it was glowing with such warmth. With one hand she flipped the CTL open and pressed a single button. I wasn't sure how I had expected this to feel. Although I had often wondered, it was just one of those unknown things that so few Gaians would get to experience. Now that I had, I hoped I would *never* have to again.

The process of being translocated from one spot to another seemed simple enough, but as with most things that seem simple, it wasn't. A small breeze blew around us and built to a gale force wind, blowing me off my feet even though I was standing still. I looked over at Mrs. Portbury who didn't seem in the least affected by the wind raging around us. It was as though we were in an invisible bubble. Every single inch of my body ached, like I was being stepped on by a team of Regionnaires from every direction. Like I was imploding. The pressure in my head was the worst part. I thought my eyes were going to pop clean out of my skull. The whole process was taking far too long when suddenly, it all stopped. The wind dissipated, the pressure had disappeared, and I was no longer in Gen's living room. I was home.

Mom appeared from the kitchen and stopped in her tracks, raising her eyebrows at the sight of me standing in the middle of the dome, one hand still on the glowing forearm of one of the most important Council members on Gaia.

"Alana! Councilor Keren!" Mom unfroze eventually to give a brief curtsey. We didn't have royalty anymore; we had the High Councilors of Avalon. And one was stood in our living room.

"Good evening, Ms. Cain. I've returned your daughter from my granddaughter's house." I let go of Gen's grandmothers' arm and stared down at my feet. "I trust you will be more aware of the whereabouts of your children in the future. It is highly inappropriate for them to be wandering around breaking our laws, especially considering your Profession and standing."

Mom's eyes narrowed, if only for a second, and she nodded. "Yes, Councilor."

"Good." Keren turned to face me, stepping back as she did. "Alana, consider this your final warning. The actions you take affect more than just yourself. I will repeat what I told Genevieve. The laws were created for a reason." She paused, frowned and stepped a little closer, looking into my eyes and then quickly stepping back again. "And you are *not* above them."

She didn't even say goodbye as she flipped open the CTL and disappeared in an untouchable typhoon breeze. Mom stared at the space where Councilor Keren had stood and then turned to glare at me.

"Do you care to explain why you were returned home by CTL, *way* after curfew, by one of the highest-ranking members of the Avalon High Council?" She spat the words out at me. I attempted to stammer out a lame excuse, what I thought she wanted to hear, but she interrupted. "And I'd also *love* for you to explain why you're sneaking out. Again! I thought you'd learned your lesson from last time!" Her voice was getting louder and louder with each word and my brothers head peered around the corner of the archway that lead from the living space to the corridor.

"Mom?" He looked bleary eyed as though he had been asleep. "What—"

"Go back to your room, Simeon!" she yelled as he skulked back into the shadows. "As for you Alana, you know what they'll do to you if you get caught again! Why would you even risk that?"

Tears were now forming in her eyes as she stood silent and looked at me, waiting for me to give her an explanation for what had just happened. I didn't have one. Her words hung in the air.

"I'm sorry, I wanted to see Gen. Just in case."

"That's your excuse? Alana, they will put you through *Processing* for being caught in the wrong place after curfew." She shook her head, exasperated, looking like she had more to say but she had given up.

I had nothing I could say to make this any better. I wished I had just told Gen I'd speak to her the next day. She sighed and pulled me into an unexpected hug.

"If anything were to happen to you…" She pulled away and put her hands on my shoulders, her eyes sad and her frown angry. "We'll talk more about this tomorrow. Go rest, you'll need it."

I felt her eyes following me as I went to my room and closed the door. I was as mad at myself as I was the last time I got caught, except *this* was worse. Caught by my best friend's grandmother who also happened to be one of the most powerful leaders of the whole damn planet. I should never have gone to see Gen the night before the Shift; it was a dumb move.

I ripped off my coat in frustration and threw it down on the floor, hearing it clunk down on the tiles. Strange. I lifted the coat back up and rummaged in each of the pockets until I found it.

A round, silver shiny ball of metal with a flat, hinged side.

And a note.

# TWO

GEN AND I SAT AT THE EDGE OF THE RIVER, watching the water rush downstream. I'd met her Hub-side this time because during the mornings 'long talk about my behavior and what is expected of me,' Mom told me I should not 'under any circumstances' go near the Village today. Shift Day. Usually I probably would have still gone to see Gen anyway, but yesterday's events had shaken me and I still wasn't sure why Gen's grandmother had let me off. I would have to be extra careful today, just in case.

On a warmer day, we might have cooled our feet in the flowing water, but today was cold enough. Almost every Region I had ever lived in—and this was my twelfth—had a river flowing through it. At least it made it feel familiar. Sort of.

Gen opened and closed the lid of the CTL over and over, peering at the tiny screen inside and then flipping it shut again. I snatched it out of her hands, sliding it back into my coat pocket. I should have left it at home. If I got caught with illegal Avalon tech, I'd be done for, and with the number of Regionnaires around today, there was an even higher chance of that happening. But if I'd left it in my room and we were chosen to leave, they would have found it anyway, and my whole family would have ended up in Processing. Because of me.

I hated the way they moved people from one Region to another. With zero thought to people's privacy, the Shift teams just went right on in to the family's dome and packed up all their belongings for them, documenting everything along the way. That was the main reason I'd kept nothing personal and never kept a journal. I hated the thought of a stranger seeing the things that meant the most to me as they pushed me out into somewhere new and unknown. I tried my best not to think of all the places I'd lived and all the things I'd loved and hated about them. The friends I'd made and lost. How much it would hurt to leave Gen behind. Perhaps today.

"So, remind me what the note said again? Sun down...?" Gen asked as she pulled her own coat tighter around her. Regionnaires were crossing the bridge over the river further down but the weeping willow trees that lined the bank hid us from their view.

"It said 'Sun down. Two hours. Find him.'" I skipped over the part of the note that said 'tell no one' because I didn't want to worry her. Gen wanted a quiet life, a farmer's life of all things! I didn't want to get her caught up in my drama, but she was the only person I could talk to.

"But where did it come from? CTLs are illegal to own unless you work for the Council. Who wrote the note? Who is 'he'?"

I shrugged. "I don't know. I'm sure the CTL wasn't in my coat when I left, so someone must have put it there, along with the note."

Gen raised her eyebrows at me. "Who would have done something like that?" She knew as well as I did that I had barely come into contact with anyone that night, except for her,

Councilor Keren, and Audelia Portbury. But I wasn't about to start accusing my best friend and her family for getting involved in something like this, even if it was the only conclusion I could come to.

"I'm not sure. Perhaps it had been in my coat before and I didn't notice it? I really don't know, Gen."

She frowned. "Well, what are you going to do with it? Are you going to use it?"

I pressed my lips together, watching the water rush past. I'd been battling that question since last night. Should I use it? An illegal teleportation device that appeared in my pocket from god knows where? I didn't know where it would take me; it could even be a trap. And who was I supposed to find?

Find him.

"I haven't decided yet." I sighed. "Can't you just tell me what to do?"

"Why me?"

"You're the sensible one out of us, you always have been!"

Gen laughed. "Only because I've had to be. Someone's got to keep you out of trouble! But, as cliché as it sounds, follow your gut." She shrugged. "I always do. Did you show it to your mom?"

"No way! You should have seen her when I appeared out of thin air in the middle of the living room with your grandmother!" I shook my head. "I'm already in enough trouble with Mom as it is. It's probably best that she doesn't find out about this."

The sirens sounded. One hour left until the Shift. The sound that told us to go 'home' and wait. I pulled my knees up to my chest and buried my face on them. If only I could freeze time and not have to face what comes next. If only it were that easy.

Gen's hand wrapped around my shoulder. "It'll be okay you

know. We've been here before loads of times and got through it. And even if they do take you somewhere else, maybe one day I can find you again. You know, once I'm at the top of the Avalon High Council."

Lifting my head up, I returned her smile. I'd never find a friend like Genevieve ever again; it was one of those things you just knew. I decided that I didn't want to say goodbye even if I would be leaving. It was too final. So instead, I gave her a big hug and told her I'd see her at school tomorrow.

She laughed again and nodded. "Sure Alana, see you at school," she said as she stood up.

She was going back home, to a home that was a home, a place she knew she wouldn't be forced to leave. I watched her through the branches that were dancing in the breeze as she crossed over the river back to the Village, and once she was out of sight, I laid myself back on the cool, grassy river bank.

I pulled the CTL out of my pocket one last time and turned it over in my hands. Such a small piece of metal and electronics that could do such an extraordinary thing. At least I knew how it felt to translocate now. Thanks to Councilor Keren, that was no longer a mystery or something to worry myself over, although I wasn't exactly thrilled at the thought of putting myself through it again. I picked myself up off the ground and dragged myself back to the dome. Mom and Simeon would already be there; they were always on time for everything.

When I arrived home, I placed my hand on the scanner at the entrance to our home-dome which scanned my handprint. Every building in the Region had one; it was the way the Avalon kept tabs on where we were. If you were found somewhere you shouldn't be, or didn't arrive somewhere at the time you should, that was when your troubles began.

Simeon and I sat, and we waited, just like we did every half-cycle. Mom rarely sat still, especially on days like this. Instead, she clattered pans in the kitchen as though it was any other day. Simeon was sitting at the round window in the living room keeping an eye out. He'd make a good Regionnaire; he had so much more patience than I did, and he noticed everything and everyone. A real people watcher. But I hoped he didn't become one when they assigned his Profession in a few cycles; it'd make my life way more difficult.

The screen in the living room was playing the Avalon Reclaim on a loop in the background, the narrator's voice echoing around the room.

"Both the Avalon and the Midorians are dedicated to bringing Gaia back to her former glory by whatever means necessary. It is of utmost importance that the Gaians, the original species of this planet, work alongside us to fulfill our goal. These new societal constructs will not feel natural to you for many thousands of Gaia-cycles, at which point you will adapt, and we will release the population out of the Region system to once again roam the lands freely.

No one knows the importance of Gaia as much as the Council of the Seven Races, and they themselves instructed this change to occur. We will make them proud as Gaia heals and we make the human race whole again..."

"Ugh, can we turn this off?" I sighed. Listening to this crap for a second time in two days was overkill. Once was enough.

Simeon looked away from the window, but only briefly. "Oh, yeah sure. It was just background noise to be honest." He was nervous; he'd always hated Shift Day even more than I did.

"It'll be all right you know," I encouraged him. "Even if we don't stay, it'll be okay." I tried my best to make it sound like I believed what I was saying.

He attempted to return my smile. "Yeah, I know. Doesn't make it much easier, but thanks," he said, and then continued to stare out of the window, waiting.

I used to be able to make my brother feel better at times like this, with a funny joke or a made-up story. I used to make him smile and laugh. But the older we got, the harder it was. He was fifteen now and acted like mister independent. Since Dad died, I supposed he felt like he should assume the 'man of the house' role. But Simeon would always be my little brother. I'd always feel responsible for him.

As siblings go, Simeon and I looked alike. We had the typical Gaian skin that changed color with the seasons, unlike the Avalon and Midorians who weren't affected by our sun in the same way. We both had Mom's deep brown eyes and dark curls, mine longer than his. The biggest difference between us was our height. Even though he was younger than me by almost two-and-a-half cycles, he towered over me. He took after Dad.

I closed my eyes as I waited, thinking back to when Dad used to be here waiting with us. This would be the eighteenth Shift Day without him. Nine cycles. Every time this day arrived, I tried my very best to hold on to the memory of the stories he used to tell us about our 'ancestral land' as he used to call it. The last time I heard them, I was only eight, but I still remembered the stories of huge cities by the ocean and sweeping beaches that stretched the coast. Mountains surrounding lakes clear as crystal. Wild horses running along grasslands in the summer heat. Dad never saw these things for himself, but his family passed the memories of his country from generation to generation. The empty hole in my chest reminded me that he was no longer here to recount the stories, so I kept them as fresh in my mind as I could. One day I'd want to tell my children where they came from. The place which should have been their home but was not. Because of the Avalon.

The Holodome on the top of the hill should be able to show us these things, but the only images of 'The United States of America' were ones of fire and dust. Of war and suffering. I knew they only gave Dad the good things to remember to pass down to his children, but I didn't see the problem with that myself. What would be the point in remembering all the awful things? Gen disagreed and told me that the Avalon showed us only the negatives so that we could learn from our mistakes. I argued that we didn't even have the freedom to make those mistakes now anyway, and we had changed the subject. Sometimes Gen's Avalon side came out more than I liked.

"It's time." Simeon's voice startled me out of brighter thoughts and brought me back to reality.

Seconds later, the final siren sounded, and I joined him at the window to watch the trucks weave in between the circles of domes. Without saying anything, Simeon grabbed my hand and held it tight, just like he had when we were little. I didn't even know how he felt about leaving here; I hadn't asked him.

The trucks stopped in our layer of the circle of domes. Simeon's hand tightened, and I realized I was holding my breath. Mom carried on doing whatever it was she was doing in the kitchen. Shift Day didn't bother her much anymore.

Regionnaires filed out of the vehicle and lined up, waiting for their instructions. The lead Regionnaire was always an Avalon, looming over the others and skin glowing bright. I saw Ableman amongst them, looking as stuck up as ever. The Avalon leader was shouting and pointing in various directions. I couldn't bear to watch, so I let go of Simeon's hand, went back to the couch, and tucked my knees up to my chin.

"You want me to tell you what's going on or what?" he asked, without looking away from the window.

"Only if it's good news."

"How I am supposed to know if it's good news or not? Do you wanna stay or do you wanna leave?" He turned to look at me, waiting for an answer I wasn't sure I could give.

"I guess it doesn't matter," I shrugged.

Sucking in a short breath, I almost told him about the CTL I had found in my pocket last night but thought better of it. My brother was one of the few constants in my life and so I told him most things, but he'd be better off not knowing about this. Just in case. Ignorance was bliss in our world. He only would have tried to convince me to hand it in to the Council, and he most definitely would have told Mom. Unlike me, Simeon preferred to follow the rules. Besides, the note had said to tell no one. I'd already ignored that by telling Gen, so I decided not to push my luck.

He returned his gaze to the window, watching intently.

"They're moving out now," he said.

I could just imagine them marching to our front door and telling us it was time. They had a formal speech they gave and everything. I hadn't heard it for many Shift Days, but I could still remember how it went. Word for awful word.

"They're getting closer." I held my breath again, my stomach twisting. "Wait... no, they're going to the Petersons' dome."

Already? The Petersons only arrived on the last Shift Day, only a half-cycle ago, in the dome opposite ours. It hardly seemed fair. Simeon kept up with his commentary of every movement the Regionnaires made. The knocks on the doors, the packing up of the belongings at the Petersons' and another dome further around the curve, the trucks filling up and moving out.

I'd rather have not known right now about who was being forced out but talking about it seemed to help him, so I let him carry on. I'd find out at some point later anyway.

"That's that, then." Simeon came away from the window and joined me on the couch, the sound of the trucks rumbling fading into the distance. "I guess we get to stay longer."

"I guess so," I replied. We simultaneously let out a long breath, and Simeon let out a small laugh.

"Hey, maybe someone new will come to the Region later who you could couple with!" He laughed again and poked me in the ribs.

"I swear, if you keep going on about that..." I said, swatting his arm away. "I've got a few cycles before they force me to couple with someone."

"That's what I mean. Better choose someone before they choose someone for you," he sang.

It lifted me to see Simeon in a lighter mood now that we knew the answer we'd been waiting for. He was always joking about me getting coupled, but it was hard to take it as a joke. If I hadn't picked someone to couple with by the time I was twenty-three, someone would be chosen for me. A stranger. And I didn't trust the Avalon's judgment, that was for damn sure.

A sharp rap on the door of our dome made me jump up from the couch.

"I thought you said they had already left!" I half-yelled at Simeon, panicked.

"They... they had!" he stammered, and I could see my own fears reflected at me in my brothers' eyes. He wanted to stay, too.

Mom appeared from the kitchen, briefly glancing at us as she went to open the front door. She looked as calm as ever. How did she do that?

"Caliza." The unwelcome voice of Archimus Ableman boomed through the doorway as I made my way to stand behind my mother to give her moral support. He was standing alone, no trucks or other Regionnaires to be seen.

"Good afternoon Archie," Mom said politely, as though she were at a Profession meeting. "Can I help you?"

"I'm here to tell you that you have not been selected for relocation this time."

Mom gave a small laugh. "Yes, I assumed that, seeing as the trucks have left and no one came knocking at our door. Until *you* came knocking at our door. I think you've scared my children half to death!"

As she said this, he took his intent gaze off her and peered around at me and Simeon, both of us staring wide-eyed back at him.

"Sorry, ma'am, I wanted to make sure you were sure and that you knew and that, well, I wondered… have you considered my proposal?"

I shuddered at the word. *Proposal.* He'd been hassling Mom to couple with him for a while now. His last coupling failed, no one knew why, and now Mom was at the top of his list of potentials for some godawful reason. Except Mom didn't *have* to be coupled with anyone now. She had children, so she had the right to choose.

"This isn't a great time to discuss that Archie, but you already know my answer."

He frowned an almost childish, sulky kind of frown and took a large step back from the door. "Ortis is gone, Caliza. You shouldn't spend your remaining days on Gaia alone."

"I'm not alone," she retorted bluntly, and before he'd even turned around and walked away, Mom had already shut the door, rolling her eyes.

We all stood in the entrance way for a moment, breathing a collective sigh of relief. I had grown to like it here, we all had. The weather was forgiving, the Profession opportunities were varied, and the people were nice. Until they had to leave. Some people got ugly when they were forced to leave. We all knew our time would run out, but this was home for now. For another half a cycle at least.

"So!" Mom clapped her hands together. "Who wants a cookie?"

Mom had been baking her 'Shift Day cookies.' While everyone else sat in dread, waiting to see if their time had run out, Mom was the type of person to keep herself busy instead of dwelling on it. Baking cookies was her current distraction, and she'd done it for the past two or three Shift Days. Last time, I made the point that we wouldn't have time to eat them if they chose us to leave, so what was the point? She'd replied that she would just leave them for the Regionnaires and wouldn't that be a nice thing to do. She thought much higher of them than I did.

Mom and I huddled on the small couch while Simeon sat at our feet with his back resting against it. The first part of the day was over, but the second part was yet to begin. Just before curfew, the new inhabitants of our Region would arrive to fill the places of those who had left. The Originators would be busy taking them on a tour of the Region, showing them how things work here and getting them settled. Mom's Profession as an admin clerk for the Region Council meant that Shift Day and the following few weeks were quite a busy time for her, too. Her job was to provide jobs for the rest of us. Though she didn't get to choose people's Professions, she notified them when they were assigned and showed them where to go.

"Mom, how come you don't tell us stories about America like Dad used to?" Simeon asked in between bites of cookie.

She shifted in her seat a little. "Life was very different for your fathers' ancestors compared to mine I'm afraid. Our stories are a little less sunshine and roses," she said, with a sad smile.

I shook my head. "I don't understand how a nation that called itself 'United' could be so divided. Even the country this Region used to be part of, what was it? The United Kingdom? That didn't sound too *united* either."

"Alana, we're not supposed to talk about the countries," Simeon whispered.

"It's all right, Simeon, they can't hear us here." Mom got up to put the rest of the cookies away before they disappeared a little too fast, it wasn't often that our rations allowed for such a treat. "Go ahead, Alana, what do you mean?"

"The Avalon go on about how 'united' we are now under their rule but... are we?" Sighing, I threw my hands up in the air, and Mom raised an eyebrow at me. "I mean, we have the one planetary language, sure, and we have one currency. But they keep us so divided in these Regions and no one would ever treat a Gaian the same way as they'd treat an Avalon."

"We're treated well here and trust me, you wouldn't want things to go back to how they were before the Cataclysm." Mom went to the window Simeon had been at before and sat in the dipped curved windowsill facing us.

"Yeah, exactly," Simeon added. "The Gaians used to kill each other over the color of their skin!"

"Don't believe everything they teach you in class Simeon," I said, rolling my eyes. "It probably wasn't as dramatic as they make it sound."

"Oh, trust me, it was as dramatic as it sounds," Mom interrupted. "Don't forget that your great-grandparents remember very clearly what life was like on Gaia before the Cataclysm. *Those* were the stories I grew up hearing."

"I'm sure it was bad but this... this can't be better. There must be a better way." My voice rose. "They pen us in Regions like animals!" I wished I hadn't started this conversation now. The whole thing made me so angry.

"Listen, I know how you feel but you can't be saying any of these things outside of this dome," she warned. "Do you understand? If they hear you or find out, you'll be sent to Processing, and I *cannot* let that happen." She stood, rigid and tense. Her sudden change in temperament caused me to tense, too. "Just tell yourself we're divided into the Regions to let the planet recover from the devastation that happened. *That* is what they tell us, and so *that* is what we must believe. That is our truth."

Judging by the stress in Mom's voice, the conversation was over. I didn't push it further as she walked back to the kitchen to finish cleaning up.

I shook off the tension and stretched myself out across the sofa, tucking my arms behind my head. I frowned at the domed ceiling. I hated these damn domes. It was like living in an inverted fishbowl. If only Dad was here to tell us stories of huge, glassy skyscrapers and roads that stretched for miles connecting one thriving metropolis to another. Stories of gorgeous sunsets across the deepest of canyons. Of celebrations and happy families.

But my heart ached. He wasn't here. And there was nothing I could do about it.

# THREE

THE NEXT DAY WAS MUCH LIKE ANY OTHER. Mom left early in the morning to get a head start on all the work she had to do. There were around one hundred and fifty new residents in the Region that were all being reassigned a Profession. Some would do the same work they'd always done, some would have to learn a whole new set of skills for a new Profession. Simeon had gone to his morning classes. I thought about maybe going to find Gen but decided that after last time, it might be worth just catching up with her after the afternoon classes that we both had. Bumping into Councilor Keren again was something I was keen to avoid.

Looking down the list of chores that Mom had left out for me, I tried to find one which would get me out of the dome and as far from it as possible considering we'd been stuck inside the day before. Collect rations. Perfect!

The Ration Center was in the Village, not as far across or as high up as Gen's house, but far enough that I'd get a decent walk out of it. Rowhill was one of the smaller Regions I'd lived in, with just over a thousand people living here. It took no time at all to walk from one side to the other, which was helpful considering there were no cars or buses like the old Gaian cities used to have. Avoiding staying in one place for too long helped it feel less... claustrophobic. And any time it did feel like the borders of the Region were closing in on me, I'd visit the Holodome on the top of the hill on the Hub side of the river.

I was always surprised with how few people used the Holodome. Being mentally transported to almost anywhere on the entire planet was a far better escape than any of the pre-prescribed books the Avalon allowed us to read. In my opinion, it was one of the best pieces of tech that the Avalon had brought to Gaia, apart from the CTLs. One small gift to Gaia-kind. It was made the same way as the home-domes but was about eight times the size. Even though it was grass-covered just like the home-domes were, to blend into the lush countryside our Region sat in, you couldn't really miss it. It had been a while since I had let the Holodome take me to wherever I wanted to go.

Before grabbing my coat, I wrapped the CTL along with the note in a t-shirt and tucked it under my pillow. It was the most obvious place to hide anything, but the home-domes were so sparsely furnished that there weren't really many options. That would have to do. The Regionnaires weren't likely to be snooping in my bedroom unless I got caught doing something I shouldn't, in which case I was screwed anyway. The only person likely to find it was Mom, and maybe that would solve all my problems. She'd probably tell me to hand it in to the Council or even do it for me. Done and dusted, decision made! Shift Day had distracted me from the CTL and the note, but I had to make the decision whether to use it or not, and soon, before I either chickened out or lost the chance. I was pretty sure which I would choose.

The air and skies were clear as I stepped out onto the stone pathway that swept between the rings of the domes. I glanced at the now empty dome which the Petersons had once lived in. Boxes were stacked outside the door, stamped with '82-1056' on each surface. Their owner wouldn't be far behind. The temperature was dropping more and more each day now that we were in the autumn quarter of the cycle. Rowhill had far more obvious seasons compared to some others I had lived in, and I liked it. There was more change which helped with the claustrophobic feeling too. The air became fresher, the colors of the trees shifted from green to reds and golds and browns, and the sunlight had a softer feel to it.

I tipped my face up to let the sunlight bounce off and warm it slightly, leaving me with lights in my eyes when I opened them again. Now that the Village had half-settled after Shift Day passing, and the fact that it was daytime instead of past curfew, I could take whichever route I wanted to the Ration Center. Instead of taking the quickest path I walked north, straight to the Region border. From there I would be able to follow the border east, all the way to the bridge that crosses the river at the hydro-station.

Much like the Holodome, not many people came this far up the Region, right up to the border. I took the opportunity as often as I could. The border fence barely looked like a fence at all because there was no fence. Every ten meters or so stood a tall metal stake, at least eight meters high, with a colorful array of blinking lights down each side. We'd been warned that if you passed between the stakes, you'd get a nasty electric pulse shock that had the potential of stopping your heart. Not that I'd ever tried. That was likely to be the main reason people stayed away. We'd all heard stories of people who had tried it, though. Not many lived to tell the tale.

Even without the long line of metal stakes, it was easy to see where the Region stopped and the Wild began. The ground on our side was neatly clipped grass, with rough stone paths only where necessary. The Wild side was exactly that; wild. The grasses stood tall and swayed in the breeze, the trees grew lofty and thick in the distance and you could sometimes see small, furry creatures scuttling about through the branches, but only if you stood still for long enough as to not frighten them.

It was bittersweet seeing out to the part of our world that we couldn't touch. As much as I wanted to be thankful that the Avalon had given us a way of letting our planet heal herself, it didn't stop me wanting to break through the barrier and see what was out there.

Before long, I was at the bridge. The hydro-station whirred loudly, the river flowing at high speed and producing electricity that pumped through underground cables to both the Village and the Hub. The river narrowed at this point as it disappeared through the mechanisms and out the other side into the Wild, and the bridge here was much narrower compared to the ones upstream. Being made of metal rather than of stone like the others, you'd think it would feel safer to cross it. But the fact that the floor was made from metal grid panels meant that you could see the water rushing past right under your feet. Sometimes I'd stand on this bridge for a while and imagine the water pulling me away, past the borders and into the unknown. If only.

I had time to spare today, so I stopped in the middle of the bridge and leaned over the railing as far as I dared. The breeze was strong, and it whipped my curls around my face. Staring down into the swirling water, out of the corner of my eye I saw movement. A man was striding through the trees at quite a pace and as he joined me on the bridge, I turned to face him. He didn't slow down until he reached me.

The narrow bridge was only a person-wide and so he

stopped in front of me.

"Let me pass?" he requested without a 'please.'

"Um, it's not wide enough to let you past." I frowned at him. Surely that was obvious? "I'll just go back."

The stranger rolled his eyes at me. "No, you don't need to. Stand sideways so I can pass you."

I raised an eyebrow at him. He was at least a foot taller than me and muscular. This was going to be... cozy. Pushing my body against the railing, I made as much space for him as I could, but he'd underestimated how much space we had. His body pressed against mine as he squeezed past. An interesting first encounter with a stranger that was for sure, especially as he had chosen to pass me facing me rather than facing the opposite way. If I'd had the space to look down at my feet, I would have. Being face-to-face, it was then that I noticed his violet eyes. Midorian. The strange purple coloring of the iris was the Midorian identifier, much subtler compared to the Avalon glow. He looked a lot like me, all the same Gaian coloring, except for those unusual eyes and his short hair.

"Thanks," he muttered. Oh, so he did have some manners at least.

"Are you new here?" I asked, even though he was already continuing across the bridge to where I had come from. I was trying hard to stifle the heat in my cheeks that had flared after being that unexpectedly close to another person.

He stopped and turned back. "I arrived yesterday."

A man of many words, clearly. I tried to guess in my head how old he must be, not much older than me, perhaps in his early twenties?

"Oh, well... I'm sure you'll like it here." I mentally kicked myself for not coming up with something more interesting to say, but those violet eyes were piercing through me. Not many

Midorians lived here, so it was almost as jarring as seeing a glowing Avalon.

He tensed, raised his eyebrows, and gave a quick nod. I couldn't help but notice the scar that ran down the side of his face. It started just below his ear, traveled across an angular jaw and down his neck. Guys with scars like that had to be trouble. Or maybe I was just telling myself that.

"You know you could get that scar sorted out at the Medical Center here?" Why was I pointing out his physical flaws on first meeting him, especially when there were so many pros I could have been highlighting instead? "Ours is in the Village, near to the old church, the one with the spire. It's not far from here."

He glared at me. "Don't you think I would have got it fixed already if I wanted to?" A deep furrow formed across his forehead making him look even more intense than before. "I don't want to."

Before I could say another word, he had turned away and crossed the bridge, quickly covering ground as he made his way towards the Hub. I thought about saying something as he walked away, just to get the last word. But I couldn't think of anything smart enough, or quick enough. He was a faster walker than I was a thinker. No doubt I'd think of something amazing to say later, clearly far too late. Or maybe Gen would come up with a witty retort when I told her all about this later. She was better at that kind of thing than I was.

While trying to decide if I was more embarrassed or angry, I realized I was still standing watching him as he reached the tree line and so I gave myself a shake down and finished crossing the bridge myself, Village-side. Way to go, Alana. That wasn't exactly the first impression I had wanted to make. Hopefully I wouldn't bump into him again.

Today's classes couldn't finish soon enough. This class was one I hated: history. Sometimes we'd learn about cultures from way back in the past, but they sounded more like myths than actual history, probably because the Avalon had something to do with them. I got the impression that the Avalon weren't always great at keeping their identity hidden before the Reclaim. I swear the whole education system seemed like one big Avalon ego boost sometimes.

History lessons were focused heavily on the shortcomings of the Gaian race, which was depressing. Today we were being reminded all about how the Gaians were created by combining Avalon and Midorian DNA for the sake of creating 'diversity within the universe' and crap about 'making advances for the betterment of each galaxy.' I tried to look like I was paying attention, but my mind was elsewhere.

I hadn't had a chance to speak to Gen yet because, as always, I was late. Ms. Haims didn't even comment on it anymore; it was just a given. I tried my best to focus on the screen at the front of the dome, with clip after clip of Avalon historians telling the woeful tale of the destructive Gaian empire and how diligently the Avalon and Midorians had watched over us since the beginning. Yawn.

The teachers we had throughout our education cycles kept notes on our progress which would go towards the decision regarding which Profession we would be put forward for. I hoped to god Ms. Haims didn't think I'd make a good teacher.

Finally, it was done, we were out, and this time Gen was waiting outside the edu-dome for me. She threw her arms around me, pulling me into a hug as soon as I was within reach.

"Looks like you're stuck with me for another half-cycle at

least," I said. She grinned at me and looped an arm in mine, leading us back down the hill. She glowed a little brighter than usual.

"Best news ever!" Gen gushed. "So, how do you feel?"

How did I feel? I was glad that we weren't leaving. I didn't want to have to leave Gen and life in Rowhill wasn't so bad, considering. But something deep inside pulled at me. There was a little voice that got louder with each passing Shift Day, saying there's more than this.

"Relieved," I replied, my chosen word not entirely reflecting the truth. "But I'm still thrown by what happened earlier."

As we slowly walked down the hill, trying to steal as much time together as we could, I told her about the man on the bridge. I thought about leaving out the part where I had told him he could get his scar fixed because frankly, I felt ridiculous, but I wanted to know what she would have said to his aggressive response. Gen laughed as I recounted what I had said to him.

"Oh Alana, only you! Don't you listen in Social Etiquette class?" I didn't listen in most classes, she knew this. "Why would you go around saying things like that to people, especially new ones? Especially someone you could potentially be coupled with!"

Coupled with? I hadn't even considered that as a possibility! Was that really what I should be thinking about when strangers were trying to squeeze past me on narrow bridges? Not that it happened often. Gen had planted a seed of thought, and it grew. I released the breath I'd been holding in.

"He's Midorian, Gen. It's highly unlikely that he'll get coupled with a Gaian like me."

By now, we were the only people left on the hill. Walking so slowly meant that everyone was long gone before we had even reached the bottom. I filled her in on the rest of Shift Day, telling her about Ableman knocking on our door and Mom getting tense when I voiced my opinion of the Avalon and the Reclaim.

"She's right though. You shouldn't talk about that kind of thing. Especially here. You don't know who could be listening."

We both automatically turned to look around us as she said it, fully expecting to be alone. But in the distance, walking fast towards us from the Hub, was the absolute last person I wanted to see today. The guy from the bridge.

"That's him!" I hissed.

"Oh really?" She squinted in his direction. "Oh, he's kind of cute!"

"Stop staring!"

He closed the distance between us in an exceptionally short time, his height made his stride way longer than most. He was going in the direction of the edu-dome, so passed us as we stood at the bottom of the hill on the path that leads up. I couldn't exactly ignore him, seeing as we were the only people in sight.

"Hello." My feeble greeting came out louder than I meant it to, reflecting my discomfort.

Without giving a verbal reply, he glanced my way, gave a quick tip of his head in acknowledgement and carried on up the hill without slowing down.

"Well," said Gen, "that was… interesting."

"Ugh, I'm done." I folded my arms across my chest. "If that is my coupling potential around here, then I'm done."

Gen laughed. "What do you mean you're done? He's a good-looking guy in a rough-around-the-edges kind of way."

"Great. It's my ideal life getting stuck with a guy that has that kind of attitude, bouncing from Region to Region forever."

There was a moment of silence as Gen flashed me a sympathetic look and put a hand on my arm. "You might find someone else before your compulsory age comes anyway."

I pulled away from her and she looked hurt at the gesture.

"I'm going home," I announced. It was best to not carry on the conversation with Gen, I'd only say something I'd regret out of jealousy for her level of freedom. "And I'm going to use the CTL."

"What?" Gen's light mood changed immediately at my bombshell. "You can't suddenly make that decision just because of one hot but emotionally stunted guy, that's ridiculous! You don't have any idea where it will take you! It's not safe!"

"I don't care anymore!" I said, flinging my hands up in frustration. "There's got to be more than... this! At least someone knows where I'm going and what I'm doing. If I don't make it back, just let Mom know what happened, okay?"

Gen stared wide-eyed at me in disbelief. "You're kidding me. You want me to break the news to your family when you disappear into thin air never to return?" Her voice reached a panicky high pitch, and she took a deep breath to calm herself. "Seriously, Alana, take a bit more time to think about this, please. Like, make the decision when you've chilled out a bit! I'm pretty sure you'd be making a huge mistake." She put her hand on my arm again, and this time I didn't pull away.

"Maybe. I'll think about it," I said, trying to reassure her. It was sweet that she was so concerned and yet again it made me thankful that I had her here. The thought that perhaps she wasn't the person to have planted the CTL in my coat pulled at me. If it had been her, she wouldn't have been so concerned. We said our goodbyes, and I made my way through the Hub, home.

I'd told Gen I'd think it over, but there wasn't anything to think about. I'd made up my mind. Back at home, we sat around the table eating dinner. Simeon had his head in one hand, pushing his food around his plate disinterested. I was doing the same thing, the weight of the CTL heavy on my mind. Mom could obviously tell there was something wrong.

"Is everything alright, Alana?" she asked. "Do you have anything you want to talk about?"

I glanced up at her briefly and then returned to poking my food around my plate. I hated lying to Mom, but it was probably safer for her if she didn't know about this. She'd only stop me. Obviously. Why wouldn't she? This was illegal and dangerous. I bit the inside of my lip nervously, but then tried to put a smile on my face.

"I'm all good Mom, don't worry. I think maybe I just need to rest." I looked out of the window, the same one Simeon had been standing at watching the Shift yesterday. The sun was starting to go down and dusk was beginning. It was now or never. "I'm going to get an early night I think," I said as I picked up my plate.

Mom raised an eyebrow at me. "As long as it's not the same kind of early night you had the other day when you were delivered home by a Councilor…"

"No, Mom, I won't try to go see Gen again. Don't worry. We already had a long chat today."

Seemingly reassured, Mom said goodnight. Simeon barely looked up at me.

"You okay, little bro?" I asked, noting his deep frown.

"Yeah, I'm fine. Just got a headache, that's all." He faked a smile just as I had, and I gave him a quick hug around his neck which he hadn't expected, said goodnight to him too and went to my room.

Sitting on the edge of my bed, my heart pounded in response to what I was about to contemplate doing. No, not contemplating. I had decided.

Retrieving the CTL and the note from under my pillow, I tucked the piece of paper into the pocket of my jeans and turned the CTL over in my hands once more. I knew how it would feel to translocate, but this time I had no idea where it was going to take me.

Find him.

Find who? I had no idea. But it was time to find out.

I stood up and moved to stand in the middle of my room. Flipping open the CTL and blindly hoping that I didn't need to change any of the settings, my thumb hovered over the same button that Councilor Keren had used when we translocated before. I had to get this over and done with before I talked myself out of it. With my heart pounding out of my chest, I closed my eyes tight and pressed down hard.

# FOUR

**T**RANSLOCATING ALONE was even more intense than when I'd translocated with Councilor Keren, perhaps because I was having to take the energy the CTL was putting out upon myself rather than it being spread across two people. As soon as the pressure stopped and the wind died down, my vision was blurry and all I could see were flickering lights in the distance. Feeling dizzy, the CTL slipped out of my sweating hand onto the ground, and I scrambled around in the darkness looking for it. As my sight returned, I found it again and got back on my feet.

I was standing beneath a towering tree that looked unlike any in the Regions I'd been in. In the place of leaves were needle-shaped spikes instead. The branches were thick with them. I tried to recall from Gaia Biology class what they called this kind... a fir tree, that was it. I definitely wasn't in Rowhill anymore.

It was darker here; the sun had just been setting at home but here it was long gone. It was colder too. Why didn't I think to put my coat on? Where the hell was I?

My heart continued pounding in my chest. Using the CTL

was a huge mistake, and I inched closer to the thick trunk of the tree, pressing my back up against it and trying to stay hidden in case anyone was around. The darkness would help with that; clouds blanketed the sky, so the light of the moon was gone. Focusing on slowing my breathing and staying calm, I tried to get my bearings.

Behind me, a short distance away, there was a dome much like the ones in the other Regions. Although instead of being covered in neatly cut grass, it was adorned with what looked like a forest floor. Mud and leaves I guessed, dark and grimy looking, but it was hard to tell in this light. It looked just like the Holodome we had on top of the hill in our Region, but much smaller. Just beyond that, the telltale tall metal poles stood in a row, fading out into the distance, so the Region border was nearby. This tree seemed to stand alone in a large clearing, but I could see others further away. Squinting into the darkness ahead of me, I could see little else except for a mud path leading towards the lights I had first seen.

A gust of icy wind blew in my direction, shaking water off the branches above me and creating a brief rainfall on top of my head. I wrapped my arms around my body to preserve what little warmth I had.

A hollowness filled my stomach. What had I done? I'd willingly and *stupidly* translocated to an unknown Region... in the dark... alone. What the hell was I thinking? With the CTL still clenched in my pale-knuckled fist, I opened it up. I was going home. Gen was right. This was a bad idea.

The screen on the small device didn't look the same as when I had opened it at home. Before, a long line of numbers and letters had filled the screen. I hadn't understood what they meant, but I had pressed the button anyway and hoped for the best. Now, there were five symbols in their place, flashing on and off. I'd seen nothing like the symbols before, but then again, I'd never carried around illegal Avalon tech before. I stepped away from the tree, took a deep breath and then released it, slowly. Taking in another deep breath and holding it, I pressed the button for the second time today, with even more trepidation than the first.

Nothing happened.

Frowning, I closed the hinged lid, opened it again and pressed the button again. Nothing. I tried a third time. And a fourth.

Nothing.

My breathing quickened once more as it dawned on me that I was stuck here, maybe forever! Wherever here was. Oh god. Once they found me, I'd be translocated home by Regionnaires and sent to Processing. Or maybe they'd not bother and send me to Processing here instead. That was if I didn't die of cold first. And it was all my fault.

"Hello?"

The deep voice seemingly coming from nowhere made me jump backwards, and I pushed up against the tree trunk again. I'd been staring at the brightly lit screen of the CTL for so long, willing it to work, that it took a moment for my eyes to refocus to see who had spoken.

Shoving the CTL into my jeans pocket, even though that didn't hide it very well, I tried to make out the figure who had now walked close enough to stand under the tree with me.

It was a young man who didn't look much older than me. He was taller than me, which wasn't hard, but not as tall as Simeon, and he was much better dressed for the weather here than I was, that was for sure.

He handed me a heavy, thick coat. "You might want this." His voice was gentle, like he was talking to a small animal which he had found wounded in the Wild.

I paused, deciding whether to take it from him. I couldn't see his face clearly enough in the darkness to see if his eyes were friendly. Another blast of wind arrived, so I took the coat from his hands and put it on, relishing the immediate warmth that flooded through me. The thick, lush fabric felt like a heater had warmed it.

"Thank you."

"It's not safe to stay here," he said, just loud enough to hear over the wind rushing past my ears. "We need to go somewhere to talk."

"I'm not going anywhere with you!" I said, pressing myself harder against the trunk of the tree. I slipped the CTL out of my pocket, hoping that he wouldn't notice, and managed to flip it open and press the button with one hand. Still nothing.

This had all been a huge mistake. I turned to look in his direction again. "How did you even know I was here?"

"Listen, we both have questions that need to be answered but please, we can't talk here. I don't know who's going to be wandering about this time of night." Don't they have a curfew here? "My cabin is just up ahead, if we're quick enough and quiet enough then hopefully no one will see us."

I gave up on pressing the CTL button over and over and shoved it back in my pocket and huffed. I didn't have much choice. It was either follow the second stranger I'd met today or stay here under this stupid tree and freeze to death.

"This is as much a risk for me as it is for you," he said as he turned his body to indicate that we had to leave, now. "Come on."

I nodded my head without saying a word, and he led the way up the path towards the lights. I pulled the coat closer to myself as the wind blew harder and was thankful that he had thought to bring it. How had he known to bring it? Did they take to carrying around extra coats in this Region?

We walked side by side, in silence, and I wondered if this was the *him* someone wanted me to find.

As we approached the source of the lights, it became easier to see where we were heading. There were five or six wooden cabins sat in a cluster, I assumed in a valley as we had been walking downhill and surrounding them in the distance were the dark shadows of more fir trees. There were no domes down here, and the cabins were set at all different angles from each other rather than in neat circles like our home-domes were. Several of the cabins were shrouded in darkness, while others had flickering light shining through the multi-paned windows. This must have been what I saw when I first arrived.

As we got closer to the cluster, the stranger I was following sped up. Now and then I'd have to jog to keep up with him. At one point he even had to stop and turn back, waiting for me to catch up. We reached the door of the closest cabin, which was facing away from the rest towards the way we had just come, and he placed a hand on the small of my back to usher me inside.

I'd always lived in a home-dome, and they were always the same construction: a single level with rounded windows and insulated on the outside with a covering of earth and whatever else would make them blend into the landscape. The furnishings inside were always basic, but often reflected the history of the country the Region used to know itself by. Everything was recycled.

This was nothing like the home-domes. The cabin I had just been pushed into was made entirely of wood, inside and out, and most of the contents seemed to be made from wood, too. It wasn't a huge space; we'd walked straight into a living room that I assumed also served as the bedroom considering it had both a couch and a bed in it. A doorway led to a kitchen on one side and what I assumed was a bathroom behind the door on the other side. In the wall's center opposite the front door was a hole lined with big chunks of stone. It held a black metal container with a glass window set into a little door at the front. A fire was burning inside, providing most of the light for the room. Piles of cut wood sat to one side. Strange, I'd never seen a fire burning in a home or any other building! I'd have to remember to ask him why it was there.

I turned back to face him as he closed the door as quietly as possible, and he held out his hand. It took a second or two to realize that he was asking for me to pass him the coat, and I stopped gawping at him long enough to take it off and pass it to him. Giving it a little shake, he hung it on a hook on the wall, just to the right of the fire. So that's why it had felt so warm when I'd put it on.

I was sure I'd stepped into a dream. I was lightheaded, with no idea where I was, who this guy was, or how the hell I would get home.

"You can sit down if you like," he said.

That's when I realized I'd been standing in the corner of the room since we got in, frozen to the spot. "You haven't even told me your name," I said, a little more aggressively than I probably should have. He was being quite the gentleman, so far.

He sat down on the couch and smiled. "Sorry, I was distracted by the whole 'strange girl appearing from mid-air' thing. I'm Aiden."

Strange? Who are you calling strange? Before I could voice my disapproval, a voice boomed through the door behind me, accompanied by a loud knocking.

"Merrick! You home?"

"Crap!" Aiden pointed at the door to the bathroom and

whispered, "Hide in there, now! I'll get rid of him."

Once I was shut in the bathroom, Aiden let in whoever it was that had arrived, apparently unexpectedly. I pressed an ear against the thick wooden door to see if I could hear what was going on, but I only heard muffled voices. All I could do was wait.

I looked myself up and down in the mirror on the wall, framed with wood just like everything else in this place. Translocating and traipsing about in the forest had done me no favors whatsoever. Doing my best to fix myself up as silently as I could, I pulled the needles from the fir tree out of my hair and brushed the dry mud from the knees of my jeans where I had been searching for the CTL. I took it from my pocket and flipped it open again. The symbols were still there. Still flashing, except there were only four of them... I could have sworn there were five before.

I tried to suck in a large breath of air without making any sound. This *Aiden* better have more answers than questions because I certainly had more questions than answers. I'd been waiting a lifetime when the door to the bathroom swung open, and I held my breath.

It was Aiden, alone.

"You can come out, he's gone."

I followed him to the couch where we both sat down this time, facing the fireplace.

"Who was it?" I didn't know why I was asking him that, considering I didn't even know who *he* was, let alone anyone who may come knocking on his door past curfew. That was, if they even had a curfew here.

"That was Mr. Hilroy. He's my Profession mentor. I don't think he saw you though."

"Oh, I see. What do you do for a Profession?"

Aiden laughed. "You're talking to me as though this is just like any other time you've met someone new."

I smiled and looked down at my hands. I wasn't good at meeting new people at the best of times, yesterday's encounter with the guy on the bridge was a testament to that. But this was something altogether different.

"Sorry, I… can't get my head around all of this." I gestured to the room around me and then to him.

"All right let's start from the beginning," he said. "Why don't you start by telling me your name now you know mine?"

"Alana Cain, Gaian."

Another smile spread across his face, which I could see much better now we were in the light. His eyes were kind, and they were just like the rest of this place: a rich brown color, earthy but bright. Dark hair framed his pale skin, the contrast making his eyes stand out all the more.

"Nice to meet you Alana Cain, Gaian," he said, copying my formality. "As you know, I'm Aiden. Aiden Merrick. Also Gaian."

"How did you find me?" I blurted out, a little more accusatory than I intended. "I mean, did you just walk past and happen to see me standing there under that tree? And you happened to be carrying a spare coat?"

"Ah, well… no." He pulled a piece of paper out of his pocket. "*This* is how I found you." He passed me the tattered handwritten note.

*One hour past sun down, the big tree next to the Holodome.*
*Two hours. Find her. Tell no one.*
*(Take a coat)*

"To be honest, I thought it was a joke or something. Some of the guys around here are playful like that and they've been mocking me recently about coupling. You know."

Yeah, I knew. It was a hot topic when you reached a certain age. Some took cruel pleasure in reminding us that the clock was ticking. He took the note back from me and I retrieved my almost identical note from my pocket and passed it to him.

"Unless they were playing the same joke on both of us..." I said.

He frowned as he read the note and then looked up at me, concern blazing in his eyes. "How did you get here Alana?"

Wondering whether to trust this stranger with the knowledge that I had somehow acquired illegal tech, I decided that I had nothing to lose now. I took the CTL from my other pocket and held it out. He moved closer towards me to look at it.

"You have a Cellular Translocator?" he asked, perhaps with a hint of worry in his voice. I nodded. "And you used it without knowing where it would even take you?" he said, apparently impressed. I nodded again. "That was kinda brave."

"Or stupid!" I laughed. I flipped open the lid and showed him the screen, the symbols flashing away. I pressed the starter-button, and he jumped back.

"Don't worry," I laughed again, "It doesn't work. See?" I pressed it a few more times for effect.

He took the CTL from my hands and turned it over in his, a lot like Gen had when I first showed it to her. He examined it, flipped open the lid and pressed a few of the other buttons underneath the screen.

"Maybe it's broken?" he suggested. "I don't know. We use these a lot here, but they're always preset for us." He laid it down on the seat between us, reached his hands up to his head and ran his fingers through his hair. "So, I suppose you're the '*her*' I'm supposed to find and I'm the '*him*' you're supposed to find."

"Well, I suppose?" I shrugged. "But... why?"

We sat in silence until I shivered. The fire was dying down. I grabbed a blanket that he had draped over the back of the couch.

"Do you mind if I use this?"

"Of course!" He clumsily helped drape it over my legs. "Sorry. We're so used to the cold here, I can imagine it's quite a change for you. Saying that, I don't know what kind of Region you've come from." Aiden got up to tend to the fire by opening the little door on the black box, putting fresh logs into it and poking it with a metal rod.

"It's a temperate climate Region. Region 82-1056. We call it Rowhill," I said.

"Oh, I know exactly the one you mean!" he sarcastically laughed. "What country did it used to be?"

I hesitated for a moment. "We're not supposed to talk about the countries."

"You're also not supposed to use an illegal CTL to translocate to a different Region without permission, yet here we are."

He had a point.

"It was the United Kingdom."

"Ah yeah, I know it well. There aren't many Regions on that island I don't think. You like it there?" He sat back down and put his feet up on a footstool, a wooden one of course.

"It's all right I suppose, though I might never see it again if I can't get this damn CTL to work. Do you mind telling me where I am now? It would be nice to know, even if it won't help a damn bit."

"Sorry," he laughed, "I forget that you most likely have as many questions as I do. But sure, this is Region 11-0111, we call it Nordlys. In what used to be Norway, Scandinavia."

No wonder it was so cold. We were much further north on Gaia.

"So, we've covered names and locations. That's as good a start as any." He smiled at me. "Can I get you a drink?"

I hadn't eaten before I left to come here, and even though it was late, I was hungry. "Yes please, if you don't mind. I don't suppose you have anything I could eat too? I was distracted by the whole CTL and translocating thing to eat much at home."

"Sure." With yet another warm smile, he set about getting me a hot drink and some food, leaving me to warm up wrapped up in the thick, knitted blanket I had borrowed. This cabin felt so much cozier than our home-dome, and even more homely than Gen's house. It almost felt untouched by the Avalon or the Midorians. Perhaps that was why I liked it.

Aiden returned from the kitchen with a steaming mug of tea and a plate carrying a thick piece of bread with some slices of cheese on one side.

"Your dinner m'lady." He performed a bow, and we both laughed. "I didn't know what you liked, but I don't have much in stock at the moment."

"It's perfect, thank you."

As we sat, I ate, and he talked. He told me about Nordlys, and I did my best to ignore the fact that I may be stuck here forever. It wasn't like the other Regions. It had a low population, and Shift Day didn't affect them. The people who lived here were only here for their Profession. There were two separate areas of these wooden cabins, about two miles apart from each other, the Holodome, and a tiny Info Center between the two cabin clusters. It was so sparse, they had to translocate to the next closest Region to get supplies. I'd never seen nor heard of a Region like it.

"So, why the fire? Why don't you have electric heaters like the other Regions do?" I asked. But before he could answer, a quiet intermittent beeping sound interrupted our conversation.

"What is that?" Aiden said.

"I don't know, this is your cabin, you tell me!" The beeping was getting faster and louder and was coming from underneath the blanket. Aiden lifted it, picked up the CTL, the source of the sound. He looked at me and then flipped open the screen. I leaned over to look at it too. All the symbols were gone, and a single word was flashing on the screen. Except it was in a language I didn't understand.

"What does that mean?" He passed the CTL to me, and I shrugged.

"I've given up knowing what is going on to be honest."

Aiden reached out for the CTL to have another look and then, it began.

A small breeze was building up around me, my hair flicking into my face. The pressure was increasing. I stood up in alarm, the blanket dropping off my legs onto the ground.

"What the...? How is this possible?"

Aiden stood up in front of me but was pushed backwards away from me by the invisible field that the CTL had created around me. The breeze blew into a gale, my body was imploding, my insides being crushed to dust.

And then, it was over.

He was gone. It was all gone.

# FIVE

THAT NIGHT, I ONLY GOT THREE HOURS OF SLEEP. Possibly because I had the CTL wedged under my pillow and who knows what kind of energies those things throw out even when they're not in use. But it was more likely to be because I couldn't stop thinking about Aiden. I couldn't figure out why someone wanted us to find each other, and I hadn't even been able to properly talk to him about what he thought it all meant.

The same question I'd asked before I had even used the CTL kept jumping into my mind... who had given me the CTL and what did they gain from me and Aiden meeting? And how come the CTL had suddenly kicked into life again?

I just had to talk all this through with someone and tell someone about *him*. There was only one person I could tell. Gen. She had one of her 'Avalon-only' classes this morning, so maybe I'd be able to catch her as she came out from the edu-dome.

There was time to kill before Gen finished class, and I considered trying to get more sleep as I rubbed my bleary eyes, but I was unlikely to rest until I'd offloaded last nights' events to my friend.

Mom was still home, and Simeon was out again. She was busying herself, as always, this time with moving the little furniture we had around in the living space.

"Did the furniture get all out of place in the night Mom?" I joked.

"Haha, hilarious dear," she said as she rolled her eyes at me with a smile. "I thought it might be nice to have a change. Did you sleep well?" she asked, dragging the side table across the room, its feet scraping along the tiles.

"Not really. I… I had a lot on my mind."

"Oh? Anything you want to talk about? Did something happen?" She stopped what she was doing to look at me.

"No, Mom, it's all right. I was actually thinking of going to the Holodome for a while."

"Sure, okay." She smiled at me. "I'll be heading into the Village soon, so I'll see you at dinner."

Mom didn't bother visiting the Holodome, she always said she'd rather focus on the here and now and what was in front of her rather than yearning after other places and other times. Maybe I got my Region-related-claustrophobia from Dad.

The Holodome was the ideal place to wait for Gen as it was right beside the edu-dome, so I'd be nearby when her class ended. I took my time walking there, the hill climb a little more taxing than usual because of how tired I was.

There were a few people around this morning hanging around the home-domes and traveling up or down the hill. One of the other classes must have just finished. As I approached the Holodome, there was someone leaning up against the wall of the dome, looking down at a small screen he held in his palm. He looked up at me, and I realized it was the man from the bridge. *Fantastic*. If I could go a full day without bumping into this guy, that'd be great. This time, I wouldn't bother saying a single word to him.

Marching straight for the door with my head held high and not looking in his direction, out of the corner of my eye I saw him moving towards me, cutting off my path to the Holodome. Damn.

"Hi, Alana, isn't it?"

How the hell did he know my name?

"Uh, yeah. Hi," I replied. There was a brief awkward silence between us, which after a while I had to break. "I'm just about to go in there so, uh…" I pointed at the door he was now standing in front of.

"Yeah, just wanted to say sorry for being short with you yesterday." He shrugged. "Should have introduced myself."

His eyes seemed half-sincere at least, but I could tell apologizing wasn't something he did often. I tried to figure out which part of Gaia he had originated from by his accent, but much like most people who were moved from Region to Region, it was very mixed.

"How do you know who I am?" I asked.

"Your Mom. I met her yesterday. She was showing me where to go for my new Profession and she noticed that we'd be neighbors. The dome opposite you?"

Oh, where the Petersons had just been taken from. That was quite a large dome for one person, maybe he was here with his family?

"She showed me a picture of you, said to keep a look out and say hi if I saw you."

"But… you *did* see me, soon after that. On the bridge. Don't I look like my picture?" I laughed. He didn't laugh back.

"I wasn't in the mood for meeting people that day."

Oh.

"So, you know my name, do you want to tell me yours?" I

asked.

"Dray Okeke."

"Midorian?" I queried, unnecessarily. The bright violet eyes gave it away.

"Half," he replied. "My father is Midorian, my mother is Gaian."

"You're here with them?" He didn't seem old enough to be force-coupled, which was often when people moved to a Region away from their blood family.

"No." He took a deep breath. "I'm here on my own."

"Oh, I see." I was curious, but I didn't want to pry. Dray and I had already gotten off to a rocky start. "Well, I hope you like it here."

"I don't."

The small screen he held in his hand beeped, and he looked down at it. Thank god for the distraction! What the hell could I have replied to that anyway? The conversation was about to die a death, with me looking like an idiot. Again.

"I have to go. Nice to meet you, Alana, properly that is." He didn't stop to wait for a reply, and he walked back across to the edu-dome and went inside.

I shook my head and wondered why he was even bothering to apologize to me and what mood the man on the bridge, Dray Okeke, would be in the next time I saw him.

The Holodome doors led to a small lobby, with three tall double doors made of metal up ahead. There were three rooms so several people could use it at once—not that many people did. Dad had told me that when these were first introduced into the Regions, the waiting list for just twenty minutes in the Holodome was crazy long. These days, people seemed less bothered by it, so I was confident that at least one room would be free. Today, they all were.

I placed my hand on the scanner in front of me which took my handprint for identification. My photo popped up on the large screen hanging from the ceiling along with my name and race. Soon after, the double doors to the left clunked open, and I stepped in. The room was empty and looked just like any other room in any other dome; the only difference being that there were no windows and there was a thin, silver coating on the curved walls, ceiling and floor. I picked up the controller which would let me choose and navigate somewhere to view.

It didn't take me long to decide where to view today. There was only one place on my mind. Region 11-0111. Nordlys.

I typed the numbers into the controller and every surface around me lit up.

At first, I was a little taken aback because the Holodome was showing me Aiden's Region in the day time. It looked so different. The trees looked more elegant than imposing in the sunlight. I did a full turn on the spot to see if I could figure out where I was in relation to where I knew. Using the controller, I moved the view until I could see the cluster of cabins. I was sure this was Aiden's cluster, but I was more interested in what was beyond. Navigating to the closest tree line north of the cabins, the trees inclined back up out of the valley. Only from perspective of course; I was still standing on the flat floor of the Holodome.

I went as far up as I could and ended up at the top of the hill where the trees thinned out. Turning around, the view was spectacular. I could see all the way back down into the valley where the cluster of cabins stood in a clearing, and even up the other side to where the lone fir tree stood next to the Nordlys Holodome. I'd only been in Nordlys for a few hours, but standing here amongst the trees, even though this was only a projection of it, I realized I missed it. Or maybe it was someone I missed.

Brushing the thought aside, I found the settings on the controller to change the time of day, to the late evening when the sun will have gone down. Just like it had been when I was there. The room went pitch black as the tech loaded the request, and as it did, the room became much brighter than I had expected it to. The source of the light was coming from behind me, away from the view of the valley, so I turned around to see what it was. My mouth fell open.

The sky was dappled with the most beautiful colors, swirling and oscillating in hypnotizing patterns. Greens, purples, blues, and pinks all danced together, like they were being painted onto the canvas of the sky by an invisible artist.

I sat down crossed-legged on the floor in the middle of the Holodome just to sit and watch the beauty of it all. If this was what Nordlys had going for it, maybe being stuck there wouldn't have been so bad after all.

After what felt like only a few minutes, though it could have been longer as I'd lost all sense of time, the screens turned off and the bright room lights came on, making me blink. My time was up. My mood turned ever so slightly darker. I'd rather have stayed in Nordlys, even the fake version of it.

I made my way out of the Holodome, back onto the hill. The sun streamed through bright white clouds which scattered strange shadows across the Hub and the river. At the edu-dome, the handful of Avalon students who lived in Rowhill were already out of the classroom and walking the winding path down the hillside. Gen wasn't with them.

A group of Avalon together looked so odd. I often wondered how anyone on Avalon ever hid from someone in the dark when they were glowing. Running down the path, I caught up with them.

"Hey, have you seen Genevieve?" I asked, short of breath. Only one of the younger girls slowed down to answer, the rest barely glanced my way. They were all tall, much like the rest of the Avalon, so I had no chance of matching their stride.

"Genevieve wasn't in class today," she answered. "She won't be in class at all from now on."

"What?" I asked. That didn't make sense; classes were mandatory until our eighteenth cycle.

"She's no longer a student. She has begun her Profession training."

"But it's not her time to start a Profession. She's not eighteen yet! Do you know where she is?" I frowned. Surely Gen would have told me that.

"They didn't tell us. I'm not even sure which Profession she began. We only assumed that starting early had something to do with her famous grandmother." The girl made a sour, unimpressed expression and one of the older girls turned to glare at her and hurry her along. I mumbled a quick thanks to her and she took no time at all to catch up with her glowing friends who crossed the bridge back to the Village.

I stopped at the bottom of the hill where Gen and I had stood just yesterday when I had told her that I was going to use the CTL. Leaning against the fence, I tipped my head back and watched the clouds floating by. I *had* to tell her what had happened last night; I couldn't speak to anyone else about it! The note said to tell no one, and I'd already ignored it. The person who wrote it obviously didn't know me very well. I'd never been great at keeping secrets. It was more than just needing to get it off my chest, too. I needed Gen to tell me what to do next.

I debated trying to find her, but I didn't know where to start apart from going to her house and asking Mrs. Portbury where she was. But that would involve talking about what happened on the night before Shift Day… no thanks. Gen's mom would either be full of apologies for letting Keren find me, even though there wasn't much she could have done about it, or she'd tell me I wasn't to visit Gen after curfew anymore. Or both. It would be best not to give her the opportunity to do either of those things, although I'd have to hear them eventually considering how much time I spent with Gen and her family.

Even though it would be far more difficult, not to mention dangerous, compared to finding Gen wherever she was, there was only one other person who I could talk this through with to figure out what was going on.

Aiden.

# SIX

**T**HIS TIME WAS DIFFERENT. This time, I knew where the small device would take me and who would be there. Or at least, I hoped he'd be there. Turning the CTL over in my hands, shiny and smooth, I remembered Aiden doing the same thing. I remembered his hands. I tried to picture his face and realized that I could, in clear detail. The slight dimples below his cheeks when he smiled. The way his brow gently furrowed when he was thinking. The strong curve of his neck and the defined collar bone beneath it that only just showed above the neck of his t-shirt. And the sparkle in his eyes that never seemed to leave whether he was smiling or not. How can you notice so much about a person in only a few hours of being with them?

When I got back to the home-dome, neither Mom nor Simeon were home. As I stepped through the door, the large screen on the living room wall burst into life with a quick video message Mom had sent from work. She had to work late because of the post-Shift Day new arrivals, so she'd stay at the workers apartments in the Village, spare rooms used by those doing night work, so they wouldn't have to break curfew by returning to the

Hub. Mom said Simeon was with her because he was going through some health assessments at the Medical Center.

I frowned; that was the first I'd heard of it. Did it have to do with his headache yesterday? He seemed tired a lot too, which was unlike him. In her video message, she told me not to worry but the older-sister-protector in me was already trying to think of ways I could help him. I'd have to talk to him once he was back. Simeon and I didn't talk all that much these days; now that he was fully in his teenage years, talking to him wasn't as easy as it used to be. Maybe I hadn't made as much of an effort as I used to.

I pushed the thought aside for now. I could deal with how to talk to my brother when we were all back at home. It was ideal timing, though. Translocating in my bedroom while the rest of my family was here came with significant risks. If I got caught, I'd rather not have Mom or Simeon involved at all. They shouldn't have to pay for my stupidity.

I knew how stupid this was. This time, it was only mildly less stupid since I knew where I'd be going; Nordlys. That was if the CTL would take me back to the same place, of course. I hadn't even considered that possibility, but I had to find out.

I flipped open the lid of the device and looked dubiously at the screen, hoping that the long string of numbers and letters would look familiar compared to yesterday. I thought it looked the same, but I'd just have to hope for the best.

This time, I put on my coat. I wouldn't make that mistake again. Although I would have preferred Aiden's fireplace warmed, thick lined coat, I couldn't rely on him being there this time. I hoped I would appear in the same place. From the big fir tree next to the Holodome, I was sure I could find my way to Aiden's cabin, attempting to stay hidden. For a moment, I was thankful I wasn't a glowing Avalon.

Holding my breath and tensing my entire body in anticipation, I pressed the button again.

It took a few seconds for my vision to settle, just like last time. If it was possible, it was even darker than yesterday, and my ears filled with the sound of heavy rain dripping through the branches of the fir tree. Within seconds, it soaked my hair, and I flung my coat hood over my head though it wasn't much use.

At least I had arrived in the same place as yesterday, so I knew where I was. It was harder to see the cabin lights in the distance with the thick rainfall blurring the view all around.

"Alana!" His voice came from behind me, from the direction of the Holodome. I turned around and Aiden was rushing towards me. He was carrying the same coat again and had an umbrella hooked over his arm.

"You're here." He smiled. One of those smiles that lights up your whole face.

"I guess I am!" I said, returning his grin. "But how did you know I would be?"

"I didn't, but I hoped you would." He looked me up and down and said, "Although I thought you'd learn from yesterday and dress for the weather."

My coat was much thinner than the ones he had, but I didn't see what was wrong with jeans and sneakers until I looked at the thick pants and walking boots he wore.

"I tried!" I said, pointing to my coat.

"You call that a coat?" he laughed, "*This* is a coat!" He draped the heavy coat over my shoulders and opened the umbrella to hold it over me. The immediate warmth and protection from the rain was welcome.

"This was the best I could do; I borrowed it from one of my neighbors. We don't use these much here as we're as used to the rain as we are to the cold."

Not to be outdone, I stepped out from under the tree's canopy and into the full-on rain. "Oh don't worry, I don't need that." Tiny drops of icy water fell onto me, stinging any exposed skin like tiny pins and despite wearing two coats, it was awful. I ran back under the tree, shivering, and he laughed again.

"You sure about that?"

"Well, it might be helpful." I had to stand close to Aiden to fit under the umbrella he was still holding. Tucking the CTL into my coat pocket I said, "Let's go, shall we?"

I knew the drill now from yesterday; we would take the mud path towards the lights that would lead us to his cabin. And there'd be no talking so we didn't attract any unwanted attention. We would have to walk side by side to both fit under the umbrella, and he stepped out away from the tree and waited for me to join him. I wondered why he didn't just pass it to me so I could use it alone if he was so used to the rain like he said he was. Instead, I stood as close to him as I dared, and he suddenly put his arm around my waist, pulling my side against his to keep us close as we walked along. Though he acted like it was the most natural thing in the world to do, my heart pounded at a thousand miles an hour and my skin tingled where he was holding me. I told myself he was just doing it to fit us both under the umbrella and that was that. Besides, I relished the extra warmth his body gave as we walked along at least, so much so that when we reached his cabin and he let go of me, the cold was unbearable.

It didn't get much warmer inside either. Unlike yesterday, the fireplace wasn't lit, and the only lights in the room were two small battery powered lamps, one sat on a sideboard next to the bathroom door, and another by the side of his bed which he had left unmade.

"Sorry it's not all that cozy in here tonight. I've been working, and I wasn't convinced you'd show up to be honest," he said as he lit another fire in the black box in the wall.

"Don't worry," I said, sitting down on the couch and wrapping myself in the same knitted blanket from yesterday. "But I was wondering yesterday... why do you have a fire in your house?"

"That's your first question? Out of the thousand questions you could ask about yesterday?" He raised his eyebrows at me playfully. "But hey if that's what you want to know! We don't have much electricity in the cabins. All the energy made in Nordlys goes into the equipment we use for the work we do. So yeah, we use fire for heat and cooking and most of our light." The fire roared into life and the temperature increased.

"That's... unusual. What's your Profession?" I asked.

"I'm a scientist. Well, a scientist in training at least. My mentor will train me for a few cycles yet, it's long and complicated so it'll take a while. I've been here doing this for one cycle now." That must mean he was about nineteen, if he had been given his Profession at eighteen like the rest of us.

Almost the rest of us.

Aiden sat on the couch next to me, closer than he had yesterday and gave a big yawn. "Sorry, I didn't get much sleep," he said. "I couldn't stop thinking about... well, about you and all of this. It doesn't make sense. Have you had any more ideas about where the CTL and note might have come from?"

I was almost a hundred percent sure that the device and note weren't in my coat before I went to see Gen the night before the Shift. If I told Aiden about Gen, I'd end up explaining that I'd told her about the CTL and that I'd already broken the *tell no one* part of the note. Besides, there was no way to tell if it was one of Gen's family members and talking about her behind her back would be best-friend-betrayal.

"I'm not sure," I said, making sure not to make eye contact in case I gave myself away. "What about you? Where do you think the note could have come from? Where did you find it?"

"Someone had slipped it under my cabin door while I was out getting rations from the other Region. It could have been anyone."

We sat in silence for a minute, staring at the fire, both deep in thought. Aiden broke the silence with a loud sigh. "Okay well, if we can't figure out who brought us together, we need to at least try to find out *why*." He turned his body towards me, facing me front on and sitting up straight with purpose. "Tell me, Alana, why did you come back? I mean, you almost got stuck here yesterday. Yet here you are, risking it again."

I stared at him. It was a good question; this was a dangerous game we were playing. "I… I wanted to talk to you. I wanted to know…"

"…what was going on?"

"Well, yes," I said, nodding.

He relaxed his body and leaned his side against the seat. He looked down at his hands and absent-mindedly picked at a nail. "Was there any other reason?" he asked, trying to sound casual but failing miserably.

"Well," I hesitated, not knowing how to put it in words without him thinking I was being weird, "I missed… this place."

He looked up at me now, directly into my eyes, and smiled. "You did?"

"I did, which is weird right?" I shrugged. "We were only together for a few hours, but it's like I'm drawn here."

"Any particular reason?" he asked, again failing at casual.

"There's an energy here, I can't pinpoint what it is but… I've never felt it before."

"Oh." His face fell. "That'll be the Aurora Borealis."

"The what?" I asked.

He grabbed a small handheld screen from the side table, similar to the one Dray had been holding at the Holodome and got a picture up on the screen to show me. "The Aurora Borealis. Or the 'Northern Lights' as they're also known. They have a strong energy signature. Science stuff."

The picture Aiden showed me was of the beautiful lights in the sky I'd watched at the Holodome. "I've seen those!" I exclaimed. "I went to the Holodome just this morning and saw them there. I've never seen anything like it, anywhere!"

"You visited Nordlys at your Holodome?" he asked, a smile creeping onto his face.

"Well yeah. Like I said, I missed it." I looked at the photo of the lights, and while they were stunning, I knew they weren't the reason I was drawn here. They weren't why I missed Nordlys.

"Did you miss *me*?" he asked, far less casually this time, and I looked up in surprise trying to suppress a blush rising in my cheeks.

"Umm… Aiden, I barely know you."

"I know. But it doesn't feel like that does it? It feels like we've known each other for forever. Or is it just me?"

The blush couldn't be kept away, and my face burned.

"Sorry, I didn't mean to embarrass you," he started.

"It's all right, honestly," I said, rubbing my hands across my cheeks and willing the redness to disappear. "These past few days have been crazy. And it was; it was you I missed. Which is insane because you're a stranger. And I don't even know why I'm admitting that out loud."

"You never know." He grinned at me. "We may have known

each other in a past life."

We both laughed. I wasn't even sure if I believed in that kind of thing. But I couldn't deny that this was different to anything else I could compare it to. I'd met several guys in a fair few of the Regions, but my only interaction with them involved holding hands under the desks in class or quick kisses behind the edu-dome.

Now here I was, sitting with a stranger who I'd been brought to by tech I wasn't meant to have, given to me by an unknown person for an unknown reason. And all I knew was that I never wanted to leave.

I shivered again as the fire had died down, and I'd already thrown the blanket off from being too warm when the fire had got going.

"Sorry, I'm still no good at this. I've just got used to the cold I think." Aiden got up and threw more logs into the black box, and as he came back to the couch, he picked up the blanket and threw it around my shoulders, draping it over my knees carefully. Holding each edge, he folded it across me so it would stay in place and rubbed the side of my arms to warm me. His touch made my heart beat faster, and I wished I didn't have this thick blanket in between my skin and his hands.

He sat down next to me, close enough that his side pressed against mine. The damn blanket still in the way. "Let's just decide that we won't be strangers anymore, all right?" he said with a lightness in his voice.

"How do we do that?"

He reached out his hand, palm facing up. "Strangers don't hold hands. So, we'll start there."

I laughed, and his eyes lit up even more than usual. I shimmied my hand out from underneath the blanket and put my hand into his.

"Not like that... like this." He lifted my hand off his with his other hand and then took my hand in his again, interlocking our fingers. "Now. Tell me about you."

We sat, hand in hand, and talked like old friends. Although the way my hand tingled and warmed in his, and the way my body responded to his body pressed against mine... we might be more than friends.

I told him about Mom and Simeon, and that Dad was no longer with us. He gently squeezed my hand when I relived the night Mom came home to tell me and my brother that Dad was gone. He explained that both his parents had passed too, and his older brother and sister mostly raised him. So that was why he was in Nordlys without his family.

I told him all about Gen, the night of the Shift when I got the CTL, and about Councilor Keren finding me and translocating me home. He was just as surprised as I was that I didn't get into trouble that night.

He told me about his mentor, Mr. Hilroy, the friends he'd left behind in his last Region, and how much he missed it there.

And I talked about Rowhill; the high hill with the domes on top, the river and the Village on the other side, that I loved to stand and look at the Wild as much as I could and how I wished I could go wherever I wanted.

He described with beautiful clarity the way the skies in Nordlys lit up with all the colors of the rainbow in the Northern Lights and told me that one day he'd love to take me there and show me. We talked and talked. And he never once let go of my hand. If only the evening could last forever.

The CTL beeped, the Avalonian word flashing on the screen with urgency. Our time was up. Again.

"Dammit! Is there a time limit on this thing or something?" he said, mirroring my frustration.

"I guess there is. The note said 'two hours,' remember?" I frowned. "Maybe that's all the time we get?"

Aiden chuckled. "Then it'll have to be two hours every day until we can figure out how to turn the timer on this stupid thing off!"

I stood up, still holding his hand and pulled the blanket off my shoulders, dropping it back onto the couch. He faced me, and I hoped he didn't want me to leave just as much as I did.

"You need to let go of my hand, otherwise I'll end up going with you," he said.

I didn't let go. "Maybe I want you to come with me."

"You know I can't. Despite what we both want."

"What do you want?"

He squeezed my hand. "More than I can have, it would seem."

The beeping continued and got faster, matching the speed my heart was pumping. He pulled my hand up to his face, gently kissed the top of it and then let it fall to my side.

"Tomorrow, same time, same place. Please?"

I smiled and nodded. The wind blew, my body imploded and then, he was gone.

# SEVEN

**A**DARK AND EMPTY HOME-DOME GREETED ME. I'd forgotten that Mom and Simeon were in the Village tonight. It was warmer here compared to Aiden's cabin at least, but colder at the same time.

A light was flashing on the living room screen, so I stood in front of it to activate whatever message was waiting. I doubted that it would be for me unless it was Mom again.

Gen's face appeared on the screen, and she looked more excited and bouncier than usual. Usually only family members were permitted to send messages to each other on the system, but I could hazard a guess at how she got around yet another 'little rule.'

Not going into detail about why she was no longer a student and had been thrust into Profession life, she asked me to meet her tomorrow morning at the Ration Center in the Village. It wasn't the best time or place for me to talk to her about Aiden, but at least I knew where she would be instead of having to trawl Rowhill for her.

I went into my room and looked myself up and down in the

long mirror hanging on the wall, realizing I had left my coat in Aiden's cabin. Dammit. My jeans and sneakers were flecked with mud, my cheeks were flushed, and my curls were a hot mess. I laughed to myself, it must be my personality that Aiden liked. My cheeks flushed even more as I remembered the way he'd looked at me before I left.

After getting into more comfortable clothes for bed, I slid the CTL under the mattress of the bed this time, hoping that would afford me a little more sleep than before. I laid in bed, my body tired but my mind awake with questions and memories. I closed my eyes and pictured him sitting next to me; the sparkle in his eyes, holding my hand for no other reason than not to be strangers anymore. We certainly weren't strangers now. I wasn't sure what we were. Friends I hoped. More than friends I dared to hope.

I would go see him again tomorrow. I would translocate to him every night, even if for only two hours at a time, until we figured this out. I simply couldn't resist.

Aiden's face and laughter filled my thoughts until I drifted off to sleep and the thoughts faded into dreams.

I wondered why Gen had asked to meet me at the Ration Center rather than our usual spot by the river or even at her house. I left earlier than I knew I had to; I'd never really liked being in the home-dome alone. Besides, I was keen to catch up with the only person in the whole of Rowhill I could talk to about Aiden. Bottling it up wasn't doing me any favors; I was antsy.

As I left home and shut the door behind me, Dray was across the wide, stone pathway that separated his neighboring dome from mine, doing the same thing.

"Alana," he said as he pulled his door shut. "You heading south?" He smiled at me, for the first time, which threw me.

I had planned on taking the north bridge, the same one I had met Dray on, so that I could pass the Wild but figured it was just as easy to take the south route. It wouldn't take much longer and the company would be nice. Or at least I hoped it would be nice. He seemed to be in a good mood for once, but only time would tell.

"Yeah, I'm going to the Village."

"All right then." He didn't bother to ask if I'd like to walk with him, he simply assumed, walking ahead and looking back, waiting for me to follow. We walked along in silence for a while. I'd already gathered that he wasn't a man of many words, but it wasn't as awkward a silence as I'd expected it to be.

"You should have brought a coat," he said matter-of-factly as I wrapped my arms across my chest for warmth.

I'd only had the one coat, which was now hanging by Aiden's fireplace. I thought to borrow Mom's, but she only had one too, and she had it with her. It wasn't as cold here compared to Nordlys, and the sun was shining but there was only a minimal amount of warmth to it this time in the Gaia-cycle. I shrugged. "I'll be fine."

"Want mine?" Unexpected. His tall frame had a huge coat to match, it would have looked more like a full dress on me.

"Thank you, but really, I'll be fine." I was kind of cold though.

"Good, I'd hate to get cold myself," he smirked. "My last Region was much warmer than this one."

"What was it like there?" I asked. The Regions fascinated me; I wanted to see all of them, but of course I only got to see the ones that were chosen for me.

"Grasslands, blue skies. The Wilds there were full of the

most amazing animals; I can't believe they survived the Cataclysm. They're more resilient than us you know. I used to watch them for hours."

Finally, something we had in common.

"The creatures here are so shy, you'd be lucky to spot them even watching for hours," I said, and he smiled.

"You just need to be patient."

"Where are you off to anyway?" I asked him.

"To the edu-dome, for work. Same as any other day." He was giving more than one-word answers today which made a change.

"Oh, I didn't realize that's why you were there yesterday."

"Yep." He sighed. "It's new to me. It's not the Profession I started with, so I have to learn all over again." He didn't seem impressed or excited at the prospect, and I didn't dare ask him if he liked it so far. That question never prompted a positive response. I got the distinct impression he didn't want to be here in Rowhill.

"So, you're in training then?" I asked, and he nodded. He didn't seem to want to talk much about that either, and I wondered what topic of conversation Dray would ever want to talk about, apart from animals apparently.

"You don't like it here do you." I wasn't sure what made me come out with such a blunt statement, but it took him by surprise and he turned to look at me with his eyebrows raised.

"It's not that I don't like it..." He paused, like he wanted to continue but was struggling to find the right words to say.

"So, you *do* like it here?"

"There are good things about it sure," he said, smiling at me again. Dray's smile changed his whole face, turning from an angry *don't mess with me* type of look to a rugged charm. His violet eyes shifted from dangerous to warm in an instant.

"Well, if you ever want me to show you around Rowhill, let me know. When you're not working that is." We had reached the bottom of the hill which he would go up and I would go around.

"Thanks, 'preciate it." He didn't slow down or stop to say goodbye. Instead, he gave a quick wave and made his way to the edu-dome.

I wondered why he had a new Profession instead of transferring with his previous one. I mean, sure, it happened, but not that often. The Avalon were far too practical to keep making people retrain.

I watched him take long strides up the winding path that led to the domes on top of the hill, his head down and hands in his pockets. It took me a moment to realize that I had been watching him walk away far too long, and I blushed and hurried along towards the Village. I remembered Gen suggesting Dray as someone to couple with, and I'd detested the idea at the time. It was less of a horrible prospect now that he'd shown a different side. A softer side. I guess you can't judge a book by its cover.

When I arrived at the Ration Center, Gen was already stood outside waiting for me, her hands clasped together in front of her and tapping her foot. I was so used to seeing her looking the way she always looked, but today was different. She usually wore short flowing dresses, tights, and boots this time of year. Now here she was, wearing a long, form-fitting dress in deep purple. Profession-wear for the High Council. Thank god she wasn't wearing the lordly cloaks that the Avalon Councilors wore. I might have just turned right back around and gone straight home if she'd rocked up looking like a miniature version of her grandmother. It made her seem much older and made me feel that much younger, and dare I think it… inferior. Still, she looked elegant as always. Genevieve Portbury could look nothing but elegant even on a bad day, and she was still the same

Gen.

She gave me the briefest of hugs when I reached her, and then grabbed me by the hand and pulled me along behind her, down the cobbled street.

"What are you doing Gen?" I laughed, trying my best not to trip on the raised stones on the ground as I was dragged down the paths winding in between the rustic buildings in the Village.

"We can't chat here, you've got to tell me everything!" she gushed in a single breath.

Eventually, she stopped at one of the larger houses, towards the top of the hill which the Village sloped down. It looked even more impressive than Gen's house, with beautiful ornate pillars sitting either side of huge wooden double doors. As traditionally Gaian as this house looked, it had Avalon written all over it. Gen placed her right hand on a scanner on the wall just to the left of the doors, and they swung open.

The Avalon had updated the inside of the house from how it had looked pre-Reclaim. Seeing a modern and technology-filled interior after the exterior told such a different story was unsettling. A sweeping staircase led upstairs, lined with panels of glass. That's where Gen led me. At the top, two corridors leading left and right led to metal sliding doors. What was this place? She was still rushing me along, and I was out of breath.

"Slow down, Gen! I've only got little legs you know!"

As we reached the third door in the left corridor, Gen again placed her palm onto another scanner and this door also opened, revealing a room not much bigger than the bedroom she had at home. Large panel lights were suspended from the ceiling, lighting up three desks fit in to the space. The door closed behind us as we entered, and we were in a different world. The ornate windows and the view out of them looking down over the Village with the river winding in the distance were the only reminder of where we actually were.

Gen stood in the center of the room, in between the desks and stretched her arms outwards with a look of triumph on her face.

"What do you think?" she breathed.

I looked around me at the high tech monitors sat on each desk and wondered who they belonged to. The walls were pure white and had large screens on them which at that moment were displaying landscape photos of another planet that looked nothing like Gaia.

"It's... great? Umm, where are we?" Some kind of crazy Avalon space station?

"This is where I work now. This is one of the Avalon High Council offices. Although it's just for the lower down in rank but, I get my own office. I mean, obviously I have to share with two others, but they're not always here so that's great right? Grandmother is here often too, mostly checking on my progress and seeing to my training." Gen was talking at the speed of light, with a hint of nerves as though she desperately wanted me to be impressed. "Here, sit down," she said as she pulled out a chair at a desk.

I sat down, and she took a seat at her own.

"So?" she began and left a long expectant pause.

"So what?" I laughed.

"So, tell me about what happened the other night!"

"No way! I'm asking the questions first!" I exclaimed. "What happened? You're not eighteen yet, why the hell have you started your Profession?" I already knew the answer.

"Grandmother decided that I didn't need to wait," Gen said quickly. "It's only a few months early, and I was doing well in my studies, so she got my training started straight away. Isn't that great?"

I raised an eyebrow at her. "I thought you weren't even that keen on working for the High Council…"

"I wasn't, but now I'm here, it's not so bad. I quite like it." She smoothed down the front of her figure-hugging dress with an air of pride.

"Umm well, okay, I guess. Better than being on the farmlands?"

"Oh absolutely! Look how lovely it is here!" She swept her arms around her, in an exaggerated gesture to highlight the glory of her most amazing surroundings. I took in the stark, Avalon-drenched room again and couldn't disagree more. I'd hate to be stuck in this small, crowded room day in day out, even more than I hated being in the edu-dome most days. I couldn't understand why Gen's attitude towards her Profession had changed so much all of a sudden. Perhaps she was trying to please her grandmother? She always did like to keep the peace.

"So, what do you do here?" I asked, eyeing her, though she didn't notice as she carried on gushing about how wonderful it all was.

"Oh, I'm being taught by my mentor in all the roles of the High Council, including the data and systems we use. Grandmother will be training me every so often too, although she oversees the entire north-west quadrant of Gaia, so she's not exactly got a ton of free time. She'll take me to Dracoa soon to show me around there too, isn't that exciting?" she enthused, bright-eyed.

Dracoa, the Avalon High Council Region-in-the-sky. Us non-Avalons weren't allowed there. They taught us all about it in class, but most of us would never see it. Set floating a mile or so above the ground in a lush tropical Region down in one of the southern continents of Gaia, it looked impressive. But seeing it on the screens in the edu-dome was the closest I would get. We weren't even allowed to view it in the Holodome.

Gen certainly hadn't been interested in Dracoa before; she'd thought it strange. The look on her face now, bright and excited, was the opposite of how she'd usually be when talking about that place.

I tried my best to be excited for her. After all, I had encouraged her to accept her grandmother's suggestion—or insistence more like—of working for the Avalon High Council. But seeing Gen's unexpected response to all of this made me uneasy. In fact, this whole building made me uneasy. Her excited voice brought me away from the discomfort.

"Alana, I'm too impatient! Tell me! What happened the night you used the CTL?" she begged.

"Are you sure it's safe to talk about that here Gen? I mean, we're in the High Council offices!"

She casually waved a hand. "We're the only ones in the office now and I'll be alerted before anyone comes in. No one can hear us, don't worry! Tell me!"

Gen continued to encourage me that all would be 'fine,' so I told her what had happened that night. How I arrived in the dark under the fir tree. Aiden appearing out of the darkness and bringing me a warm coat. Going to Aiden's cabin and almost being caught by his mentor. The CTL beeping and taking me back home before we'd even got to know each other.

"The CTL just brought you home without you doing anything? I didn't know they could do that," she said.

"Apparently they do. It must be some kind of setting but I'd have no idea how to change it. It happened the second time too."

"You used the CTL a second time, even though you almost got stuck there the first time?" she gasped. Gen already thought of me as the irresponsible one, so it amused me that she was surprised by that.

I blushed a little. "I had to go back, I... I couldn't resist."

"Oh... oh, I see," she said in a sing-song voice. "You like him!"

"I mean, he's nice..."

Gen tilted her head and narrowed her eyes as she examined my rosy-cheeked face. "No, there's something more to it than that, isn't there."

I looked down and pulled at the edges of my sweater sleeves. It was hard trying to explain to anyone else what it was about Aiden Merrick. I barely understood it myself.

"There aren't words for it Gen, I'm drawn to him. Like a moth to a flame." I glanced up at her, her eyes sparkling with delight.

"Love at first sight?" She practically swooned in her chair.

"I'm not sure I'd go that far," I laughed. "I hardly know the guy, but it feels like I've always known him. Does that make sense? And I miss him. There's an energy about him, when I'm with him it makes me feel..." I tried to search for the right word, "... powerful."

"That's unusual considering you'd only just met," Gen agreed.

"It is." I shrugged. "I don't know what it is about him, but it's not puppy love or anything like that. I'm pretty sure I've grown out of that."

"Maybe he's your Mirror Soul!" She swooned again, as though this were a love story she was reading in one of her books.

"My *what*?"

"Your *Mirror Soul.*" She spoke the words slowly as though I was hard of hearing. As though saying them any clearer would mean I knew what she was going on about. "They taught us about them in the Avalon classes, recently actually."

"What's a Mirror Soul?" I asked.

"Oh, it's something to do with two people born with connected souls. They reflect each other perfectly. Some things they have in common and some things they are the complete opposite with, like mirrors. Something like that anyway, I didn't listen to much of it as it seems far-fetched. But the Avalon seem to believe in them."

"So, it's like, a myth?" It seemed far-fetched to me too, but I began to think of things that Aiden and I might have in common or not.

"Yeah, something like that. It was just a joke. Is he hot?" We both laughed, and I blushed even harder this time.

"I'm not even going to lie, he really is."

The metal sliding door beeped, alerting us that someone was about to enter the room, I jumped up from the desk and moved away from it, standing in front of Gen's again. She greeted the Avalon woman who entered, presumably the third person who shared the office, the other desk being for Gen's mentor. The stranger eyed me, greeted only Gen, and sat at the desk I had been at.

My conversation with Gen had to end, so we left the room and headed back down the glass paneled stair case into the lobby. At the bottom of the stairs stood an all too familiar figure, cloaked in the same color purple that Gen was wearing. Councilor Keren.

Gen gave a small curtsey. "Good morning, Grandmother."

"Genevieve, good morning. Ah, and Alana. Once again I find you in a place in which you do not belong." Councilor Keren seemed unimpressed with me for a second time. Her expression at a constant static, the glow of her skin was the only thing that seemed to give away any emotion.

"Don't blame her, Grandmother, it was my idea to bring her

here. I wanted to show her my new Profession workplace. I apologize, it'll only happen this once."

Keren turned from me, her eyes narrowed. "Forgiveness granted," she said in a robotic fashion. "I came here to see how your training was going Genevieve."

"It's fine, Grandmother, we've only just begun but I'm very much looking forward to visiting Dracoa soon."

"All in good time my dear." She smiled a faux smile that wasn't reflected in her eyes nor her glow. "Now, hurry along, Councilor Writt is waiting for you at the Holodome."

Councilor Keren kept her eyes on me as we said goodbye and left. I wished I knew what she was thinking when she looked at me with that curious, piercing gaze. I was glad to get out of the High Council office and be back on the streets of the Village. In fact, I'd be much happier being back on my side of the river where I 'belonged.' As far away from that place as possible.

# EIGHT

I DIDN'T NORMALLY LOOK FORWARD TO CLASS, but today was different. Although it would be strange without Gen there, being talked at by my teacher would help the time pass faster. I couldn't guarantee I'd focus much though. As soon as the sun had set, I'd be translocating back to Aiden. I still had so many questions for him. And I still missed him.

Piling into the classroom with the rest of the students, I sat in my normal seat and glanced over at where Gen should have been sitting. I know she had only been given her Profession a few months early, but it didn't sit right with me.

Only mere seconds after I had sat down, Ms. Haims stood at the front of the room calling my name.

"Alana Cain." I looked up in surprise. "Outside please."

Geez, what had I done wrong this time? All eyes were on me as I stood and exited the room behind Ms. Haims. A woman waited in the lobby, someone I recognized but wasn't sure where from.

"Good afternoon, Ms. Cain," the woman said, bobbing her head at me in greeting, "I have news for you."

At that point I remembered how I knew her, she worked with Mom at the Profession offices. What did she want with me?

"Is everything okay? Did something happen to my mom or brother?" I blurted out.

"No, nothing like that." She smiled sweetly. "My name is Rahila Tenor. I'm here to present you with your Profession."

I froze to the spot, and my stomach turned. Seriously? This couldn't be happening. She continued, despite the shock on my face and my inability to speak.

"This is an unusual circumstance considering you are still a half-cycle away from turning eighteen. But it has been decided that you will begin your Profession training before that happens." She glanced down at a screen in her hand. "Now, actually. Immediately."

"*Who* decided?" I asked once I found my voice again. It came out with a squeak. It had been less than a week since Shift Day and finding out we'd be staying here, and now this? Rahila looked at me with a hint of impatience but attempted to reply with an air of kindness.

"The same people who make all the decisions, dear. Now, let's see, I'm to take you to your mentor, so if you'll follow me please."

I stood rooted to the spot. This wasn't supposed to happen. Everything in the Regions ran like clockwork; the Avalon always followed the rules. Why were they being changed now? I understood why they'd be flexible for Gen, but for me? I was just a plain Gaian like the rest.

Rahila frowned at me, the kindness fading. "Now, please, Ms. Cain. The consequences for refusal to follow the orders of a Council official are high, as I'm sure you know."

I shook my head as though that would reset the day and put everything back to how it should be, and I followed her out of the edu-dome and towards the path that would lead us back down the hill. I hadn't even asked her what Profession the Council had selected for me or where we were going. It didn't really matter anyway.

I glanced back at the edu-dome as we walked around it. The place I once despised coming to for all its monotony and propaganda now seemed a haven compared to the uncertainty of my current situation. Passing the large rounded windows of the classroom opposite to the one I had been in, the classroom I should still be sat in, I saw Dray's face watching as I left. If only I could communicate a thousand words with just a look, I'd tell him I hated it here too. I'd tell him I wished that Shift Day *had* taken me somewhere else.

I followed Rahila down the hill and east across the river to the Village. Instead of walking deeper in the Village like I did this morning to meet Gen, we were walking away from it. I hadn't been to this part of Rowhill before, though it didn't seem like there was much over there. The trees on this section of the river looked older and were in a tight group which didn't help with feeling trapped. That was probably one of the reasons I avoided this place.

The path narrowed and wound its way through the woods. The sun had gone in now, hidden behind a blanket of gray cloud. Even if the sun shone, I imagined it would struggle to penetrate the thick branches above me. I shivered. Going without a coat in autumn wasn't the best idea. I should have taken Dray's offer of one, even if it had been half-hearted.

We reached a small clearing, though the trees were so thick surrounding it that the overhanging branches left no opening to view the sky. A cabin similar to Aiden's sat in the middle of the open space. A pang of longing shot through me.

Rahila hadn't said a word during the walk here. To be fair, I wouldn't know what to say to me, either. She rapped on the small wooden door three times and stood back. An older man, perhaps in his sixties, answered the door. The frown on his face wrinkled his forehead and turned down his mouth.

"What is it?" he barked at Rahila.

"Mr. Lefroy, this is your new trainee, Alana Cain," she said. He glanced at me without breaking his frown even for a second.

"No one told me I was getting a new trainee. Did no one think to tell me?" he shouted in her face.

"Umm... I'm just following orders, sir." Rahila took another small step back, put her arm around my back, and pushed me forward. "If there's a problem, you must contact the Profession offices. Good day!"

Her final words smacked of false cheer as she gave a little wave, turned around and practically ran back down the path to where we'd come from. Mr. Lefroy invited me in, with zero warmth, and I stepped inside.

It was clear once I was inside that the cabin was very different to Aiden's. While his had been cozy and homely with its warm fireplace, this one had none of that charm. The main living space looked more like an office, with two large desks lining the wall in front of the door, covered in complicated looking equipment. All flashing lights and beeping sounds. Above the desks were two huge screens, one showing fast-scrolling lines of what looked like conversations and the other showing a checklist of tasks.

Mr. Lefroy broke the silence, bringing my attention back to him. "So, I'm sure they have briefed you all about your new Profession. We'll get started straight away."

"Actually, sir, no one told me what my Profession is," I replied. "I'm not meant to get one so soon. I won't be eighteen for another half-cycle."

His face dropped the frown, and he laughed. "Looks like the Avalon have it in for you then, girl! Does that mean you don't know what this place is, who I am, or what we do here?"

I shook my head. "No, sir."

"Goodness." He rolled his eyes. "I'll have to catch you up, then."

A very lengthy explanation of this hidden cabin in the woods followed. Mr. Lefroy explained how he had been here all his life as he was an Originator for Rowhill. I couldn't think of anything worse, never getting to leave. Which was ironic considering how much I wanted to stay on Shift Day a week ago. I wondered if he ever used the Holodome, to experience more of this world than this small patch of it. Perhaps it was easier when you didn't know any different.

His job for all those cycles was 'Region Maintenance.' What seemed like a security office was just a way for him to keep on top of what needed checking on in the Region. His job involved fixing things, cleaning things, and 'keeping it pretty,' he said. And that was now my job too. I had to shadow him and help him where needed.

"I'm not getting any younger, am I? Going to have to pass on all my knowledge to some youngster at some point, aren't I," Lefroy said.

"I won't be in Rowhill forever, though," I said. "I'm not an Originator like you."

"Ah, well." He leaned back in the chair at the desk, putting his hands behind his head. "They probably have other plans for you, young lady. You never know with these Avalon folks. But for now, you help me."

"Right."

This was madness. I should be coming out of class now and going home for dinner, just like any other day. I glanced out of the window, and even though there wasn't a single patch of sky in view, I could tell that it was getting darker outside. It wouldn't be long until the time I was planning on translocating to Nordlys. I hadn't been here with Lefroy long, but I'm sure he'd continue his lessons in the morning.

"It's getting late Mr. Lefroy, I should get home. It's just the one path from here that leads back to the Village, yes?"

"Oh ho ho!" he guffawed, making me jump. "No, no, little one. You're staying here for now. Here, we work at night. No one wants things fixed, cleaned, or sorted out during the day time, do they now? We'd only get in their way, wouldn't we now!"

My face fell. Night work? How would I get to see Aiden? Lefroy didn't notice my devastated expression, either that or he ignored it, and continued blabbering on.

"All right, these here texts," he waved his hand towards the screens, "they come from a feed from those fancy High Council offices. That's where them Regionnaire lot oversee the Region. Keep people in check and so forth. These are what tells us what's going on and whatnot."

I stared at the screens, line upon line of Regionnaires' conversations flying up the screen, making me dizzy. I didn't know how he could even keep up with this lot.

"Don't worry about that one," he said, nodding his head at the fast-moving text on the first screen. "It's that other one we gotta worry about. I've got a whole list of jobs to do as you can see, so let's get to it. Get your coat."

"I don't have one, sir," I said, still staring at the screens, my vision blurring.

"I meant one of those coats." Lefroy rolled his eyes and pointed towards the tan coats hanging next to the door, each with the Region number embroidered across the back. "They'll be a little big for you, I reckon. Didn't think I'd get such a dinky lass for a trainee."

My Profession life had begun, and I started to regret wishing away all my years spent in the edu-dome. Student life was luxury compared to this, even counting all the essay writing, homework, and boring Avalon lectures. The hours dragged by slowly as we walked what seemed like the length and width of Rowhill, doing this and that. We fixed a leaking pipe in one of the original buildings in the Village and checked the electrical connections to the new domes that had been built at the Hub. We hadn't even achieved much considering how much effort it had all been. I wondered why he wasn't given the option to translocate around the Region instead of having to walk it; it made far more sense to me.

As the sun reappeared over the horizon, Lefroy dismissed me and told me to be back at the cabin the next day at sundown. I was already dreading it. Walking back home was slow going. I was exhausted, and my calves and feet ached like crazy. If only I could press a little button on a CTL and be home in a few seconds. It would be worth the discomfort of translocating over these aches.

When I got back to the home-dome, I expected Mom to be concerned, not knowing where I had been. As I collapsed down onto the couch, she did have a look of concern but not for the reason I expected.

"How was it? Your first day," she asked.

"My first *night* you mean," I replied. "You knew about it?"

"Yes, Rahila told me what was going on when she came back from taking you to your workplace."

"That dusty cabin. Yeah, great. Do *you* have any idea why they've given me my Profession a half-cycle early?" I demanded. I didn't mean to sound like I was accusing her, it wasn't her fault. She sat down next to me and wrapped an arm around my shoulders so I could lean into her and close my eyes.

"I don't know, sweetheart, I wish I did." Something in her voice didn't sound right, like there was a delicate mistruth placed there. But I was so tired, maybe I was just reading her wrong. "You best get some sleep."

"But it's morning!" I complained.

"You'll have to get used to that I'm afraid."

I made my way to my room, and after pulling the curtains across the rounded window in my room, I climbed into bed. With no time for thoughts nor dreams of Aiden to form this time, I was out like a light.

# NINE

**D**AYS AND NIGHTS PASSED with everything in reverse. I now had to sleep all day and work all night. It seemed like punishment, but I wasn't sure what for.

Lefroy told me he'd seen my Profession file and that the teachers had listed me as a hard worker—seriously?—and used to staying up later than usual during the night. Well, at least they got that part right, though I wasn't sure how they'd know that.

I asked Lefroy when I'd get time off, and all he said was that the Profession Office set my schedule. It had been a week since I'd been presented with my Profession by Rahila. One week since I started working with Lefroy, and for the whole week, I worked every damn night. He called it intensive training. I called it bullshit.

Aiden was on my mind every single day. I'd told him I'd be back. No, I'd promised him. He'd probably given up by now, and I couldn't blame him.

I didn't see Gen much now either. When she was working, I was sleeping and vice versa. She'd sent me another quick message via the screen in the home-dome, but she couldn't say much about anything in case Mom and Simeon might overhear. I thought about skipping sleep to see her at the High Council house, but to be honest, I didn't want to go back there. There was something about that place I didn't like, and as always, avoiding Councilor Keren was on the top of my list of priorities. Every time I was around her, my body launched into danger mode. Although Gen's grandmother had never done anything to me, my heart sped up and my body tensed. The potential for danger was there.

I arrived at Lefroy's cabin for my next night of work. Night after night of working without a break was taking its toll on me. My body was still adjusting to the change. In between working and sleeping, I was trying to spend as much time outside as I could, but in autumn the sun set early and the clouds were thick most days, so I still didn't get enough daylight.

I'd looked at myself in the mirror before I left and I looked a mess. Huge bags were forming under my eyes, and my skin had a slight grayish tinge to it. Every day was like walking through thick mud, just trudging through the night and waiting for it to pass.

I missed Gen. And I missed Aiden. Hell, I even missed my Mom and Simeon since I hardly saw them now. Was this what life would be like? Spending all my time with a grouchy Region-keeper?

Lefroy wasn't so bad; he was kind when he wanted to be.

Today was one day he decided to be kind. He took one look at me as I stepped through the door and tutted at me.

"Dear me, little one, I'm not sure this job here suits your fragile little self."

"What makes you say that, sir?" I asked tiredly.

"You look like shit."

Thanks, so much.

"Did next week's work schedule arrive yet?" I asked.

"Err, yeah it did… you're working every night again this coming week."

What? That had to be a mistake! Collapsing down on the seat in front of the monitors, defeated, tears formed in my eyes. I rarely cried in front of anyone, not even when Dad passed. I avoided it; I hated anyone seeing me cry. I tried my best to shove the tears back down and turned my face away from Lefroy so he didn't notice.

"I'm sorry, lass. I'm not sure why they're working you to the bone. It ain't my choice to make, you see?" The sympathy in his voice was genuine.

I didn't know why they were working me to the bone either, but my bones were feeling it.

"Listen, why don't you take tomorrow night off?" he said, and I looked up at him in surprise.

"Really?" I hadn't expected Lefroy to be the one to throw me a lifeline.

"Yeah, really. You're no good if you can't hardly walk nowhere or get nothing done are you. Maybe it's just an error on them Profession people's computers or something." The look on his face told me he didn't quite believe that. The Avalon tech was never wrong.

"Are you sure, Mr. Lefroy? We'd both get into a lot of trouble if we're found out. I don't want you to end up in Processing because of me." I bit my lip, worried that he'd change his mind. But I needed to be sure he understood the risk he was taking.

"Don't get found out then," he said, as though it were that simple. "Stay home. Don't get found by no one. The end. Now, time to work."

The night went extra slow, now that I'd have the next night off. I knew exactly what I would do with it too. I would go see

Aiden. He wouldn't be waiting for me under the tree when I got there, but I knew where to find him.

When my work night came to an end, I breathed a huge sigh of relief. My body desperately needed rest. We'd walked so far tonight; to the top of the hill in the Village to one of the Avalon Councilors' homes to fix a wiring problem, and then all the way back down to the far side of the Hub where they had started to build even more new domes and Lefroy needed to check on their progress, and back again.

I wondered if Lefroy worked at night because of what he'd first said, staying out of people's way, or if he was just trying to avoid talking to anyone. I wasn't sure that was it, because he liked to talk. He talked all the damn time to me. In hushed tones when we were out and about and in loud booming guffaws when we were in his cabin.

I waved a brief greeting to Mom when I came in and headed straight to my room to sleep. I wanted to get as much sleep as I could before tonight. It would have been nice if I'd have fallen asleep as quickly as I had every other night this week, but I was too jittery. Would Aiden even care that I'd made my way back to him?

There was a quiet knock at the door.

"Come in."

Mom cracked the door and peered around it. "I'm just making sure you're okay," she said.

I sat up in my bed and pulled the covers up around me. The tiredness coursing through me made me that much colder. "I'm tired, that's all, Mom." I sighed, the heaviness of the week catching up with me. "And I don't get it, I don't get why they're making me work through the night. Every freaking night. I'm not even eighteen yet!"

"I don't understand either." She walked into my room and sat on the edge of my bed. "I tried to speak to the head of the department at work about it, but he wouldn't discuss it with me because of resident confidentiality." She rolled her eyes. "They really are treating you as though you're eighteen now."

"Lefroy gave me the night off tomorrow. Well, tonight. Even though I'm scheduled to be working," I told her.

"Are you sure that's wise? If you're caught—"

"I know Mom. Processing," I interrupted. "That's always your biggest worry, but from what I've heard, it's not all that bad. All they'll do is change my DNA or brain structure to be more compliant. Perhaps that's what I need!" I laughed, but Mom didn't laugh with me.

"Alana." The darkness on her face was unmistakable. "You need to avoid it, at all costs." She looked me deep in the eyes with a sense of urgency and put her hand on top of mine, which was still clutching the bed covers to my chest. "I mean it. They might... I mean, you... you won't be the same person if they Process you."

Now my laughter seemed rather misplaced. It was that bad?

"Don't worry Mom, I'm just going to stay home and catch up on sleep," I lied. "No one will even notice. The only people who will know are you and Lefroy."

She tried to lift her mouth into a smile, but the worry stayed etched on her face. "Okay, just don't climb out that window again," she said, followed by a half-hearted laugh. "Otherwise I'll have to keep all of them locked!"

She said goodnight, or good morning rather as the sun was coming up, and left me to attempt to sleep.

# TEN

SEVEN HOURS OF BROKEN SLEEP was nowhere near enough, but it was all I could manage. Every time I laid down to close my eyes, Aiden's face appeared, and I'd be trying to remember how he looked down to the little detail and wondering if my memory of him was all wrong. I would find out later this evening. If I could find him. Mom's ominous words hung around me like heavy chains too. If Processing was bad enough to cause Mom such concern, was leaving Rowhill via CTL an acceptable risk?

I'd woken up only moments before Mom came back from the Village and Simeon came back from classes. I was huddled up on the sofa with a mug of hot tea when they returned. Simeon looked paler than usual as he slumped down onto the couch next to me and Mom went to the kitchen to start on the dinner.

I gently bumped Simeon's shoulder with mine. "What's up little bro? They not fixed you at the Health Center yet? Useless bunch."

He smiled and rested his head back on the seat. "Nah, not yet."

"What's up with you anyway? You've still got the headaches?"

"Headaches and problems sleeping. It's a miracle if I can get to sleep these days, and when I do," he took a deep breath, "I get nightmares."

"Nightmares?" I repeated. The Avalon had all the races pretty much healthy since they arrived here with their fancy tech. It was unusual to hear of someone being unwell. Why weren't they sorting Simeon's issues out?

"Yeah," he replied. "Bad dreams. Dark stuff. Anyway, it doesn't matter. They're doing more tests and connecting me up to machines and all that. If anyone can figure me out, it's the Avalon."

Before I could reply with something condescending towards our overseers, there was a short rap at the door. Mom called from the kitchen for one of us to answer it, and I figured as I was the one in good health, I'd jump up and do it. I opened the door to find Dray standing there, the strong autumn wind blowing his coat around him.

"Can I come in or are you just going to stare at me?" he asked with a laugh. I stood back to let him through the doorway as he slammed the door behind him.

"The weather here is awful, how can you stand it?" He shuddered and took his coat off as Mom came out of the kitchen to greet our unexpected guest.

"Good evening Dray, I'm so glad you could make it."

*Oh, not unexpected then?* I glanced between Dray, Simeon, and Mom.

"Didn't have much else to do to be honest Mrs. Cain. Thanks for inviting me."

"Call me Cal, please."

Simeon didn't look as surprised as I was, so perhaps Mom

had already told him she'd invited our new neighbor to dinner. I kept quiet, not wanting to seem either rude or idiotic yet again.

"Did you find your coat yet, Alana?" Dray asked. *Oh great, small talk.* "Looks like you'll need it," he said, nodding to the blustery view out of the window.

"Not yet," I replied. "But hopefully soon."

Dinner was more awkward than usual, for me at least. Mom used to invite people over for dinners when Dad was still around, especially newcomers to whatever Region we were in at the time. But since he died, it was usually just the three of us. Mom chatted away to our guest, and Simeon kept to himself. I still couldn't figure Dray out. Every time I'd seen him, he'd acted differently towards me. Who knew what he'd be like tonight? My mind jumped between the conversation around the table and thoughts of translocating to see Aiden again. I hoped Dray wouldn't stay long and make me miss the opportunity.

"How are you finding it here in Rowhill, Dray? Have you settled okay?" Mom asked, ever the polite hostess.

"It's cold, but it'll do," he replied, and I noted the gentle lilt in his voice that I hadn't noticed before. "I'll get used to it though, I'm sure."

"It's only going to get colder," Mom said. "The days are getting shorter and the nights are darker."

"You're right. They are."

Mom and Dray continued their dinner-time conversation as though they'd known each other for years rather than little more than a week. I answered when spoken to, but otherwise I simply observed. Dray really was like a different person every time, and I wondered which was the real him. The brusque guy I met that day crossing the river? Or this friendly, small-talking guy sat at the dinner table with us. I determined that he was the type of person who didn't hide how he was feeling, and tonight it was clear that he was much more relaxed than when I'd previously bumped into him. He had a deep, rumbling laugh that you couldn't help but smile or laugh along with. Dray told us about the other Regions he had lived in and how he had spent a good number of years in one Region. A warmer one, as he loved to keep reminding us, where he had been lucky enough to grow up surrounded by quite a few family members. He'd had a few cousins he grew up with there, which was extremely rare. He described it so beautifully, I could practically feel the heat of the sun beating down on me from the way he talked.

As Mom got up to clear the table and Simeon joined her, still quiet and pale, Dray turned his attention towards me.

"Tell me, Alana, which has been your favorite Region so far?"

"This one," I replied without hesitation, "Rowhill. I wish we never had to leave." My mind flew to Nordlys, and it surprised me that I didn't think of there first. Even if I had, I couldn't have used that as an answer anyway. No one could know I had been to Nordlys, I was never meant to have been there.

"I think Rowhill might end up being my favorite too."

"Didn't you just say it was too cold here?"

"There are things about this place that make up for the terrible weather." My eyes met his, and he looked at me with an intensity I hadn't expected. Perhaps it was just the violet that made it seem that way. Regardless, the heat rose in my cheeks, and I smiled at the man from the bridge.

Mom and Simeon came back into the room, breaking the moment, and a twinge of guilt hit me. Had Dray been flirting with me? No, surely not. I brushed the thought aside as I sat down on the rug on the floor next to my brother. We only had the one two-seater couch, which Mom and Dray sat on. Simeon sighed a sad sigh which must have been almost involuntary as he genuinely looked surprised when we all stared at him.

"Is everything all right Simeon?" Mom asked. He shrugged and took a minute to reply.

"Yeah, I just… don't feel great," he said, hesitating. We all naturally left a gap for him to continue. "Things feel tense around Rowhill recently."

"What do you mean?" Mom responded.

"With all the Regionnaires around, even during the day. The teachers start our classes with the Region-rules now, and they never used to do that. They practically make us chant them," he groaned.

"There are definitely more Regionnaires in Rowhill than in other Regions I've been in," said Dray.

"Yeah, well, it makes me nervous." Simeon wrung his hands together, staring down at them. "And," he took another big sigh before he continued, "my friend Elodie, they took her for Processing yesterday."

Mom sat more alert than before, her tension filling the space between us all.

"They did? What for?" she asked.

"She didn't get home in time for curfew. She only arrived back at her home-dome five minutes late, and they found her and took her straight away. Why would they do that? She's just a kid, she's only fourteen." Simeon shook his head, in both sadness and anger.

I knew how he felt, and my heart ached for him. I'd had a friend who had been Processed in our Region before Rowhill, and it had been awful. One day, they're the person you know. The next, they're almost someone else. It's rare for kids to go through Processing, so it surprised me that both of us had experienced that happening to a friend.

"She'll be fine, Simeon, I'm sure she will," Mom said, giving quite a different message to my brother compared to the one she gave me about Processing. "Though it serves to remind us, we *must* follow the rules here. They're stricter here compared to the other Regions we've been in, but if we keep our heads down and do as we're told, it will be okay." She stood up again, never one to sit down for long at all. "We'll be okay," she finished.

Dray shifted uncomfortably in his seat and then stood up too. As much as he wore his feelings on his sleeve, I don't think he was used to seeing it from other people. Curfew was about to begin, and so he said his goodbyes and made his way back to his dome. It didn't make sense to me that he'd been given a family sized dome for just one person, and I wondered if he was lonely there by himself.

The evening was over, but for me it was just about to begin. I turned back to Simeon, who was still sitting on the floor, with his head in his hands massaging his temples. I reached out a hand to him, to help him up.

"Don't worry, Simeon. You'll see your friend soon," I reassured him as I only just about managed to heave him up from the floor. I wanted to give him a hug, but a distance had grown between my brother and I in the past few years. A distance that sneaked up on me without us realizing. We were such different people and dealt with life in such different ways, it was hard to relate to him.

"I don't know if she'll be the same, though," he replied, sadness creeping over his face.

Simeon didn't do so well with change; he didn't find it easy to go with the ebb and flow like Mom and I did. Dad's death was hard on all of us, but it was especially difficult for my brother. He had spent a lot of time with Dad; he even wanted to follow in his Profession footsteps as a medical expert, if they would let him. I wanted to comfort Simeon, but I didn't know how. Mom was better at that than I was; she always had the right things to say. Or a plate of cookies to make life a little sweeter.

Simeon sucked in a sharp breath through his teeth as he pressed his palm to his forehead.

"Geez, how long have you been having these headaches? Can't the Medi's fix you up?" I asked him, a concerned frown forming on my own face.

"Only a few weeks or so. They're getting worse all the time, though. Mom is taking me back there tonight; they're going to monitor my brain activity while I sleep or something. That's gonna be fun, trying to sleep in a lab room wired up to a load of machines." He dramatically rolled his eyes and smiled. "Don't worry about me, honestly. You've got your own drama going on. How does it feel to be eighteen before you're actually eighteen?"

I laughed. "Being 'eighteen' sucks! They couldn't have given me a Profession that suited me less, it's crazy."

"You never know," he said. "If they've given you your Profession early, they might force you to couple with someone early too." Simeon grinned. "Some old, bald dude who no one else wants." We laughed together, something I'd missed over the past few weeks, and I gently elbowed him in the side.

"Just let them try!"

"Well you better pick someone quick then! How about Dray?" Simeon smirked.

"God, why does everyone keep suggesting that?" I said, making a face at my brother.

"Because he's the right age and not a bad guy maybe?"

"You think so?" I asked. "I can't work him out."

"Mom seems to trust him and get on with him. That's a good sign, right?" Simeon laughed. "I'm just messing with you, Alana, don't be so sensitive. You've got loads of time."

The seed planted by Gen a few weeks ago began to grow,

and I hastily shoved it back down with my cheeks burning. I was going to see Aiden tonight; I couldn't have thoughts of Dray in my head! Not in that way at least.

Mom and Simeon left for the Medical Center for his tests, and I hoped that he'd come back with answers this time. I hated the thought of my little brother having to endure more nightmares or pain.

At least I had the perfect opportunity to translocate to Aiden without my family getting caught up in it. Although Mom would be back at some point, I'd told her that I would be sleeping again by the time she returned, so I crossed my fingers that she wouldn't check up on me.

I peered out of the round window in my room. The sun had already gone down. I had passed the *sun down* window the note had said I should follow. Though it wouldn't make much of a difference; the time had only been set the first time so that Aiden would find me.

I dressed for the weather this time. Nordlys would only get colder as the weeks went by, just like Rowhill was. I wore thick socks inside walking boots and a cozy sweater underneath the coat Lefroy had given me. I didn't know how far I'd have to walk to find Aiden, if he wasn't in his cabin. Where would I look if I didn't find him there? My legs protested at the thought of walking more after over a week of traipsing the Region for work.

My heart fluttered and my chest tightened as I rummaged for the CTL under my mattress. The talk at dinner had worried me. More Regionnaires checking up on what we were doing was a bad thing. What if I got caught this time? What if I got there and couldn't find Aiden and I had to sit in the rain and hide for two hours? What if I got there, found him, and he'd changed his mind about his feelings?

I tried to suppress the negative thoughts bombarding me. It wasn't like I was going to give up and not go back to Nordlys; that wasn't even an option. My determination kicked in, and I flipped the lid open once I had retrieved the CTL. I'd been checking the device every morning after my Profession shift to make sure it was still working. Today was no different. It still displayed the same line of numbers and letters on the screen. This would be my fourth translocation, and I was thankful that it got easier each time. At least, the actual translocation got easier. The situation surrounding it didn't. I didn't waste any more time in worrying as I hit the button once more. As long as I could get to Aiden, it would all be fine.

# ELEVEN

**M**Y EYES REFOCUSED; I was back under the tree in Nordlys. It wasn't raining, fortunate since I hadn't considered preparing for that despite last time. I looked up at the clear sky. There wasn't a cloud in sight, and the entire expanse was full of stars. No Region I had lived in had ever had a sky covered in stars like that. It took my breath away. Distracted by the beauty above me, I almost missed the sound of leaves being scuffed around on the bottom of boots.

I turned around and there he was. Waiting.

Aiden.

He stood leaning against the trunk of the tree, looking down at the ground.

Looking up as I appeared from nowhere, his face lit up, reflecting the same smile that was also on my face. I threw myself forward towards him in a half-run. I couldn't believe he was here! His arms wrapped around my waist as mine flung around his neck and he pulled me close to him. My breath was taken away again. What should, in theory, have been awkward, this kind of close encounter with a man I've only spent mere hours with, was the most natural and beautiful thing in the world.

Not letting go of me, he nuzzled his face into my hair. "You're late."

I laughed and pulled backwards. His arms stayed locked around my waist and so I kept my arms where they were. With his body and face closer to mine than ever before, I tried to compose myself and not stumble over my words like an idiot.

I smiled. "I can't believe you're here."

"I've been here every single night since you left. It's been kind of cold."

"Warmer now?" I asked.

"Much warmer." He rested his forehead on mine and closed his eyes.

And it was. In fact, there was a strange warmth that had started in my chest right where my heart was, and it was spreading, spiraling outwards through the rest of me like an electrical current. I put it down to this being the closest I'd been to a guy in, well, ever. And Aiden was no ordinary guy.

"We can't stay here," he murmured, releasing me a little.

"I wish we could."

In one smooth movement, he let go of my waist and spun me around so I was at his side, grabbing hold of my hand. "Come on." He put his finger to his lips to remind me to be quiet in case anyone was around. It was unlikely there would be as it was much later than normal, but then I wasn't sure of the curfew rules in Nordlys. Everything was different here.

When we arrived at his cabin, Aiden was still clasping my hand, as though making sure I didn't disappear again.

"You'll have to let go at some point," I laughed. He smiled, lifted my hand up to his face to kiss it like he had last time I was here and let go.

"Make yourself at home, I have to go check on something."

He disappeared out of the front door before I could say anything or even ask where he was going. His cabin didn't look much different compared to my last visit, although he'd made the bed this time. I smiled. Maybe he was trying to impress me.

Stoking the fire in the black box in the wall, though I didn't know what I was doing at all, kept me occupied for the shortest time as I was waiting for him to come back. Now that Aiden wasn't here commanding my attention, I noticed more about his home. It was clear that he'd been living here a while, this place just felt infused with *Aiden*. As I wandered around the room, I noticed a frame holding a photograph by the side of his bed which I picked up. The image showed a man and a woman standing behind three small children. The woman had Aiden's warm eyes and the man had his dark, wavy hair. These were his parents. The smallest child of the three was him. He looked shy and reserved as he tucked himself close to his mother, letting his brother and sister take the spotlight. He looked happy, though, and his smile hadn't changed a bit.

The door opened, and I returned the photo frame before he had walked through it, I didn't want Aiden to think I was going through his things. Even though I kind of was.

"Sorry, I had to make sure the others were in their cabins and not outside. They got chatty." He reached out his hand again. "Come with me, I've got something I want to show you."

Taking my hand in his, he led me out of the cabin, and we walked in the opposite direction to the fir tree and the Holodome. Skirting around the edge of the cabins, far away enough that the dark enveloped us, I wondered why this felt so familiar. Of course! I'd been here before; in the Holodome. He was taking me up the other side of the valley through the thick trees. We walked further along the tree line than I had when I was in the Holodome, which brought us to a narrow path that led through the trees. Now we were far away enough from the cabin cluster to not be overheard, we could talk.

"This is the way I go to work most days. Trying to get through the trees is hard work, so we always take this path even if it takes a little longer," he said.

This place reminded me of home, of the trees hiding Mr. Lefroy's cabin. I threw a little gratitude up to the heavens for that man, who was the only reason I could make it back here.

"Where are we going?" I asked, without an ounce of apprehension. I knew wherever Aiden would take me, I'd be safe.

"You'll see." He smiled. "I'm sure you'll like it."

"I'm sure I will, too." I'd like *anywhere* if it was with him.

The trees thinned out as we reached the crest of the hill. I looked behind me, remembering from my time in the Holodome that I'd be able to see down into the valley from here. He stopped as I did and looked back, too. The Holodome stood out, standing alone. I could see our tree, too. Beyond the valley that the cabins stood in were more trees. It was a dense forest, beautiful but with an air of danger. I wondered how far you'd have to walk to come across another Region.

"We're almost there, come on." He started walking again, and I followed, still holding onto his hand. I knew where he was taking me now. To the lights.

As we passed over the top of the hill and could see into the valley on the other side, again full of trees, the sky had burst into life on the horizon. It was even more beautiful than it had been at the Holodome. The Northern Lights danced across the sky, in all the colors you could possibly imagine. They ran in gentle oscillating waves, with such grace that I couldn't believe what I was seeing. When I turned to look at him, he wasn't watching the lights; he was watching me.

"I knew you'd like it," he said.

"What are they?" I asked, entranced.

"It's the Aurora Borealis. It's complicated, science stuff," he answered, and he winked at me.

"Excuse me? 'Science stuff?'" I tore my eyes from the sky and put on a mock offended tone. "You don't think I'd understand 'science stuff?' I'm terribly smart, you know!"

Aiden laughed. "Oh, so you already know all about atmospheric gases, the ionization and excitation of atmospheric constituents, geomagnetic storms and the solar wind disruption of the magnetosphere?" He smirked.

I stared at him with a blank look for a moment and then we both laughed.

"All right, all right," I said, "so maybe I don't understand the science stuff. How do you know so much about it?"

"Our work here revolves around these lights."

He pointed into the distance where sitting atop the hill was another dome. It surprised me that I hadn't noticed it when I was at the Holodome viewing Nordlys, but I supposed I had been so distracted by the beauty of the… what was it again? The aurora?

"That's where we work. The lights aren't just pretty, they're full of energetic information we have to extract." I looked at him, confused, and he laughed. "Yeah, I don't fully understand it yet either. I'm still learning!"

"It's more pretty than science-y, let's leave it at that," I said with a smile, and I watched the aurora dance again.

"Although, fun fact, they never used to be this bright or colorful. Before the Reclaim and before the Cataclysm, they were much dimmer. Sometimes they were barely visible," he said.

He was the teacher, and I was the student. I wondered why they could be seen here and not in other Regions, but I didn't ask. I didn't want the science to overshadow the beauty and romance of it all.

Aiden let go of my hand and moved to stand behind me. He wrapped his arms around me, crossing my chest to rest on my shoulders and I leaned back into him. I could have stayed here forever. But we didn't have forever. We only had two hours.

I yawned, which made him laugh again. "Time to rest?" he asked.

"I can't even tell you how tired I am. No matter how much sleep I get, I'm still tired."

We headed back down into the valley, towards the cabins, hand in hand again. I told Aiden about being given my Profession early and how unexpected it was. About Lefroy and how, even though the Profession Office were trying to destroy me by working me to the bone, he let me have a night off.

"So, half a cycle early they give you your Profession that just so happens to be night work?"

"Yeah," I answered, wearily.

"Which happened to be just after you translocate here to meet me, which stops you coming to see me again."

"Yeah?"

"Doesn't it seem a little strange?" he questioned.

"What do you mean?"

"What if they're doing it to you on purpose, to stop you seeing me?"

"It can't be that. No one knows I've translocated here." But that wasn't true. There was one person who knew. Gen. But she wouldn't have told anyone... would she?

"Does anyone know you're here?" he asked.

I considered bending the truth, I didn't want to make him worry. But more than that, if I told him about Gen, I didn't want him to think I had been lying to him the whole time.

"Well, yeah, I told my best friend. Genevieve. But I'm sure

she wouldn't have told anyone else. She knows the risks!"

Aiden looked unsure, which I understood. But he didn't know Gen like I did. Saying that, she didn't seem quite so... Gen-like these days. Especially the last time I saw her at the High Council house.

"I hope she didn't tell anyone. I can't bear the thought of you getting hurt because of this. Because of coming to see me."

"Hurt? They won't hurt me. The worst they'd do is put me through Processing."

"Processing can hurt," he interrupted, his tone serious and concerned. "It changes who you are deep down. I've seen it."

"I'll be careful. We'll both be careful."

As we reached the perimeter of the cabin cluster again, we had to revert to silence once more. We crept to his cabin where the fire had gone out. Aiden switched on one of the battery powered lights and collapsed down on the couch. It had been a long week for him too.

"I'm sorry it's cold," he said. I sat down next to him, lifting my feet up and tucking them underneath me as I leaned into his body. As I placed the knitted blanket across us, his hand was on my shoulder and he pulled me closer.

He kissed the top of my head, which sent dancing waves of happiness right through me. We huddled together, sharing each other's warmth.

"I'm glad you came back Alana," he said sleepily.

"Me too..."

Laying my head on his chest, my curls spilling across him, I closed my eyes. I didn't care where in the world anyone tried to send me. I knew this, right here... this was my real home.

# TWELVE

**M**Y EYES SPRANG OPEN. What was that beeping sound? My head was foggy, and the sound was getting faster. My head still rested on Aiden's chest, his eyes still closed. One of his hands rested on my shoulder, the other intertwined with one of mine.

The CTL! I took it out of my pocket, lifted the lid, and peered at the screen with my bleary eyes. Surely our time couldn't be up already.

It *was* time. The CTL screen jumped to life, and the translocation began. I hadn't even been able to say goodbye.

"Aiden!" The breeze swirled into a gale, by which time he had woken up from his sleep too and was looking at me wild-eyed.

"What?" was all he managed to say before the pressure built and the translocation was complete.

We were back in my room at the home-dome.

Both of us.

We sat in silence for a minute, taking in what the hell had just happened. He had translocated with me. We had been holding hands. Skin contact; we had been cellularly connected. Panic immediately set in.

"Where are we?" Aiden exclaimed.

"Shhhh!" I hushed, "Mom and Simeon are probably here!"

"We're in *your* Region?" He seemed panicked, and I needed him to be the calm, strong one right now. "How am I going to get back?"

Looking around my room, I wished that I had at least cleaned up. I hadn't been expecting guests! He laughed at me frantically picking up clothes from the floor and kicking shoes under my bed and then covered his mouth as my eyes flew up at him. I put my finger to my lips telling him to be quiet. I stayed quiet in Nordlys; how come he wouldn't stay quiet in my Region?

I stood still, facing him, and took a deep breath. "We'll figure this out, I'm sure we will. It will be fine," I whispered, unconvinced.

The door to my bedroom flung open. It was Mom. Oh god, how was I going to explain this? "Mom! I… I errr…" I mumbled, racking my brain for a logical explanation to give her.

"There's no *time* for that Alana. He's not supposed to be here. What were you thinking?" she shouted.

*Wait, what?*

"Give me the CTL, now!"

I couldn't move quick enough for her as she was waving a hand out in front of me. How the hell did she know about the CTL? Passing her the device, she flipped open the lid and frantically pressed buttons in what seemed like a random order.

"Mom?" I leaned in towards her, trying to get her attention, but she was engrossed in whatever it was she was doing, pressing buttons like a woman possessed.

When she stopped, she faced Aiden, who was standing

silently, looking rather uncomfortable. She grabbed his hand and shoved the CTL in it, still open.

"I wish there was time to explain, Aiden, but you must leave, *immediately.* Speak to Hilroy, tell him Cal said to tell you everything. Go!"

She pressed the activating button as I fought the urge to snatch the CTL out of her hands so that she couldn't send him away. Grabbing me by the shoulders, she pulled me backwards away from him. Leaving Aiden had never been easy, but this time it was me who had to watch him disappear rather than the other way around. *So this is how it feels.* And this time, I didn't know when I'd see him again, or if I ever would. Our one small mistake had changed everything. His eyes met mine as the wind blew around him, mirroring my misery, and my heart lurched. If I could just jump into the invisible bubble with him and grab his hand, I could translocate back to Nordlys with him.

Mom's grip on my shoulders was strong enough to resist the urge and stop me being reckless. If I had been alone with him, I would have done it. Without hesitation. I clenched my fists at my sides. It wouldn't solve anything even if I did go with him. It was a cruel joke for the universe to bring Aiden and I together only for us to have to be separated constantly. Tears filled my eyes, but I did my best to hold myself together rather than fall apart entirely. I would have given anything to go with him. Anything.

But in the briefest of moments, he was gone. The only thing left behind was the knitted blanket laying on my bed, the one that had been keeping us warm. Standing watching the aurora seemed like forever ago.

"Alana. ALANA!" Mom shouted, snapping me out of my trance as I'd been staring at the spot where Aiden had stood. "Follow me, we need to talk."

By the time Mom walked through to the living room, she had already calmed to her usual serene self. I wish I knew how she did that. Was she actually calm or just well-practiced at putting on a front? My heart was still pounding, ready to run. We sat down, but I didn't know what to say to her. I had a thousand questions. How did she know I had the CTL? Why wasn't she surprised to see a boy in my room? She even knew his name! How did she know about Mr. Hilroy? But I didn't know how to begin. I stared out of the window, in a state of shock, until Mom's hand found mine.

"Alana," she started, and I looked at her. I'd been hiding all of this from her, how did she know? "This will be quite a lot to take in."

"I don't understand, Mom. The CTL, how did you know I had it?"

"Because I was the one who gave it to you."

My mind flew back a few weeks to the day I had found the CTL, the day before the Shift. It had appeared in my coat pocket out of nowhere. It had to have come from somewhere, but from Mom? I thought Councilor Keren or Audelia Portbury had put it there, but I hadn't taken any time to investigate it further because I was so keen to get out. To have an adventure.

The adventure just got way more complicated.

"*You* put it in my coat?" I asked. "But... why?"

Mom gave a big sigh, laid her head back on the seat and rubbed her hands down her face. She was stressed. "Because it was my job to."

"What does that even mean?" What the hell? Mom wasn't usually this vague.

"I don't know how much to tell you without causing you too much of a burden. Or without... making things... difficult." She seemed torn, it was written all over her face. But I wished she'd give it to me straight and stop treating me like a child.

"Please Mom, tell me. Why did you give me the CTL? Why did I have to find Aiden?"

"We believe he is your other half, your Mirror Soul."

Gen had got it right? Did she already know?

"I thought Mirror Souls were a myth. And who is *we*?" The questions wanted to roll out of me now like an avalanche, but I held them back, trying to keep a level head. If Mom could do it, then so could I. But I felt shaky, I needed information that would steady me. I doubted any answers she gave would provide that.

"By *we*, I mean the Midorians," she answered, one of my questions at least.

"You're working with the Midorians?" I yelled, and she shushed me, looking uneasy.

"Yes. I'm part of the Midorian Intervention. We're determined to make the Avalon accountable for what they've done and what they're doing."

What the Avalon were doing? Midorian Intervention? This was wrong, all wrong. Mom worked for the Avalon Council; she was an outstanding citizen without a blemish to her record. Unprocessed. Never in trouble. Perfect wife, perfect mother, perfect neighbor. And now I'm finding out she's a *rebel*?

I tried to suck in a deep breath, but the air seemed thin. My heart was racing, and my muscles tensed. I stood up and paced the floor, trying to stifle the need to run out of the home-dome and never come back. Maybe I could find a way through to the Wild and live out there. Perhaps Gen would come with me; she couldn't be happy working with her grandmother. No, that was a dumb idea. I'd never survive out there, even with Gen with me. I tried to push the irrational thoughts to the back of my mind.

Mom had given me the CTL. Mom made me find Aiden. The news was slowly sinking in, but the questions kept coming.

"Why though? Why are you working with *them?* Why am I only just finding out about this now? Were you ever going to tell me any of this?" I sickened at the thought. My stomach turned, and my heart hurt. Were my feelings for Aiden real or had they somehow been, I don't know, manufactured? I didn't know what Mirror Souls were, or *how* they were. "So, I'm being used?" I asked.

She stood up, too. With hurt from my accusation all over her face, she stood in front of me and put her hands on my shoulders.

"Anything I have ever kept from you has *only* been to keep you safe. Things aren't what they seem. It may seem like we live in a utopia with everything perfectly laid out for us, but there are deeper things at work. Things that affect all of us."

"You're talking in riddles, Mom. You haven't even answered my questions!"

"Alana, you needed to find Aiden on your own. It would have happened eventually, but we gave you a little push." She released my shoulders and stepped back. "To be honest, I'm surprised you used the CTL by yourself. I wasn't expecting you to be so brave and jump straight in."

"I surprised myself." Her compliment calmed me a little, but I wasn't sure why. From what she was saying, it sounded like they've dragged me into an uprising against the Avalon. Oh god! I hadn't signed up for that! My heart rate that had calmed slightly peaked again. I wondered if anyone had outright asked me to sign up for that whether I would have. No!

"Does anyone else know about, you know, this Midorian business you're involved in? Does Simeon know?" I asked.

"The only person who knew was your father." She paused and stared down at the ground.

So my father had secrets, too. Was that why he was gone? They told me he had died in an emergency surgery at the

Medical Center. They hadn't let me see his body, but I was only nine cycles old, so of course they would lie to me. I couldn't bring myself to ask Mom about what had really happened to Dad. This day had been stressful enough.

I sat back down, and Mom followed. I shut my eyes tight and took a deep breath.

"What is a Mirror Soul?" I asked, the question weighing heaviest on my mind now. Aiden and I were only just getting to know each other, and now we had this label over our heads. Except I had no clue what it meant.

"That's quite the question, and I won't have all the answers, but I'll do my best." Mom mirrored my deep breath and clasped her hands in her lap as though to compose herself and pull up knowledge that was rarely spoken of.

"No one knows how Mirror Souls came to be," she started. "They've always been around, to some extent, we believe. In the past they've been known as different things. Soul mates. Twin flames. But since the Cataclysm and the Reclaim, with the Avalon taking control of Gaia, they've been appearing exponentially. Mirror Souls are two people who share an exceptionally strong energetic connection. One that cannot be broken, and one that has profound effects on both the Souls, and on the people around them. It's not always a romantic thing, there are sometimes Mirror Souls who are friends, or even family members. But often, it's the way you have experienced it with Aiden."

"How do you know what I've experienced with Aiden?" I interrupted.

She smiled. "I see it on your face, and the way you are. How torn you were when I made him leave. I've seen it before. No, I've felt it before. I was a Mirror Soul too."

"You and Dad?" Surely I would have noticed something like

that? Even as a child! She looked down at the floor again and nodded. My father was gone too, and unlike Aiden, there was no chance of him coming back.

"Your father and I kept our Mirror Soul secret well hidden," she said. "But you and Aiden have to be careful."

"What do you mean?" We'd already tried to be careful, but not careful enough considering I had accidentally translocated back here with him.

"When two Mirror Souls are together, they create an energy surge. Unseen, but very much detectable if someone is looking for it. If you're together too long, that energy surge *will* be noticed, and they will come for you. That's why the CTL was configured to bring you home after two hours, to avoid the surge."

Confused, I shook my head. "Mom, you're not making any sense. Energy surges? And who will come for us?"

"The Avalon. You're a threat to them."

Great, so not only was I now being dragged into an uprising, I'm now a threat to the enemy?

"What kind of threat could we possibly be? We're just... we're just friends. We just hang out!"

Before she had the chance to answer, there was a fast, heavy knock at the door. Mom glanced at me, eyes full of worry, and went to open it. It was Ableman, again. Mom's body relaxed a little, this was one visitor she was used to getting.

"Listen Archie, I can't talk right now —"

"Caliza Cain, you are to come with me. Please." He added the request on the end, as though he were trying to appease her, but he was here for another reason. He was doing his job.

"Oh." Mom tensed again.

"The High Council demands your presence."

"But it's so late, can't it wait until morning?" she asked.

Pleaded.

"I'm afraid not."

Our conversation was over, and the rest of my questions would have to wait.

"I'll get my coat." She shut the door on Ableman, leaving him to wait outside. She looked panicked, and seeing that look on my mother's usually calm face ramped up the tension in my chest. She took both of my hands in hers.

"There's a spare CTL, I hid it in the large yellow jar at the top of the right-hand cupboard in the kitchen." We had CTLs hidden all over our home-dome now? "It's already pre-programmed to get you to Aiden. Go there. Now. As soon as I've gone."

"But what about Simeon?"

"He's fine, he'll be in the Medical Center until the tests are done." She grasped my hand. "Don't worry about Simeon, he's in… good hands. You need to focus now. Get to Aiden. Speak to Hilroy, tell him the High Council have taken me in. He has to protect you now."

"Protect me? What? Mom, you'll be okay, won't you?" I stammered, heart racing.

"I don't know." Ableman knocked on the door again, louder this time. "Get to Aiden and Hilroy, hopefully they can help. But *don't* stay with Aiden for longer than two hours Alana, they'll find you. Just like they found your father."

My heart stopped as she hugged me tight, took her coat, and left with Ableman.

I stood in the living room for a few minutes. Part of me wanted to go back, back to the day before the Shift. Where all I had to worry about was if we would stay in Rowhill. Where I'd sit in Gen's room and wonder what life had in store for us. What the Avalon had in store for us.

Now I knew what life had in store for me. Or at least, I had a vague idea. And I wasn't sure I liked it. But there was no going back, I just had to move forward and hope that somehow, I wouldn't take a wrong step.

# THIRTEEN

I RUMMAGED THROUGH JARS in the kitchen cupboards until I found it, the hidden CTL. I wasted no time in using it to get back to Aiden. There were no nerves this time, no apprehension. Just pure panic.

Aiden wasn't waiting for me under the tree, but I already knew he wouldn't be. He wouldn't have a clue that I'd be coming back, considering he'd only just been sent back to Nordlys. Alone.

Pulling my hood tightly over my head, I ran down the path that led to Aiden's cabin cluster. There were no lights shining through his windows, no sign of life at all. I tapped lightly on his door. No answer. I tapped once more, louder this time. Nothing. Dammit, I didn't have time to be searching Nordlys for him! Surely he couldn't be asleep by now, not after everything that just happened. I peered through a window, but there was only darkness.

The moon shone brightly, making it easier for me to find my way but also making it easier for anyone to spot me. I kept close to the shadow of Aiden's cabin and walked around to the other side to see the rest of the cabins. Most of them were in darkness like his, except for one.

Keeping to any dark spots I could find, I made my way over to the lit window. Pressing my body against the dark, wooden wall, I angled my head so that I could peer inside. It took a while for my eyes to adjust to the brightness of the room but once they did; I saw him. Aiden was pacing the room, talking to a man sitting in a large armchair, legs crossed and holding a screen in his hand. Maybe this was Hilroy? If it wasn't, and I knocked on the door…

I had to take the risk. I only had two hours; there wasn't time to wait around for Aiden to finish talking and come out. I knocked on the door and held my breath.

The man opened the door and sucked a breath of air in through his teeth. "Quick, quick, in you come," he whispered, ushering me into the cabin. "You must be Alana."

As the man said my name, Aiden practically shouted it at the same time. It was music to my ears. The time we had been apart had been the shortest so far, but it had felt like the longest. He pulled me into an embrace that made all the anxious tension in my body disappear with relief.

He put a hand on each side of my face, sending waves of warmth through me and making my skin tingle. "Are you all right? Is everything okay? What happened?"

"I'm okay, I think." Pulling his hands down from my face, I rested my forehead against his, just for a moment. If only we had more time. I turned to the man. "Are you Mr. Hilroy?"

He nodded. "Just call me Hilroy. Why did you come here?" he asked. "It's not safe for you here."

"It's not safe at home either," I replied sadly. "A Regionnaire took Mom to the High Council. She told me to come back here."

"How did you get back here if Aiden used your CTL?"

I pulled the other CTL from my pocket, which he snatched out of my hand.

"Dammit, they can probably track this," Hilroy said.

Before I could reassure him that it wasn't trackable, he took a screwdriver from the small wooden side table and pried the back of the device open, yanking at the wires inside. There went my way out of Nordlys!

Aiden took hold of my hand and squeezed it gently as Hilroy sat back down in the armchair and put his head in his hands.

"This wasn't the way this should have played out. This is not good… not good at all," he mumbled to himself.

"Why do I get the distinct impression that we've been dragged into some kind of messed up game?" I demanded. "These are people's lives you're messing with! We want nothing to do with a fight between the races. They've probably taken Mom for Processing, and I still have way more questions than answers!"

Aiden put his hand on my arm to calm me, but fear for my mother coursed through me like a raging river. I'd already lost one parent; I wouldn't lose the other.

"This is not a game, Alana, we realize that! Don't underestimate how complex this all is." Hilroy stood up again. He was as troubled as Aiden and me. As he stood closer to the fire, his eyes glowed violet in the light.

"You're Midorian," I stated.

"Yes," was his brief retort.

"Then tell me, why are you dragging Gaians into your rebellion against the Avalon? Why can't you leave us out of this?" I fumed.

His face flashed with anger, but he suppressed it.

"Because this affects all of us, the whole of Gaia. You don't understand what's going on, and I can't even begin to explain it all, especially being on a time limit. You two are a ticking time bomb. If you stay here together too long, they'll come for you. I need you both to understand that we *need* you. The Midorians need you. You can change the future of this planet."

Tonight had taken such a turn. I thought back to how it had begun, with Aiden holding me close as we watched the aurora filling the sky. His body warming mine and feeling like there was nowhere else I'd rather be.

And now... now we were weapons in a war. Except we didn't understand how or why.

I turned to Aiden. "Do you understand any of this? Did you *know* about any of this?"

He put his hands up in the air in defense. "I don't have a clue about any of it! I know as much as you do. I wouldn't have lied to you!"

I didn't know what to believe anymore. My own parents had been keeping secrets from me; who knew how deep the lies would go. Sheer exhaustion hit me so I sat down on the closest seat I could find, a small wooden stool, and sighed heavily. All I wanted to do was be at home, fall asleep, and wake up to realize it had all been a dream.

"What do you want from us?" I asked Hilroy.

"As I was just explaining to Aiden, the energy surge you two can create together would be useful to—"

Exasperated at the general lack of sane answers I was getting tonight, I interrupted. "For god's sake, energy surges? Mom mentioned those too. I've never heard of anything like that!"

Hilroy opened his mouth to answer when there was a knock at the door. Could we not just be left in peace for once today? Aiden took me by the hand and pulled me into the kitchen as Hilroy gestured at us to hide and stay quiet. We stood by the closed door, trying to hear what was going on.

"We have to get out of here," Aiden whispered.

"And go where?" I whispered back, frustrated.

"Away from here. We need to leave, now."

I pressed my ear up to the door to see if I could hear anything. As soon as I recognized the words '… take a look around…' I knew exactly what or who they were looking for.

"They're here for us!" I hissed.

"How do they even know we're here?" he whispered, panicked.

I pointed at the window, which Aiden took no time at all in opening, letting me climb through first. He followed and took my hand again, and we ran, getting a decent head start before they spotted us. The moonlight was doing us no favors tonight, and there was a shout behind us.

Regionnaires!

"Where are we going?" I shouted at Aiden as we continued to run towards the thick gathering of trees.

"To the dome… on top of the hill…" he panted. "We might lose them through the trees… but… there might be another… another CTL."

Even if Hilroy hadn't pulled apart the one I had used to get here, it was probably on a timer like the other one had been, so wouldn't have gotten us back to Rowhill for another hour and a half at least. This was our only option.

My legs were violently protesting everything I had put them through today on top of the week of walking the Region, and I slowed down. "I can't Aiden, I just can't!" Tears formed in my eyes. I was desperately worried about Mom being taken away to the High Council. I was worried about Simeon being in the Medical Center with nothing getting better for him. I was worried about Gen who wasn't acting right and wasn't taking any time to see me. But most of all, I was worried they would take Aiden, and I'd never see him again. Ever.

"Please, keep going," he begged. "It's not far. I need you to just keep going. We'll rest soon, I promise."

Pushing my body as hard as I could, we kept running, slower now. Voices were still in the distance, but they were having trouble finding us as we had wound our way through the trees rather than taking the path. The trees cleared, and the crest of the hill and the aurora came into view. It had dimmed now but was still shimmering with intense beauty. There was no time to enjoy it this time, though. As we reached the dome where Aiden worked, he scanned his hand to open the door, and we rushed inside. Closing the door behind us, I hoped the restricted access to this dome would afford us some time at least.

"We have to get out of here," he said again.

"You've said that," I replied shortly, rubbing my calves which were burning from the effort. Aiden rummaged around in cupboards and boxes, throwing out expletives here and there when he couldn't find what he was looking for.

"Aha!" He held the CTL up in the air in triumph. "Let's go!"

"We can't re-program it, where will it take us?" Going to yet another unknown Region was just the icing on the cake for tonight. For this whole damn week!

"It'll take us to the nearest Region, remember I told you? Where we get our supplies from. It's the only thing I can think of doing right now. And this is wasting time!"

I frowned at him. "I'm tired and stressed out, there's no need to talk to me like that!"

His face softened. "I'm sorry," he said as he held out his hand towards me, with urgency. "But we really have to go, now!"

He flipped open the lid of the CTL he had found and pressed the button as soon as my hand touched his. As the translocation began, I heard voices at the door of the dome, and then the booming sound of them trying to break it down reverberating around the inside the dome. But before they'd even had the chance, we were gone.

# FOURTEEN

I T WAS STILL THE MIDDLE OF THE NIGHT in the Region we translocated to, which was more than helpful considering the CTL brought us directly in the center of what seemed to be a huge town square. This must have been the marketplace where Aiden and the rest of his team picked up supplies. I could imagine that during the day it would teem with people, but for now, it was deserted.

Even though no one seemed to be around, Aiden guided me towards one of the tall buildings standing at the edge of the square. We ducked down into a large doorway, both crouching down to avoid being seen. The town square was surrounded by buildings of all shapes and sizes, including a huge church, bell-tower and all, with steps leading up to it. A stone fountain bubbled in the center, drowning out our voices for others to hear but also making it harder for us to hear if anyone was approaching.

"What now?" I whispered. He knew this place better than I did, but not by much.

"We need to find somewhere to lie low for a while."

"And then what?" My voice rose with the panic bubbling in my chest. "How are we going to get back?"

"I don't know if we *can* go back…"

I stared at him. I knew he was right, but what could I say? I had to get back to Mom and Simeon; I had to make sure they were all right. But I also knew Aiden couldn't come with me, that the Regionnaires would find me, and I'd be sent to Processing. If I had to choose between living on the run with Aiden, my Mirror Soul, and being with my family but having to be Processed, which would I choose?

I swallowed the thought back down, doing my best to focus on the here and now. We had to make sure we were hidden from sight. That was the first step. It was even colder here than in Nordlys, and I shivered. Aiden put his arm around me.

"We should find somewhere warmer than this at least," he said.

We stood up, my legs once more protesting with burning and aching muscles, and skirted around the edge of the town square, staying in the shadow of the buildings until we reached the steps up to the church.

"There are rooms inside the church that aren't used much," Aiden said. "We can hide in one of those until we can figure out what to do."

"What if someone in the church sees us?"

"They're compassionate people, maybe they won't ask questions."

I was doubtful but decided to leave him with his optimistic thought rather than destroying it with my realism. We ran up the steps and slowly opened the heavy wooden door at the front of the church building. I kept my back to his, keeping a look out as he tried to open the door with minimal creaking, and we slipped through the small gap he had made.

As Aiden tried to close the door quietly once more, I looked around inside the church. It was stunning. A large collection of candles had been lit atop an alter at the back of the cavernous room, with others spaced down the sides. With no other light source, the flickering lights cast strange shadows across the empty floor. The effect was eerie. Most buildings like this had been destroyed before the Cataclysm had even occurred, but few were used for their original purpose these days.

With the door now shut, Aiden headed towards the back of the building, looking in each side door he came to.

"What are you looking for? Aren't they pretty much all the same?" I asked. He stopped at a door and held it open for me to enter.

"I wanted to see if I could find one that had a door leading back outside. If anyone comes into the church, it's handy for us to have another way out, you know?"

I smiled a tired smile at him, glad he was on the ball at least. I was just looking forward to at least sitting down but hoping with all my heart that there was a huge, soft, cozy bed inside this room, covered in pillows and thick blankets.

There wasn't. Obviously. Apart from a damaged wooden table laying on its side with a leg missing and a few candles sitting on the windowsill, the room was empty. The Avalon wouldn't leave luxuries lying around in a room like that; everything useful had to be recycled or reused.

Aiden went back into the main room to get a candle to light the ones in this room, shutting the door once he was back inside. "Help me move this table to block the doorway."

I tried to help him, but I was more of a hinderance than a help. My body had had enough. I sat down in a corner of the room on the rough floor and drew my knees up to my chest, partly to keep myself warm and partly to stretch my overworked muscles.

Sitting beside me, Aiden put his arm around my shoulders, and I leaned into him for the second time today. Last time we had been like this, it was in a much cozier setting in his cabin, warmed by the fire. Falling asleep together was our mistake. Things would have turned out very differently if only we hadn't fallen asleep, but we couldn't change that now.

"We need to figure out what to do next," he said.

"I'm so tired. Let's rest for a minute okay? We'll figure it out but... I need a break. Please?"

He nodded as he looked down at me, and I rested my head on his chest again. I didn't dare close my eyes even though they were desperate to. Bad things happened the last time I did that.

"So," he said. "Mirror Souls, huh?"

I laughed lightly. "Yeah, who'd have thought."

"Do you think it's true? Do you think we're really Mirror Souls? With energy surges and whatever else they say we can do?" he asked.

I sat up and turned so I could see his face. He looked at me expectantly, and I wished I could answer his questions.

"I don't know," I said honestly. "It's the first I've ever heard of them. Well, until Gen mentioned it, that is. They teach the Avalon about them in their 'special classes'."

"Well, if the Avalon are teaching it in class, it can't just be a myth."

I hadn't thought of it like that. We sat in silence for a second, just looking at each other.

"It feels different, being with you I mean. Compared to anything else," he continued. A pang of jealousy ran through me, the thought of him being with someone else gnawing away at me like a rabid animal. I tried to ignore it.

"I know what you mean. It's... electric." As soon as the word left my mouth, I felt ridiculous. But Aiden's face had lit up, a smile spreading across it.

"I'm glad you agree," he said softly. He brushed a rogue curl from my face and tucked it behind my ear, his hand resting on the side of my neck afterwards. "I know this has all been crazy, and quite dangerous actually, but... I'm glad we met. I'm glad we found each other and that we're... together."

My heart jumped at the word. We *were* together, and I couldn't ever imagine a time where we would not be. No matter what happened from this point, together is where we'd always be. If not in person, then always in spirit. I would always want just him.

His lips pressed against my forehead, like he had done once before. I sat still and closed my eyes, inside willing him not to leave it at that. He must want more; I certainly did.

As though he was reading my mind, his hand reached under my chin to tilt my head back, and he kissed my lips, gently as though I would break or disappear under his touch. It didn't matter where we were, or what had happened tonight; in that moment, everything else faded away. He kissed me deeper, and as my body responded to his, it felt like an explosion going off inside my chest. With my eyes still closed, lights as bright and beautiful as the aurora were filling my dark vision, swirling in beautiful motion that matched the rhythm that my heart was beating.

Suddenly, my eyes burned, painfully. An unwelcome distraction from this kiss that I never wanted to end. I pulled away from him suddenly and sharply, pressing my fingers to my closed eyes and shaking my head.

"What's wrong?" he asked, his voice tinged with both concern and surprise. I guessed he wasn't used to kisses feeling like that, well maybe he was... but he probably wasn't used to them ending like that at least!

"My eyes are hurting, I don't know why," I replied. Maybe it was because I was tired. It really *had* been a long night. But it felt like something was wrong with them. I moved my hands away and carefully opened them, blinking over and over.

The pain had stopped now, but they were blurry and watering.

"Let me look." Aiden once again put his hand under my chin, but this time only to twist my face to be facing his. Looking into my eyes, he frowned.

"What is it? Did I get something in my eye? Or... eyes, they both hurt!"

"No," he said, perplexed. "Your eyes, they look different."

"What do you mean different?"

"They've... well, I think they've changed color."

I looked around the room for a mirror, but there wasn't one here. Maybe he was mistaken; the room was only dimly lit by these candles. It could have been a trick of the light.

"I'm sure they haven't." I laughed. "But what terrible timing for my eyes to start hurting."

Aiden gave an adorably shy smile. "You enjoyed that as much as I did, then?"

"Most definitely. Although," I said, as I shuffled myself into a different position on the floor, "there are probably nicer places in the world to have a first kiss, that's for sure."

We laughed together, and he pulled me back in towards him, with both his arms wrapped around me.

"It doesn't matter where we are—"

He didn't have time to finish what he was saying. A blast of wind swept through the room despite all the windows and doors being shut, and suddenly, there were now four extra people with us.

Regionnaires.

Aiden and I stood up, bodies tensed, ready to run. We both looked around, but there was nowhere to run this time. Being in a room with two exits hadn't helped us in the slightest as they immediately blocked them.

"Alana Cain," said the only glowing Regionnaire, with clear authority, "Aiden Merrick. You are both under review for breaking Region protocols and disobeying the divine word of the Avalon High Council. Will you come without force?"

There was no point resisting them. We looked at each other, defeated and then simultaneously turned back to the Regionnaires and nodded. I only hoped that wherever they took us, they took us together. I reluctantly let Aiden's hand slip out of mine, and one of the Regionnaires grabbed me by the wrist. One had Aiden's wrist, too, and in that moment, I knew they'd never take us together.

"No! No, no, no!" I yelled out as I lunged forward, reaching out for him. The Regionnaires grip was too tight.

Aiden's eyes locked onto mine, and he mouthed the words *I'll find you*, with pain and longing all over his face as the Regionnaires triggered the CTLs in unison.

For the second time today, Aiden, my Mirror Soul, had been taken from me.

# FIFTEEN

I WAS BACK IN ROWHILL. It was eerily silent and bathed in darkness. We had appeared in front of the tallest building in the Village, the Avalon labs. I'd always noted this as the least beautiful of the old Gaian buildings; it looked opposing and angry and out of place. The Regionnaire's hand was still on my wrist, and he dragged me along behind him as he made his way to the doors. My eyes darted around to take in my surroundings and to see if they had, by some miracle, brought Aiden to the same place. But they hadn't. The courtyard in front of the Processing lab was empty.

Beyond the gates, the sun was just about to peek over the horizon. It had been the longest night, and I almost wished that Lefroy hadn't let me take the night off. Although, there was one thing about it all that had very much been worth it.

Hauled through the doors into a large atrium, I tried my best to keep going.

"Stop resisting!" the Regionnaire snarled, my wrist aching from where his grip was cutting into it.

I wasn't even resisting; what would be the point? The only

reason I was going so slow was because my body was damn near collapse. I didn't have the energy to argue, but I didn't have the energy to push myself any harder than I already was.

We walked down corridors sporting identical doors with zero identification on them, each with a scanner pad to the right-hand side. How could anyone find their way around in a maze like this? We stopped at an unassuming door. The Regionnaire opened the door with a hand roughly placed on the scanner and pushed me inside.

"Someone will come for you later." He scowled. So strange how he looked Gaian but sounded so Avalon.

The room was almost as empty as the one in the church apart from two mattresses on the floor, against each of the side walls. And apart from a girl, huddled up in a corner on one of the mattresses.

She looked up at me expectantly as I entered but looked dejected again as soon as the Regionnaire slammed the door shut. She said nothing.

With my legs pushed to their limit, I collapsed down on the unoccupied mattress and lay flat out on it. The mattress was adorned with a pillow and blanket, both thin and barely worth having. My mind flew back to Aiden's couch, with the thick knitted blanket and plush cushions, and my heart ached just that little more.

Without moving my body, I turned my head towards the girl, who now had her head tucked into her chest, hiding behind her knees.

"Hi," I whispered. She looked like a timid little mouse, afraid but with no hole to run and hide in. She lifted her head to peer at me over the tops of her knees with big, round, blue eyes. "I'm Alana."

"I know," she whispered back. That wasn't the answer I was

expecting.

"You know?" I asked.

"You're Simeon's sister, I've seen you before. He talks about you."

I tried to search my brain to remember who this girl was but failed. "You know my brother?"

"We're friends. Or… we were friends. I'm Elodie."

Simeon had told me about his friend who had been taken for Processing for only just missing curfew, this must be her. She looked terrified as I stood up on shaky legs and collapsed down next to her. "He's told me about you too. Are you okay?"

"No… I'm not. They did something to me, the Processing." Tears filled her eyes. "I'm so scared. I want to go home." She began to cry, and she hid her face again, her whole body trembling.

The poor little thing. What had they done to her? I hated seeing her in such fear and pain, so I put my arm around her shoulder. She needed a big sister right now.

"It's all right, Elodie, it's all going to be okay," I said as she cried and shook.

It was at that moment, I felt strange myself. Inside and out I was warm, very warm. I fanned my face with my hand from the sudden heat. The electricity in my chest, the same that had built up when Aiden kissed me, had returned. Except it was building and becoming damn uncomfortable. I held my breath from the pressure of it, wondering if I was about to translocate somehow. It was a similar sensation, except there was no gale force wind. Maybe this was what having a heart attack felt like. I clutched my hand to my chest when the electricity suddenly rushed out of my body in one huge pulse.

I could breathe again.

Elodie stopped crying and looked up at me wide-eyed in

surprise, tears no longer in her eyes but cheeks still wet from them. "What did you just do?" she whispered again, in awe. Had she felt that?

"What do you mean?" I asked.

"What... what *did* you do?" She looked down at her hands as though she'd see a change in them and then put her hands up against each of her temples.

The door opening made us both jump, and I stood up away from Elodie. I didn't want to get into any more trouble than I was already in. A Regionnaire entered, a different one this time.

"Elodie Durand," he said, "your father is here to collect you."

A man, Elodie's father, walked in behind the Regionnaire and took his daughter into his arms as she got up and threw herself into them. Once they had embraced, he took his daughter's face into his hands.

"Are you all right, cherie? Did they tell you what they'd done? Did it hurt? Are you okay?"

"Papa, I'm okay. She fixed me." Elodie turned her head to look at me, and both her father and the Regionnaire followed suit. I gave a quick, subtle shake of my head, and she frowned at me, then smiled. "Let's go, Papa. Let's go home." The two of them left the room while the Regionnaire lingered. He half stepped out of the door and turned back.

"No funny business, Cain," he said, frowning. He looked as confused as I was, but exited the room, shutting the door behind him.

What had just happened?

I lay back down on the mattress and covered myself with the thin blanket. My eyes wouldn't stay open much longer, and I'd need to gather as much energy as possible for what lay ahead of me.

✦

After only a few hours of sleep, the door opened again, and a basic breakfast was presented to me. As much as I didn't want to accept anything from the people who were about to mentally edit me, I was starving and ate every crumb and drank every drop as though they were my last.

An hour or so later, another Regionnaire led me to a lab which looked nothing like I expected it to. No one had ever talked about what it was like inside. Perhaps they didn't remember, but I thought it would be more… lab-like. White interiors with hard cornered surfaces. Test tubes and computers and lab coats. That kind of thing. Okay, so they had lab coats and computers. But the rest of it was more like a living room than a lab.

In the middle of the wooden paneled room was a large chair which looked soft and inviting after barely sleeping on a hard mattress on the floor. The only alert to danger were the wrist and ankle restraints on the arms and footrest. A screen hung from the ceiling in front of the chair. Around the edges of the room were a bank of ornate wooden desks with high tech computers and equipment sitting on them. The walls were adorned with screens, blinking with images, graphs, and words I didn't understand. Us Gaians would never be taught the Avalon language, and any Avalon caught teaching a non-Avalon was taken away and never seen again.

The room had been made to make the recipient of the 'treatment' be at ease, but I was anything but relaxed. All my muscles, still aching from yesterday, were tensed. Ready to run. Except there was, as always, nowhere to run. The Regionnaire led me to the chair, strapped me in, and then left the room. Behind the desks were two lab technicians, I assumed, from the white lab coats. Both Avalon. Both glowing.

"Alana Cain?" one technician asked. Her voice rang like a

bell. The Avalon voice had a different quality to the Gaian voice, it had an odd clarity to it that was difficult to explain. Midorians had a rougher edge to their tone, like they were tougher than the rest.

"Yes," I replied, trying to shake off my distracting thoughts.

"Please watch the following announcement." She nodded to the screen hanging in front of me, as it switched on. It was the same video we were made to watch the day before every Shift Day, a glowing Avalon woman filling the screen.

"The Gaian race has grown over millennia and has developed character flaws that are detrimental to progress and to the way of life we are promoting on Gaia. We have created a way to help you on your journey towards greatness alongside your creators, and we call this 'character-enhancing Processing.'

Avalon technologies have the ability to edit your brain structure, thought patterns and DNA strands in order to accelerate the development of your race.

There is no need to fear. Processing is painless and non-invasive. You can rest assured in the knowledge that we have performed this many times, over many thousands of Gaia-cycles and only to the betterment of the race, and therefore, the betterment of the galaxy."

The screen automatically switched off.

Without saying anything else, the technician stood up and brought a tray containing a needle and syringe over. My heart raced. I'd only had an injection once, and it was so long ago, I'd already placed it as an unwanted distant memory in my mind.

"This won't hurt. Please stay calm," she said. Calmly. She wasn't the one about to have a needle shoved in her so of course she was freaking calm!

Lifting the arm of my shirt up, she wiped the skin with a thin cloth and injected a sickly green substance into my arm. I couldn't help watching as it disappeared out of the syringe to begin its intended purpose inside me. Whatever that was. I clenched my fists and my teeth simultaneously.

"What's that for?" I asked with a grimace, the liquid flowing into my muscle. My question was met with silence as she stuck sensors on me, sticky pads with wires trailing from them, which disappeared into a panel on the floor just next to the chair. One on each of my upper arms, the same place she had just injected me, one on top of each hand, one on both temples and one on each ankle. I must have looked ridiculous connected to all these wires, and for a second, I felt much less human.

The technician sat back down at her desk, and we sat in silence, with only the sounds of them both tapping away on their keyboards to break it. Apparently there was no point in asking questions.

"Alana?" the male technician asked this time.

"Yes?" I replied again, hesitantly.

He frowned and walked over to the chair, standing in front of me. It was unsettling being strapped in this chair, unable to defend myself if the need arose.

"State your name, date of birth and race please," he asked.

"Alana Cain, fourteenth day of the fifth month of the two one eight one cycle, Gaian."

"And you are well?" he asked.

What a stupid question, I was about to be Processed, why the hell would I be well?

"Umm... yes, I'm fine," I lied, not wanting to give him the satisfaction of knowing how terrified I was.

He turned to his female colleague. "Call Councilor Keren."

Seriously? The last person I wanted to see. The female

technician spoke into a device I had never seen before, in a language I didn't understand. Avalonian, I assumed, but it rarely got spoken in the Regions. The only words I understood were my name and Keren's.

Within minutes, Councilor Keren was striding through the door, glowing brighter than ever. Without looking at me or even acknowledging that I was in the room, she stood in front of the technicians' desks as the male one spoke to her in Avalonian again. I wanted to say something, to scream and shout at her for taking Aiden away. But I was helplessly strapped into this damn chair. What good would it do?

"Have you taken a blood sample yet?" she snapped at the technicians. They looked shaken that she'd changed the language so that I could understand, and they followed suit.

"Not yet, Councilor."

"Do it, then."

Another needle drew out blood out of my opposite arm. It stung, and I wasn't even able to reach it to apply any pressure to make it hurt less.

Machines launched into life and they inserted my blood into a chamber which made whirring sounds and clattered about inside carrying out an unknown process. They stared at screens and shared whispers I couldn't hear.

Keren walked over to me this time and now looked me in the face. I opened my mouth to speak, but she placed one long fingered glowing hand on top of it so that as well as not being able to move, I now couldn't speak. Her face was mere inches from mine, and she stared at me, right into my eyes, so close that I saw my reflection on the surface of hers.

"Interesting," she said. "I wonder how that escaped our notice."

The female technician spoke over the growing silence as

Keren stared at me and I stared back with as much hatred I could convey with just a look. She didn't seem to notice or care what I thought about her.

"Councilor, you realize now why the sedative has failed. It won't work on—"

"Get it done without the sedative. Immediately." Keren interrupted.

"But the increased risk of—"

"I said immediately!"

The finality in Keren's voice made the technician sit down straight away and duck her head down below the screen in front of her. Keren took her hand away from my mouth, and I sucked in a breath of air. Before I could say anything, the Councilor left without looking at me or saying any more to the technicians.

Then, the Processing began. Both technicians gave me a look of sympathy, then glanced at each other with concern as they started their work.

It wasn't long until I would understand why they performed Processing under a sedative. The pain started in my head, low level at first but intensifying into the worst headache, ever. The pressure built behind my eyes and I desperately wanted to press my fingers to them to give even the smallest amount of relief.

"Stop… please!" I whimpered through the agony, as it spread through the rest of my body. From my head, it wound its way down my neck into my chest and then down into my stomach. From there, it radiated out into my arms until every cell in my body was screaming.

I was screaming.

Loudly.

The pain. I couldn't breathe because of the pain.

Then, it went dark.

# SIXTEEN

**W**HEN I WOKE, my eyes took longer than usual to refocus, and they were full of tears as though I had been crying despite passing out. I looked around the room. Only the male technician had stayed, and he looked concerned.

Something was wrong.

I tried to breathe a full, deep breath, but it wouldn't come. It wasn't enough. Every muscle in my body tensed and ached from the strain of it even though I was barely moving. I was still strapped tight into the chair. My chest lifted as I try to suck in more air, but it did little good.

"What have you done to me?" Desperation filled my voice, which broke slightly. Speaking was a luxury I couldn't afford when I was using all my energy holding myself together.

"Just a few character adjustments, that's all." He looked over at me, and I couldn't tell if he was looking at me with sadness or with curiosity. Maybe it was both.

"What character adjustments?" The words were shaky, and I swallowed as I waited for the answer, my palms sweating. He sighed and looked back at the screens, probably to avoid looking at me. I must have looked a mess as sweat dripped down my forehead. Why was it so hot in here? Why do I feel so *hot?*

"Most people are sedated for this. I'm not acclimated to being questioned. However, I can't refuse an answer, it's against *my* character." Typical Avalon. "You have been Processed with an increase in fear. It will manifest as anxiety which often takes on a physical form. I'm sure you are experiencing it right now, are you not?"

I tried to keep my breathing calm and even just to prove him wrong. But it didn't come easily like it used to. Sweat continued to bead on my face; my hands were hot. I was trapped, like an animal in a cage.

"Why? How is that character enhancing Processing?" I tried to yell, to show my anger, but the words came out with unintended weakness.

He laughed a short but precise laugh, taking me by surprise. "I assume it is a punishment or a means of control. I do not know which, nor will I presume. We work on character flaws that are pre-existing. It is simple to manipulate someone prone to worry into full-blown fear." I half expected him to flash me a cruel smile, but instead he looked at me blankly. "We're finished here. I will fetch a Regionnaire who will arrange for your return to your home-dome."

Fear. Punishment or control. It was both. Councilor Keren knew me better than I thought.

There was no one to come and collect me like Elodie's father had collected her. Not Mom, nor Simeon. They could have asked Gen at a push, but I supposed they wouldn't have. After seeing how weak I was looking, a discussion between the female technician—who had finally come back into the room but wouldn't look me in the eye—and one of the Regionnaires led to the decision that I should be translocated back to the Hub rather than walking.

At this point, I had translocated a handful of times in the past few weeks and it had become easier every time. But *this* time, I was terrified. What if something went wrong? What if it didn't work properly? What if it took us to the wrong place and we were stuck there? What if… what if… something. Something bad. Anything could go wrong.

The Regionnaire held me by the wrist again, and as he pushed the button on his CTL, my stomach filled with cramping pain like I was going to throw up.

They brought me back to the Info Center in the middle of the Hub and left me there. Dumped like garbage. All the Regionnaire told me was that I had to make my way back to my home-dome on my own, and that I better hurry because it would be curfew soon. That was it. I must have been passed out for longer than I realized. My heart pounded out of my chest and wouldn't slow down no matter how much I tried to calm myself.

The Hub would be full of people finishing up for the day and making their way back home before curfew. The quickest way back home was to cut through the circles of domes surrounding the Info Center, but that would take me past the market and the other high traffic buildings in the Hub. I couldn't bear the thought of encountering so many people on my way, so instead I walked north towards the border. Away from home. At least I'd only have to pass more home-domes and most people would probably be already inside by now.

I walked slower than usual thanks to the exhaustion and stress from this godawful day. Even though the thought of missing curfew should have made me move quicker, my body wouldn't cooperate. I stopped once I reached the Region border and sat right in front of it. Before today, the times I had looked out into the Wild had given me a perfectly balanced combination of calm and adventure. Before, I'd have given anything to explore what else was 'out there' on Gaia. Now? The only reason I wanted to pass the border was because passing through those stakes in the ground would give me shock so strong it would stop my heart. And that seemed the easier option. The dark thought consumed me.

I gazed at the line of trees past the tall, breeze-filled grasses. They were darker and more dangerous looking than normal as the sky had clouded over, thick and gray, and there was no sunlight to penetrate the canopy of the woodland.

I felt uneasy. Like I was being watched. Not able to shake it, I stood up and continued my path just as slowly as before. It stayed with me all the way home, and each step was like a mountain to climb.

My home-dome came into view, and I breathed a sigh of relief. It was close to dinner time, so it would almost be like things had gone back to normal. Almost.

I hoped Mom had come back from her chat with the High Council by now. Surely she had. And Simeon's tests at the Medical Center should be done by now too. If she was home, Mom would make things better. Perhaps we could finish off the leftover cookies. Hopefully she wouldn't ask too many questions, at least until after I had slept. And I was sure Simeon would have something funny to say to lift my spirits.

I prepared for the possibility of them not being back yet as I opened the door ready to greet them if they were, and my heart dropped into my stomach.

It was empty.

My home was empty. Everything had gone.

My breath quickened as I tried to stifle the panic. No! No, this couldn't be happening. *This day cannot get any worse. It can't!*

"Hello?" I shouted, my desperate voice echoing off the

ceiling back at me. Hollow inside, just like the room I was standing in, I ran to Mom's room. Empty. I ran to Simeon's room. Empty. I hesitated in front of my room before I reached the door and took a deep breath as I opened it and stood in the doorway. All my belongings were as I'd left them, including the knitted blanket from Aiden's cabin, which I had left in a heap on top of my bed.

They were gone. My family were gone. I should have walked right through that border fence when I had the chance and ended this nightmare.

"Hello?" a deep voice called from the front door which I had left wide open in my panic at seeing the dome empty. I prayed that it wasn't Ableman or any other Regionnaire. I'd had enough of them to last me a lifetime.

I made my way down the corridor and back into the living room, and the man who had called out was standing filling the doorway at the entrance of the dome. It was Dray.

I stared at him blankly, not sure what to say. Not sure what to do. He peered behind me at the empty space.

"What on earth happened?" He stepped past me into the middle of the now empty living room and turned around in a circle.

There were no words. How could I even explain what had happened over the past twenty-four hours? How could I explain that Mom had been taken away by the Regionnaires and had never returned and I had no idea why or where she was now? How Simeon hadn't come back from the Medical Center. How my family's life had been packed up and shipped away. How I'd been left here alone. Why should he care anyway?

He stopped turning and faced me. "Are you all right Alana?" He took a hesitant step towards me as my eyes filled up and my legs weakened.

Inside I was screaming *no, I'm not all right!*

Inside I was just… screaming.

"I'm fine."

"No, you're not," he stated.

"What are you doing here anyway?"

"Your mom invited me for dinner again tonight when I left yesterday." He gazed around the room again, contemplating, the furrow appearing on his forehead again. He looked exactly the same as the day I'd met him. "This isn't good. Why would they have done this? Where's your mom? Where's Simeon?"

I couldn't get words to get in the correct order in my head, let alone get them out of my mouth. So instead I shook my head and shrugged. He had to leave. I couldn't hold myself together any longer.

"I need to be alone," I said, more bluntly than I should have.

"I'm not leaving you here in an empty dome." He folded his arms across his chest. If there had been a couch, I would have collapsed down onto it.

"Just go Dray, I'll figure this out. I need time to figure this out."

He raised his eyebrows at me. "If that's what you want." He made his way back to the door and put his hand on my shoulder as he passed me. "You know where I am if you need me." The worry shone through in the way he looked at me, and his hand left a warm spot that I missed as soon as it had gone.

The dome was cold, stark, and empty. I shut myself in my room. The desperation of the situation rose up in me like a tidal wave that started from the pit of my stomach and rose up into my throat making me nauseous. Everyone was gone. They could all be dead for all I knew. I couldn't undo any of this. This was all my fault. All my fault.

Suddenly, my body had forgotten how to breathe as the pure

panic hit me hard. A floodgate of tears opened, and I crumpled down onto my bedroom floor, pulling myself into a ball, sobs leaving me but without enough air to sustain them. My whole body shook as I gasped deeply, my heart beating irregularly as it tried to keep up with my breathing. What was I going to do? There was nothing I could do. My ears started to buzz with a high-pitched ring, and my vision blurred. *Am I dying?*

There was a gentle knock at my bedroom door. Dray had come back. He said my name quietly from the other side.

"Go… away…!" I half-yelled between airless sobs. He opened the door and peered around it. If I had the energy, I probably would have cared about how much of a mess I looked. But I'd stopped caring. I looked up at him, tears soaking my cheeks. He was the same guy I had met on the bridge; tall, strong, and with eyes that seemed to penetrate your soul, but he had lost the hardness he had back then and gained a softness that made me feel safer. He didn't say a word as he sat down on the floor next to me and put an arm around me, yet another unexpected move from Dray.

"What did they do to you? They've done something to you, haven't they?"

"It's that obvious?" I replied with an edge of sarcasm. I didn't want anyone to see the dark thoughts inside my head, least of all Dray.

"You can tell me, you know…"

I burst into tears. "They've broken me," I said in between even more sobs. "Everyone I love has gone and there's nothing I can do. I'm broken!" As I continued crying into my hands, Dray cursed under his breath. I doubted he expected this to be happening to him today.

"We'll find them somehow, I'm sure. Don't worry. You need to rest right now though."

"I can't rest here!" I nearly shouted. "How can I? They've taken everyone and everything. What have I done to deserve this?"

"All right," he said, standing up suddenly, "if you can't stay here, then come stay with me."

I hesitated and glanced up at him, weighing up my options. Stay here and suffer alone or go with Dray and suffer with someone else around. Mom had trusted Dray, even Simeon had said so. Regardless of only knowing him a short time, he was my only option right now. I would have gone to the Portbury's if I could guarantee it was safe. But the thought of being anywhere that Keren could appear at any time… no. I would go with Dray. It had to be better than being here alone in a mostly empty dome.

Inside, my heart told me to get over it, get up! Find Mom and Simeon! Find Aiden! But my head was telling me the exact opposite. A fight raged between the two Alanas inside me, and the weakest one was winning. I reached out a hand. With a firm grip that anchored me back to reality again rather than floating away from it, Dray took it and helped me stand.

I packed the bare essentials from what was left in my room, including Aiden's blanket. We dashed through the pouring rain from my home-dome to Dray's. He set me up in one of the spare rooms without trying to get me to talk anymore and left me to rest.

As I lay in the narrow bed, I wrapped myself up in Aiden's blanket. It smelled like his cabin, woody and earthy, which made me crave him even more. *He* was the one I had to find. I knew deep down that the only person who could help put me back together was him. Except I had no idea where they'd taken him. I squeezed my eyes shut, focusing on thoughts of Aiden and letting all the other thoughts float away. The day we met. Watching the aurora. Falling asleep with him. My muscles finally relaxed for what seemed like the first time in days.

Before they took Aiden, he told me he'd find me. And I trusted him.

So, I would wait until he did.

# SEVENTEEN

**W**AKING UP IN THE SPARE ROOM IN DRAY'S DOME, I didn't recognize where I was at first and I panicked. As my brain slowly processed what had happened over the past few days and I remembered where I was, I calmed myself. I was safe. For now.

Dray crashed about in the kitchen. It reminded me of Mom. She always did that. Maybe she was doing that somewhere else. I *hoped* she was doing that somewhere else, that all they had done was move her to a different Region, and that something worse hadn't happened to her and my brother. Yet another thought I had to push as far back into my mind as it would go. That thought might tip me over the edge.

I got out of bed and carefully folded the blanket I'd wrapped tightly around myself last night and got dressed. I looked out the window at another gray sky, the rain still falling heavily from the clouds. Without the sun shining, it was hard to tell what time it was, and there wasn't a clock in this room.

I made my way to the kitchen. Dray had been tidying up; his dome was spotless.

"Morning." He dipped his head in a greeting and smiled. "I'm not used to having guests, it was quite a mess in here to be honest. I tried to make it better…"

"You didn't have to do that for me," I said.

"Don't worry, I've got to learn to stand on my own two feet somehow!" He laughed. "I'm not used to any of this."

Nor was I.

Dray came across like nothing could phase him and that he knew everything. So, seeing him struggle with domestic tasks made him even more approachable on top of the softness he gained last night when he came back to my home-dome. I still wondered why he had come back.

"I'm not used to this either," I admitted. I wasn't used to any of the things the past few weeks had thrown at me. The Avalon *and* the Midorians had thrown me in the deep end without teaching me how to swim.

The clock on the kitchen wall showed six in the morning. I'd gone to sleep so early the evening before and slept all night long, so I was up early. That gave me a whole eleven hours before I had to be back at Lefroy's cabin and sign in for work, which gave me plenty of time to find out where they had taken Aiden. I considered finding Gen to ask for her help, but the thought of going anywhere near the Village, the High Council house, or the labs made my skin crawl. My entire body tensed at the thought.

The fire of determination to face the task ahead rose out of me, but before it made its way into action, the rain of doubt and worry came pouring down on top of it and snuffed it out. My hands trembled as all the negative thoughts poured into me, unwanted and without end. Dray noticed the change in me and seized my hand. He lowered his head to my level and looked me deep in the eyes.

"We'll find your family. I promise."

I hadn't told him who I really needed to find first. I would have to tell him about Aiden soon. Perhaps he'd heard of Mirror Souls before and understood more about them than I did, then *he* could fill *me* in.

The thought of telling Dray about Aiden made me feel uncomfortable, and I wasn't sure why. There was no reason for it to, and it knotted my stomach. He passed me a mug of hot tea, but then looked at me with a strange expression, his head tilted to one side.

"Your eyes," he said, frowning, "they're brown, aren't they?"

"Umm, yes?" I replied. Why did everyone keep talking about my eyes?

"Go look at them, in the mirror in the bathroom." He pointed the direction I needed to go, although I knew the way; his dome was an exact copy of mine.

I did as he suggested and looked closely at my eyes. Aiden had been right, they *had* changed color! They were still mostly brown, but they looked lighter than normal with an odd purple tinge to them.

I blinked over and over as though that would revert my eyes to the color they'd always been. Dray stood in the doorway, leaning against the frame, arms folded across his chest.

"Told you so," he said.

"I don't understand, what could cause this? The Processing?"

Dray frowned again, his brow furrowed in deep ridges, deep in thought. "Tell me, how did your Processing go? Was it normal? You know… where they sedate you and you sorta wake up a while later not really remembering much about what just happened?"

My skin crawled again, and a darkness grew in the very

depths of me as I recalled my Processing experience. *If only* it had been that simple.

"No, it wasn't normal." I swallowed, my mouth going dry at the thought. "The sedative didn't work. They called Councilor Keren in and she told them to go ahead without it." I shuddered, and my eyes prickled with tears. "It hurt. It hurt a *lot*."

"Come with me."

I followed Dray back out into the living room, right next to the window. The sun wasn't streaming in, but it was lighter in here. He moved me into position via my shoulders, then put his hand under my chin and tilted my head upwards.

His face was close to mine as he examined my eyes. This was the second time I had been this close to a guy in the past few weeks. I wished my heart wouldn't race so much, especially this time. Doing my best not to look directly back at him, I focused on the scar running down his neck instead. Following it down his jaw, my gaze ended up on his muscular chest and then flitted away, heat filling my face. I looked out of the window instead. *Dammit Alana, stop looking at Dray like that.* I scolded myself and my heart skipped a beat as yet again, I was having to push away thoughts about Dray that I shouldn't be having. Surely Mirror Souls should automatically have zero thoughts about anyone else! That would have been way easier than this. Hopefully he was too lost in thought about the color of my eyes to notice.

"Alana, you're Midorian. Or at least part Midorian."

"Excuse me?"

"That color in your irises, that's the Midorian identifier. How come you didn't know?" He let go of my face, and I took a step back away from him.

"I'm Gaian," I stated. I'd always been Gaian, no doubt about that! I wasn't stupid.

"No, you're not. Well, not one hundred percent anyway." He

smiled. "Hey, that gives us yet another thing in common," he said, as though there was already a long list of things.

I stood at the window, shaking my head, lost for words. Again. There was no way I could be Midorian. Both my parents were Gaian… right?

"Midorians are rarely put through Processing because the sedative doesn't work on us." He emphasized the *us*. "You and your Mom need to have a chat."

The heavy tightness in my chest started out small, but soon grew to be unmanageable, quicker than I expected. My ears started to buzz again, and I wasn't convinced my legs could hold me up anymore. I couldn't breathe. Why the hell was my body doing this to me? Why can't it just give me a damn break? It was just like when they had strapped me into that chair in the lab. I sat on Dray's couch cross-legged and buried my face in my trembling hands.

On top of everything why this? My parents lied to me my entire life? How were my eyes reverting to a Midorian state now when they'd always been Gaian eyes?

Aiden's face appeared in my mind and I focused on it with all my might. The kindness in his eyes, the warmth in the way he held me, the electricity in my chest whenever we were close. My body calmed, and my breathing evened out.

*Focus, dammit!* The question about my race would have to be answered another time.

"I need to find Aiden," I blurted.

Dray raised one eyebrow at me. "Who?"

"Aiden. He's my Mirror Soul. It's a long story," I replied. I didn't have the energy to answer Dray's questions when I had enough of my own to contend with.

"Oh. He's your… boyfriend then?"

Well that was quite a question! Clearly he knew what a

Mirror Soul was, otherwise he would have asked. But why was he asking me that? I glanced at him. Was that disappointment I saw on his face? As much as Gen and Simeon had joked with me about being coupled to Dray, surely he didn't think of me in that way? Perhaps he did and I was too inexperienced to notice. Aiden had made it quite clear how he felt about me from the get-go, but our situation was different. You lose all inhibitions when you're with your Mirror Soul. With Dray it was subtler, but there was undeniably something there.

"Well, I suppose he is? I'm not sure to be honest. We only met a few weeks ago."

"Oh." He looked both dubious and hopeful at my response. "Sorry, I didn't mean to be nosy, I just wondered…"

His voice trailed off, leaving a strange silence with unspoken words hanging in the air. After a while, he shrugged and turned away to look out the window.

"Well, if you want to find anyone on Gaia, the Info Center is where you'll want to start. Not a great day for a trip through the Hub, though."

"Right," I said, trying deep down to find an ounce of fire or drive that would make me leave the safety of Dray's dome and face the outside world again. Especially in the pouring rain.

Dray turned back to me, noticing my hesitancy. "Come on, I'll go with you."

He reached out his hand yet again, as though I were incapable of getting up from the couch myself. At this point I probably *was* incapable so I took it, ignoring the tiny dance of guilt gnawing at my heart.

# EIGHTEEN

I'D BEEN TO THE INFO CENTER BEFORE, but not for a long time. I didn't really have the need to, and I hated the crowds of people there. My parents told me all about my other family members—my grandparents, aunts, uncles, and cousins—who lived in other Regions across Gaia. This was the place you came to if you wanted to find or contact someone, but I didn't see the point when I'd never met any of them and most likely never would.

The Avalon restricted access for communication to family members only, but on the rare occasion, they'd let you stay in contact with friends. However, you could search for anyone on the entire planet. Mom would come here to send messages to her parents and sister, but she didn't invite me along. I'd never asked why.

The Info Center was in the heart of the Hub, and for me it had only ever served as a reference point so I knew the way around the Region. It was twice the size of the Holodome and had four entrances rather than one. The doors stayed open all day, sheltered from the rain by overhanging balconies, and closed at curfew. If you were bad at time-keeping or listening to warnings, you might end up stuck in there overnight.

The Info Centers were the same in all Regions and the only domes to have two stories. Four spiraling staircases stood at the right-hand side of each of the four doors, which led up to a circular mezzanine that looked down into the center of the dome. The Hub was busy today, and there were crowds of people hanging around in the Info Center. It was always like this for weeks after the Shift as people tried to find out where their friends or family had been moved to and make sure they were okay.

I instinctively grabbed Dray's arm as we entered the dome. I'd never been a fan of crowded places, even before they'd Processed me, and now it was even more overwhelming. The muscles in his arm flexed under my touch, and he put his hand on top of mine and gave it a gentle squeeze. It was a small amount of reassurance, but it was enough to keep me putting one foot in front of the other.

As we reached the center of the dome, we stopped in front of the four huge banners that dropped from the ceiling. Each banner was facing the doors, and each showed a different image. One, a glowing Avalon, regal and tall. The second, a bright-looking Midorian, violet eyes dominating her face. The third, a Gaian, plain and simple, just like me. Or at least, it had been just like me. And the fourth, Gaia itself. A spinning ball of green and blue, an image of hope that we might someday heal her back to that state instead of the patches of gray and black desolation we had left behind after the Cataclysm.

Looking up at the banners made me feel dizzy, so I held Dray's arm all the tighter. If he minded, he said nothing about it. All the info screens that stood around in clusters in the bottom layer of the dome were all occupied with people searching the

Gaia-database for their loved ones or sending video messages to them, the only connection we were allowed between Regions.

We headed upstairs to the mezzanine where the crowds were smaller, Dray letting me traverse the staircase ahead of him, and found an unoccupied screen. He tapped the screen expertly, navigating all the various options with ease and without hesitation. He'd done this before.

"Name?" he asked.

"Aiden Merrick."

"Date of birth?" It seemed like that was something I should know, and I felt a little stupid having to tell him I didn't.

"I… I don't know."

He raised an eyebrow at me again. "Most recent known location?"

"Region 01-0111."

He swiftly punched the info into the touch screen, and my heart skipped as Aiden's face popped up. Dray moved aside so I could get a better look. All of Aiden's data was there. The name of his parents, his brother and sister. His date of birth; I made a mental note of that one. His place of birth, the map showing it was one of the other Regions on this island.

And his current location. Region 01-0111, Nordlys.

"They haven't moved him." I breathed a sigh of relief. Perhaps they'd let him off, blamed me for the disturbance and just let him get back to his work with Hilroy. I closed my eyes and pictured him sitting in front of the fireplace in the cabin, safe and as though nothing had ever happened, and I smiled properly for the first time since being in the church. He was probably biding his time, trying to find a way to get to me. Like he said he would.

"That's good, I guess?" Dray said. "Shall we go?" He put his hand on the small of my back to guide me away.

"Let me check one more thing. Show me how to search for someone else?"

Dray tapped the screen again, leading back to the search, and I typed in my mother's name. "Caliza Cain." My eyes flitted past the information I already knew and rested on 'current location'.

"Region 82-1056, Rowhill," I read aloud.

"She's still here?" Dray asked.

"She can't be," I said. It didn't make sense; why would the home-dome be empty if she was still here? "Maybe the systems haven't updated yet?"

"That's not likely, that's not how these things work. They'll have been updated by now."

"How do you know so much about the Info Center?" I asked.

"Now that is just as long a story as the one you won't tell me," he replied with a knowing smile. "Let's get out of here, though. Too many ears."

We left the Info Center via the Midorian-banner facing door and followed the path through the circles back to Dray's dome. Frustration filled me from top to bottom. So much for being an 'Info Center.' I'd left with more questions than I had arrived with. Yet again.

The rain was falling even heavier, and the pointless journey to the Info Center had taken up most of the time before work began. Dray and I couldn't talk as we walked through the downpour, so it had to wait until we returned.

Taking off our soaking wet coats, Dray turned the dial up on the heater in the living room.

"Now you can tell me," I said as I shook droplets of water from the front of my hair, "how come you know so much about the Info Center?"

He took a brief pause, as though weighing up how much to tell me or whether to tell me at all, before he answered my question.

"I used to work in one, in my last Region."

"But they changed your Profession when you came here?"

"Yeah. They took me from my other Region because... I got into trouble." He sat down, putting his feet up on the small table in front of the couch, sadness clouding his face.

"Your family, they're still there?"

"Yeah, they are. I probably won't get to see them again. They won't let me contact them either." His eyes darkened to a deeper shade of violet as he spoke of his family.

"I'm sorry," I said, not knowing what else to say to comfort him, still processing what I'd found out from the Info Center.

"Don't worry about it. They're better off without me, and I can still do what I need to do from here."

"What's that supposed to mean?" I asked, confused at both the statements he had made.

He pointed at the clock in the corner of the large screen on the wall. "You'll be late for work if you don't go now." He was avoiding the question, but he was also right. "Want me to go with you?" he offered.

"No, don't worry. I'll have to stand on my own two feet at some point," I said with a small smile.

"Good," he replied and smiled back. "I hate the cold and rain."

# NINETEEN

THE DAYS AND NIGHTS FADED INTO EACH OTHER, passing slowly and painfully. Autumn was fading into winter. Each day I had to fight the demons inside my head and each day, I lost. It had been two weeks since Mom had been taken, since I had been brought back to Rowhill and Processed. I'd tried to go to the Medical Center to see Simeon, but they flat out refused to tell me anything about him. I couldn't have even guaranteed he was still there. The neighbors avoided me except for the odd sympathetic glance. When someone went missing in a Region, most people avoided asking questions. They stayed out of it. I suppose I didn't blame them, but it made me angry. The only person I had now was Dray, who had put himself out to take me in. He knew what it was like to be alone.

I had to go back to work, which was the absolute last thing I wanted to do. My mind and body both went into autopilot for work days, pushing through each hour until it was over. I'd lost the ability to laugh along to Lefroy's jokes, and the tension emanated from me. Simple tasks were more like mountains to climb since the Processing. Walking through Rowhill in the dark at night used to be something I loved doing, but now it left me panicked and shaking. Lefroy must have noticed the change in me too, but he didn't say too much about it. If anything, he was just a little gentler with me, a little less demanding because of it. I was thankful that they had given me more nights off now, so work wasn't so relenting at least.

I'd moved most of the stuff from my room to the spare room in Dray's dome, leaving my home-dome practically empty. I was pretty sure staying with him was a bad idea, especially now that there was a strange and unspoken tension between us. He liked me, even if he hadn't said it out loud. It was clear from the way he acted around me, the flirtatious comments he'd made, the effort he'd go to just to make me smile at least once a day. And I was trying not to like him. Not in that way, at least. But being alone led to my thoughts spiraling into oblivion, so I spent as much time around him as I could when he wasn't at the edu-dome. And that definitely wasn't helping the 'trying not to like him' thing.

Gen still hadn't contacted me, nor had I reached out to her. I missed her, a lot, but I'd avoided speaking to her because I wasn't sure how she would be. Our last meeting, the way she'd been gushing over her amazing Profession, had left me reeling. There was something so off about it. In my current state and after everything that had happened, I couldn't bear to come to the realization that I had lost her too. Though it felt like I already had. She would have known I was back. She would probably know all about my Processing, too, considering the information she had access to at the High Council. So, why hadn't she bothered to speak to me about it?

With a day off work ahead of me, I sat in the same spot that Gen and I had been in on Shift Day, under the draping branches of the willow tree. At least it seemed safer here, tucked away from the world. I watched as the river flowed by; the water drifting downstream and the tree sheltering me from the bitterly cold wind. So much had changed since Shift Day and almost none for the better. The Gen I knew had gone, becoming more and more like her grandmother every day, working at a Profession I had encouraged her to take on. Mom and Simeon were god knows where doing god knows what. I didn't know if they were even safe in a Region somewhere. Or even alive.

And Aiden. My heart skipped a thousand beats. Aiden was out of reach, and I had no way to get to him. There was the biggest hole in the very center of my being just screaming to be filled, and there was only one person who could close the gap. And he was entirely out of my reach, in so many ways.

The branches of the tree parted, making me jump. Only Dray knew I was here, but it wasn't him. It was Gen. She didn't sit down.

"Alana!" she said, out of breath. "I've finally found you. I came as soon as I knew! Why didn't you reply to my message? I asked you to come see me."

"Message?" I asked. "I didn't get a message."

"I sent it to your home-dome screen weeks ago," she said with a frown. Clearly she hadn't cared enough to find out why I hadn't replied.

"Oh, I haven't been there for a while." I shrugged. "I've been staying with Dray."

She raised her eyebrows in surprise. "So that's why he knew where you were. I went to your dome, but you weren't there. I bumped into him as he was leaving, and he told me you'd be here."

"You know I come here when I need to think." Or hide.

"I'm sorry about Aiden. It must be heavy on you." She sat down next to me now, and we both stared at the river.

"So, you knew about it all? And you've only just taken the precious time out of your important day to talk to me about it?" I narrowed my eyes at her, the jealousy rearing its ugly head yet again. Why should she have such a perfect life?

"Like I said, I sent you a message…"

"Wonderful. Anyway, you don't know the half of it. He said he'll come find me," I said, "so I'm waiting."

There was a long pause.

"I doubt he'll be doing that Alana."

I looked at her and shook my head. "And why's that?"

"I thought you knew already, that was what I meant before when I said this must be heavy on you. Aiden has been coupled."

I laughed out loud, and it felt forced. I rarely laugh these days. "What on earth are you talking about?"

She looked down at her hands as she twisted her fingers around each other. "It's not like I wanted to be the person to tell you this. He's with someone else now. I checked this morning on the Gaia-database. I don't know what made me think to look him up. I wanted to make sure he was okay for your sake I suppose."

"I don't believe you." I said each word clearly and with absolute defiant and angry purpose. Gen raised her eyebrows and looked down at me as though I was a child who was beneath her, just like her grandmother did. An attitude I could have done without, considering my heart had either stopped or broken or leaped out of my body.

"Why would I lie to you about something like that?" she asked.

"I visited the Info Center with Dray less than a week ago and it said nothing about him being coupled. He wouldn't do that. He… he wouldn't do that to me."

"You don't believe me?" She shook her head and sighed as though I was taking up her precious time. "Well then, I guess I'll have to prove it to you. The screens in the High Council won't lie, will they?"

She stood up and parted the branches, holding the gap open waiting for me to get up and follow her. We walked across the river and through the Village in silence. A few weeks ago, before the last Shift Day, we would have walked arm in arm, giggling about something or the other. Talking about what had happened in class, worrying about how much longer we had to spend together before I was relocated. But now, only silence. She even walked differently, her head held high with an air of superiority. My friend had definitely gone, and I didn't understand why. I blamed myself. I should never have encouraged her to accept the Profession in the High Council.

As we approached the High Council house, my heart rate increased yet again, and I felt sick to my stomach. The last time I was here, I bumped into Councilor Keren. It was bad enough back then when all she was to me was Gen's controlling grandmother and a leader of the Avalon. Now? She was the woman who had cold-heartedly caused me more pain than I'd ever experienced before and taken a part of my soul from me. In more ways than one.

We reached Gen's office, and she opened the door with one hand gracefully hovering over the scanner. We wouldn't be alone this time. A glowing woman, Gen's mentor I assumed, was sat behind a desk. She greeted Gen and ignored me, and Gen returned the greeting in parrot fashion.

Sitting at her own desk, Gen pulled up the Gaia-database search on her screen and typed in Aiden's full name and Region. I'd never told her his full name.

"Here," she said shortly, as she pointed at the screen.

Under the 'family' section, before the names of his parents and siblings, it was stated plain and clear.

*Coupled to: Corah Lindmann.*

I died inside. My body, already pushed to the absolute limit since the Processing, was now completely ready to give up. A lump rose in my throat as my stomach dropped. When I'd previously thought of Aiden, my heart had ached from longing. Now, my heart was aching because it was tearing into pieces. Surely he wouldn't do this to us. He wouldn't.

I fought back the tears that were threatening to spill out and never stop. Usually I wouldn't have cared about crying in front of my best friend, but she wasn't that any more. Plus, there was a complete stranger in the room with us. Hold it together Alana. I tried to talk but the words wouldn't come out without my voice shaking.

"I..." All I could do was shake my head and try to keep breathing as steadily as I possibly could.

Aiden's Region had changed too; it was no longer 01-0111. He wasn't in Nordlys anymore. Everything had changed. Except the photo on his profile. The warm eyes and the gentle smile... that would now be directed at someone else. Some... Corah.

With the nausea even stronger than when we arrived, I asked her to print the image off for me.

"If it makes it sink in, then sure," Gen said bluntly.

The printer flashed brightly once to burn the image, and there on the piece of paper it was immortalized. The man who was my Mirror Soul, the man who said he would come back for me. He was gone. And he was never coming back.

# TWENTY

I SAT IN DRAY'S DOME, staring at the piece of paper I held in my hands. Gen had been blunt with me, telling me I should move on from all of this and pretend none of it ever happened. It was at that point I realized my closest friend was gone. My heart broke a little more.

The combination of despair and outrage caused a huge amount of conflict within me. My head told me *it's okay to be sad for a while, and then you'll get over it. Maybe he wasn't your Mirror Soul after all. He can't have been if he moved on so quick. You'll find someone better. It'll suck, but it'll be okay.* But that logic didn't win out when I imagined him with someone else. With Corah. My mind pictured it in way more detail than was necessary; his arms around her, his lips on hers, saying the same things he'd said to me. Looking at her the way he used to look at me. My chest ached and my stomach clenched, nausea rising. While my mind was trying to bring me back to reality, my heart was telling me with a fierce rage, *how dare he do this to you! Did the past few weeks mean absolutely nothing? Why would he do this? I need to know!* My head felt fuzzy, almost dizzy, with the battle raging inside of it.

Wrapped up in my thoughts, I barely noticed as Dray returned from work.

"Hey." He greeted me with a smile, placing the boxes of rations he'd collected down on the dining table. "Good day? Bad day? Somewhere in between?"

I didn't have the heart to explain to Dray that every day was a bad day now. I didn't want him to think that I didn't appreciate everything he was doing for me.

"Bad day," I answered. "I saw Gen."

"Oh, she found you! She came looking for you a while back. What did she say?"

I hesitated. Talking to Dray about Aiden was getting even more awkward these days. "She told me that Aiden has been coupled." I swallowed, slow tears appearing in my eyes, and passed him the piece of paper that Gen had printed for me.

"I see."

"We were supposed to be… I mean, I know we hadn't spent much time together but—"

"The whole Mirror Soul thing, yeah?" he cut in, his words edged with jealousy.

I nodded. "And Gen, she's changed so much, and I can't figure out why. It's like she's a different person! Cold and way more… Avalon." I spat the word out. I couldn't deny that the past month had caused me to detest the Avalon. All of them. Gen's change wasn't helping matters.

I bit my lip, trying to keep it together, but as Dray sat down next to me, I gave up. Tears rolled down my cheeks as I sobbed. "I don't know what to do anymore Dray."

He took me in his arms and hugged me close, which should have taken me by surprise, but it didn't. I lay my head on his chest in defeat, and the muscles in his arms flexed as he held me closer.

I shouldn't have liked this, but it was safe here with Dray. I knew where I stood with him, and he stood with me through it all, no questions asked. If we were both part Midorian, it made sense. We had that in common. Maybe I should stay here. Like this. It would be easy, and safe.

The instant the thought entered my head, the electricity in my chest returned with a sharp burst that shot through my whole body. Muscles tensed, I jumped backwards out of the embrace and he looked at me in surprise.

"I have to get to Aiden," I said, out of nowhere.

It wasn't what he wanted to hear as his face switched from surprise to a deep frown. "You're kidding me. After all this?"

"I *have* to."

"That's not a good idea."

"Why not?" I demanded, standing up. "He owes me an explanation."

Dray stood up too, picking up the piece of paper that I had left on the couch and waving it in my face. "It's plain as day, he's moved on already! You wanna hurt yourself more?" I folded my arms across my chest and twisted away from him. "I'm only trying to protect you, Alana. Don't do it." He dropped the piece of paper onto the floor and took both of my hands in his, his bright eyes looking deeply into my changing ones. "Please, don't go."

"You can't protect me," I said. "It's not your job to protect me."

"Stay here," he urged. "With me."

I pulled my hands away and tried not to notice how hurt he looked. "I have to find him. I have to find out why he's done this."

Dray leaned against the wall and rubbed both hands down his face in defeat. We stood in silence, with Dray staring up at the dome ceiling and with me staring down at Aiden's face looking up at me from the printout. The guilt consumed me. I had considered staying here and forgetting all about him. Then I realized that he had forgotten all about me.

Dray broke the silence. "Fine. You wanna put yourself through more heartache? That's your choice."

"I don't have a choice," I snapped back. If only he understood.

"Yeah, you do."

"It's not that simple!" I yelled. "Mirror Souls—"

"Yeah, yeah, I get it. If you're that determined, then I guess I'll have to do all I can to help you."

All I needed was a CTL, and someone who knew how to program one so it would take me to where I needed to go. At least I had half of what I needed; part of Dray's prior Profession at the Info Center had involved learning how to code CTLs. As reluctant as he was, he said he would help me in any way that he could. I would never have been able to do it on my own. Getting the actual device would prove to be the difficult part. Mom may have had more of them hidden in our home-dome, but the Regionnaires had cleared the place out and there hadn't been one left in my room. I'd already checked.

I arrived at Lefroy's cabin, again with the awful feeling I was being watched. Exactly like I had the day they dropped me off at the Info Center and told to find my way home. I wasn't in the mood for working, not while I was trying to formulate a plan in my head. But if I didn't, I ran the high risk of getting Processed again. That was not a risk worth taking.

At least Lefroy was a constant; nothing about him or the way he acted towards me had changed in the slightest. Even if he was a constant grouch, I needed sanity right now.

"Time to get going," he said as he took his coat from the hook on the wall. I didn't move straight away, still lost in thought. "Oi!" he yelled at me. "What's wrong with you these days, lass? Snap out of it, won't ya!"

"Sorry, I have a lot on my mind."

He rolled his eyes at me but then sighed and softened again as he sat down next to me. "Gals your age always have a lot on yer mind. You need another day off or something? I mean, you did just have one."

"No," I replied, "I need something else. I need... I need to see my mom." I swallowed to fight back the tears.

"Oh? Where is she?" he asked.

"They took her away." I could see the sympathy and concern flow over him in a wave. "They won't let me see her, but I need to. They didn't even let me say goodbye."

"They're not meant to separate you from yer family until you're coupled. You didn't go ahead and do something like that did you?" he frowned.

"No, sir. I don't know why they've done it. Just like I don't know why they started my Profession so early." I paused. I could practically see the cogs turning in his head. Lefroy had been here a long time; he might know a way out of the Region.

Deep down, I somehow knew I had to get to Aiden before I could find Mom. It was the only way. At least I knew where Aiden was. The image of him somewhere other than Nordlys, coupled to someone else tore at me yet again. Of course, I couldn't let Lefroy know anything about Aiden. I'd have to play on the premise of finding Mom, tug at the old man's heartstrings.

"Do you know a way I can get to her?" I asked.

"Not a legal one... but... the Avalon haven't exactly been

doing you any favors recently have they. Or any of us for that matter." It was the first time I'd heard him talk about the Avalon like that, but he continued before I could ask him what he meant. "Well d'ya know where she is?" he asked, rubbing a hand across the creases in his forehead.

"Yes," I lied. "Why?"

"Then all you need, little lady, is one of those silver ball shaped device thingies." A deviant and bright-eyed look came over him as he said, "And I know just the place to find one."

Lefroy led the way as he always did when we were working. Most of the time, I blindly followed along behind him, uninterested and tired. But tonight, an extra spring in my step propelled me forward. I hadn't expected him to offer me help. I didn't dare ask why he was bothering to help me, just in case he'd change his mind. All I focused on was Aiden and getting the answers I deserved.

Lefroy thought I was going to find my mom, and he must never find out about Aiden. I hated lying to someone who was taking a massive risk to help me, but there was no other choice. I hadn't asked him where we were going, but we were walking up the hill through the Village. The stars were shining brightly that night, just like they had been the day Aiden took me to see the aurora. They weren't as bright here, though, with all the streetlights shining and interrupting their twinkling. Lefroy stopped, and I almost walked right into him seeing as I had been walking while staring upwards at the sky. Once I realized where we were, and where he intended to get the CTL from, my stomach tied itself into a thousand knots.

We were stood in front of the High Council house. Oh god.

Anywhere but here!

"There are loads of them devices here," he whispered. "They won't miss one little one will they. I've seen 'em before. I know exactly where they keep 'em."

"Mr. Lefroy!" I hissed, as he made his way to the gate. "You can't go in there!"

He had already placed his hand on the scanner, the gates swung open, and he held his arm up in triumph. "I can go anywhere me!"

He smiled a huge grin and beckoned me to follow. Of course he could go anywhere, it was his job to go everywhere, like it was mine. But now they'd know he had been here. And when they found a CTL missing, they'd know who to blame. Why would he do that for my sake?

Lefroy had a way of moving around the buildings and streets like a shadow. You'd never hear him coming. It was a skill I was trying to learn from him, but it would take me many Gaia-cycles of practice like it had for him. We crept into the lobby of the house, walking through the hallway between the two sweeping staircases, until we came to a door on the right. His hand reached for the handle, but before it got there, he paused and turned his head.

"You hear that?" he whispered.

"No?" I couldn't hear anything except my heart pounding in my ears.

"There's not usually anyone here this time of night, you don't hear them voices?" Curiosity got the better of him, and he walked away from the door, towards the source of the sound.

We peered around the corner, down the hallway that led off to the right. A door about halfway down was wide open, light pouring out. Lefroy put a finger to his lips. I didn't need to be told to be quiet, but I nodded anyway.

As we neared the doorway, the voices became clearer, and I froze as I recognized one of them. Councilor Keren.

I stood frozen to the spot, but Lefroy urged me forward. I wanted to yell to him we should go back, we needed to get out now. If they found me here, I would have to go through it all again. What would they do to me next? What 'character enhancement' would they inflict on me the next time they caught me doing something I shouldn't? Would it hurt as much as the first time, or perhaps even more?

I shook my head frantically, but he kept moving and I kept following. We reached the door and pressed ourselves against the wall so we couldn't be seen. And we listened. There were three voices. One was Keren. She was angry, and I bet she was glowing fiercely again. That was probably why the light coming from the door was so bright.

"I've asked you over and over Orson, make it *work*," she raged.

"Councilor, we've been working on this for weeks now, the equipment here isn't as good as in the labs. If you would let us transfer him there, or better still to Dracoa, I could —"

"No!" Keren's voice boomed out through the doorway, the finality of her response making my blood run cold. "I've told you already, countless times. This *must* be kept confidential. *No one* can find out about this," she urged. "If we do this in Dracoa, the Council of the Seven Races will find out and that'll be the end of us."

Keren was above us all and feared nothing and no one on Gaia. But right now, she sounded scared, and that filled me with even more fear.

There was a long pause, and a man whimpered.

"We can't keep him sedated for much longer, Councilor. We may have to start again tomorrow. He needs to rest or else this might inflict more damage upon him," yet another voice pleaded.

Keren sighed with an angry impatience. "Find a way, both of you. Giving up is *not* an option. The fate of the Avalon depends on this working. We must find what gives Mirror Souls the ability to manipulate energy the way they do. And when we do, we need to erase it *and* them. The stakes are high if we fail."

There was a moment of silence where all we could hear was the man breathing heavily. Whatever they were doing, it did not sound like fun. My heart rate tripled as I had a flashback from what had happened in Processing. I dug my nails into my palms inside clenched fists to stop myself from freaking out completely.

Keren spoke again. "Try once more, then let him rest. I'll return tomorrow."

Lefroy moved away from the door, back the way we came, upon hearing the conversation was over. He probably thought Keren would come rushing out of the door and spot us. But I knew better. She preferred to translocate rather than use ghastly Gaian concepts such as doors. I followed him down the corridor until we reached the closed door he had almost opened before we got distracted.

"They're experimenting on people here," he said, breathing faster than before. "Mirror Souls none the less!"

"You know about Mirror Souls?" I whispered, surprised.

"I know about everything that goes on here," he replied. *Except for the Avalon carrying out experiments on innocent people!* Everyone around me had a secret. "Let's get this thing and get out of here."

# TWENTY ONE

"**A**RE YOU SURE THEY CAN'T TRACK THIS?" I asked Dray dubiously. "If they catch me again…"

"Come on, I know CTLs like the back of my hand. They won't track this, trust me."

I wrung my hands as I stared at the silver ball sitting on the table. The CTL that Lefroy had literally risked his life to get for me. This unassuming device had started all of this, and now I couldn't be without it. I couldn't be stuck here in Rowhill, not again. It wasn't an option.

"It's ready to go whenever you are," Dray hinted, noting my hesitancy. He dipped his head so he could look me in the eye. "You don't have to do this you know. You can change your mind."

My eyes met his and the same thought from yesterday flashed through me like a bolt of lightning. I could stay here. With him. Maybe I *should* stay here. Doing what the Avalon wanted me to do was the wise choice, even if I hated them. After all, doing the opposite hadn't brought good things my way. But as quick as the thought arrived, it disappeared again. If I didn't find out what had happened to Aiden, I'd forever be wondering. And that was almost as painful as having to force myself to press the button on the CTL and attempt to find him. Almost.

"I *do* have to do this." I lifted my head, trying to push through all the self-doubt and negative thoughts that pummeled my confidence. I failed miserably but made sure to not show it on the outside. "I'm going to do this."

*Fake it 'til you make it.* I stood up quickly before I could change my mind and grabbed the CTL from the table. I turned it over in my hands and fought to push the nausea rising in my throat back down.

Taking one last look at Dray, I attempted a genuine smile. I was so grateful for him. He'd given me more than I deserved, but I knew what he wanted from me. I knew what he wanted me to say when he asked me not to go. But it was more than I could give him.

"I'll see you soon," I said, and as Dray took a small step towards me, longing filling his eyes, I pressed the button and he disappeared from sight.

That sight was replaced with a blinding brightness.

And heat. Scalding heat.

I blinked against the intense sunlight as my eyes adjusted from the dim light in the dome. Dray set the CTL so it would translocate me to an unpopulated part of Aiden's new Region. Far away enough that no one would notice me appearing out of thin air, but close enough so I wouldn't have to walk miles to find him. He'd done more research in the Info Center than I would have thought to do, so we even knew what time of day I'd have to leave Rowhill to hit midday in this one. We'd found out his new Profession and where he had to sign in for work. It was all in my head, I knew where to go.

It was just a case of going there.

This Region was so unlike Rowhill or Nordlys, the climate being the most obvious difference. The sky was bright and cloudless, the hot sun blazing. I'd worn a coat, just in case, thinking I'd learned from my visits to Nordlys and that I was being smart. So much for that! I definitely didn't need it here, so I folded it up and tucked it behind a bush with long spiked needles for leaves which left angry red scratches down my forearms.

There was very little green here. The ground was stark and bare, mud and grit. Rocks jutted out in odd places across the flat landscape and now and then, you could spot a solitary tree or a small cluster of spiny bushes. I lifted my arm above my head to shield my eyes from the sun and in the hazy distance, I could see the huge stone wall surrounding the city I needed to reach. As I got closer, the wall loomed taller. Beyond it through huge wooden gates swung wide open, there were a combination of sand-covered domes and rough stone buildings with square edges. They hadn't kept the domes separate from the original buildings here like in most other Regions; they'd crammed them in amongst them instead. Aiden was working at the Ration Center, which should be easy to find in any Region. So, I walked.

I wasn't used to this. Not the walking, god, I was definitely used to the walking, but the walking in this sweltering heat. As sweat beaded up on every inch of my body, I realized that choosing to arrive here at midday was probably a mistake.

It would be hard enough facing Aiden, let alone looking like hell and soaked in sweat.

Once I had passed through the gates, the closer I got to the town, the busier it became. They had many people here, all packed together in quite a small space. It made me grateful for Rowhill, with its meandering river, tall hills, and green lushness. The claustrophobia almost made me turn right back around again. I reached the Ration Center with the help of some passing residents who answered my questions, which was in one of the original Region buildings that stood tall with intricately carved stone pillars on either side of the entrance. Before I'd even looked inside, I could hear it was busy from the buzz of collective voices.

I took a deep breath, as deep as I could with the air being so dry, and stepped inside. Boxes were stacked in racks that covered three of the four walls, and there was a large crowd of people standing in front of the request desks. I'd picked a bad time; maybe new stock had come in today. I hoped it would be quieter so that Aiden was easier to find. I looked around, trying to spot him, but he wasn't here. Unless he was in a stock room somewhere, stacking shelves. I felt sorry for him in that moment; he loved his job working on the 'science stuff' of the aurora. He couldn't possibly be happy here.

Dammit. If he wasn't here, then I had no idea where he'd be. One of the other workers passed me, and I tapped her on the shoulder. "Excuse me, do you know where Aiden Merrick is?"

"Who?" she shouted over the noise of the crowd. Another of the workers overhead my question.

"That's that new guy, remember? He keeps to himself, but I think he said his name was Merrick, right? Anyway, he's not in today miss. Got a day off."

"Do you have any idea where he might be?" I asked hopefully, more like desperately. If they didn't know then I'd have to trawl this hot-as-hell Region looking for him. Thankfully the CTL that Dray had programmed wasn't on a timer like the other one.

"Uh, I suppose he'll be at home? His place is near to here, I think. He said something about being opposite the water tower."

"Thank you!" I called over my shoulder as I had already

turned to leave the building. These crowds were making me nervous.

"Hey, are you new here too?" The first worker I had spoken to shouted after me, but I was already out the door and searching for something that resembled a tower that would hold water.

There were too many buildings blocking my view from outside the Ration Center, so I wandered through narrow streets, looking up and around corners, until I came to a large marketplace. It reminded me of the one with the church where Aiden and I had hidden. That felt like such a long time ago. This marketplace was full of people, just like the Ration Center had been, all surrounding carts and stalls hung with colorful banners. Out of the corner of my eye, I saw a group of Regionnaires standing in a huddle together. One of them caught my eye and after a moment, leaned over to the others and pointed in my direction.

My heart stopped.

If they caught me now, I wouldn't get to speak to Aiden. And I knew exactly what would happen when they returned me to Rowhill. Now I'd heard what Councilor Keren was trying to achieve with the Mirror Souls, if she found out I *was* one... it didn't bear thinking about.

Being one of the tallest buildings around, the water tower was easy to spot now that I wasn't surrounded by stone facades and closed in roads. If I could just get there...

Why were the Regionnaires pointing me out? Surely I looked like everyone else here. And then I realized that no, I didn't look like everyone else. Looking down at my clothes, I was wearing dark blue jeans, a gray t-shirt and sneakers - my usual. The people here were dressed in light-colored clothing; whites and beiges and tans, flowing fabrics to keep them cool in this disgusting heat. I stood out. I stood out a lot.

One of the Regionnaires spoke into the communicator fitted into his ear and headed towards me. I turned around to face the direction I had just come from, doing my best to act casual. I took the CTL out of my pocket and holding it in my hand in case I needed it as an escape plan. Then I walked away. Fast.

With my heart pounding hard, I knew I was at a huge disadvantage. They knew these streets and I didn't. Turning left away from the courtyard, and away from the water tower, I took one of the narrower streets which was empty and broke into a run. I had to put as much distance between myself and the Regionnaires as possible.

I heard a shout which made me run faster, not even paying attention to the direction I was going. I almost ran into several people who had to press themselves against the wall to get out of my way, shouting a breathless apology over my shoulder as I shot past.

Running in this heat was killing me, and I was sweating more than ever. Sure I had lost the Regionnaires, I slowed down and eventually stopped. Hands on my thighs and bent over, I panted hard, trying to catch my breath. I needed water. I needed Aiden.

Once I had caught my breath, I looked around me. I was stood in the water tower's shadow. Thank god! After weaving my way through streets, I had ended up on the other side of the courtyard at the foot of the tower. I had to be quick, though; I was too easy to spot.

Skirting the tower in one full circle, there were only three home-domes facing it, and I had to pick the right one. If I knocked on the door of a stranger and they saw me looking out of place and on the run, they would alert the Regionnaires, no doubt about it.

I closed my eyes, took a deep breath in and pushed it slowly back out. *Time to follow your gut, Alana.* Time to follow my heart. I walked towards the first dome.

*No, that's not right. Keep walking.*

I kept my head down and picked up the pace as I continued to the second dome.

*No, keep going.*

Third time lucky? Perhaps I shouldn't be following my intuition after all.

As I reached the third dome, the electricity flared in my chest. This must be it, he must be here! I could feel it. I stopped outside the door and froze with my hand on the handle. My heart rate shot through the roof. This was it; I'd finally get to get answers from Aiden. The overwhelming thought to turn around and go straight back home filled me. Was I making a mistake? Would this make anything better? What if *she* was here, and I had to see them together? Oh god. Before I could decide what to do, there was a shout in one of the alleyways that I had come down to get here. Without even stopping to knock on the door, I opened it and went inside, if only to hide from the Regionnaires who were looking for me. Aiden was standing inside the dome with his back facing the door I had just entered.

"You're home early," he said, still facing away, "did they give you a half day off?"

"Aiden."

He spun around on the spot and stared at me, and his jaw dropped. I wasn't who he expected to see. He didn't smile. Why wasn't he smiling? My heart ached, and my stomach turned over with nerves.

"Alana? What are you doing here?" he asked.

I stood tall and forced myself into a faux confidence when really, I knew I had made a huge mistake in coming here. There was no warmth in his eyes or his voice.

"I'm here to ask you that exact question. What are *you* doing here?"

"I live here." He was looking at me with such a blank expression now, and I became hyper aware of how much of a hot mess I looked.

"You got coupled." There wasn't much point in skirting around the subject. This was why I was here.

"I asked to be," he said.

Definitely *not* the response I was expecting.

"What? Why?" I wanted to yell at him, to grab him by the shoulders and force him to explain himself, but my words were weak. Like my legs were.

He looked down at the ground frowning and then back up at me with the same blank expression. "I went to the High Council and asked them to couple me. I didn't even have to think about it. It was all sorted out for me."

"You're not answering my question." I stepped towards him, but he held his hand out.

"Don't, Alana, I'm no good for you. Society is how it is, this is how it has been constructed for us, and it won't change. Ever. We need to get on with it and that's exactly what I'm doing. With Corah." He dropped his arm back to his side. "You should leave."

I folded my arms across my chest.

"I'm not leaving. You're not making any damn sense at all. What happened after the Regionnaires took you from the church?"

"What church?"

My entire being shattered into a million tiny pieces. He didn't remember. The Avalon had taken one of the most beautiful memories we had from the man I was supposedly destined to be with. I wanted to scream.

"They Processed you, didn't they? What did they do to you? What did they take from you?" I slowly stepped towards him again, but he seemed afraid of me being close.

"Don't. Don't come near me. It will hurt us both."

"I need you to remember, Aiden. Please try to remember. We're Mirror Souls, you remember that part at least, right?" I took another step, and he put his hands up onto his temples.

"I'm coupled now, you should leave. You shouldn't be here." He shut his eyes tight, and I took yet another step.

"Aiden, try to remember. Remember watching the aurora. We ran from the Regionnaires. We hid in the church. You... we kissed."

The pressure built in my chest again with intensity, the electricity wrapping around my heart, which was beating faster now. He threw one hand onto his chest. He could feel it too. He looked up at me.

"Don't," he said, breathless, "it'll hurt us both."

"No, it won't." And I knew it wouldn't. "We need each other. We need to repair what they've done to us, and we can only do that together." I reached out both of my hands. They were trembling; my whole body was terrified and shaking. "Take my hands," I pleaded.

He held his breath and reached out to me as we both stepped forward to close the gap between us. As our hands touched, the electricity became almost unbearable, and it burst outwards from us both in an invisible shock wave.

We stood in silence, reeling from the energy surge we had just somehow created. It had blurred my eyes, which flashed with bright lights and were burning again, like last time. I shook my head to clear it. When I looked up, his expression was no longer blank but full of confusion.

"What the hell?" he said. He grabbed my chin and stared at

me. "Alana, your eyes!" I stared at him. It was happening again? "They're even more violet than before. You're… are you…?"

I rubbed my eyes again and blinked over and over. I didn't need a mirror to see what he was seeing; I'd already seen the beginnings of it and Dray had planted that seed of doubt.

"Midorian," I finished for him. "Maybe?"

There was nothing more I could say to him about it; there was only one person on this planet who could answer that question. Aiden smiled at me, his face lighting up like he was seeing me for the first time and it made me forget everything else if only for a second.

But we weren't alone anymore, and the smile faded.

"Aiden?" Corah said his name with a coarseness, not the way it should be said. Not the way I said it. It should roll off the tongue like it's the most precious word you've ever uttered. "What are you doing?" She was looking at us as we were standing closely facing each other, with both my hands in his. He took longer than he should to pull away from me and explain all of this to the girl he'd promised a lifetime to.

I hadn't asked him if he'd told Corah about me yet. Judging by the look on her face, I guessed he had not.

# TWENTY TWO

"ALANA." AIDEN BREATHED MY NAME. He said it the way he used to, and warmth ran through me. He looked down at our hands, still entwined.

"What just happened?" he exclaimed.

"That's what I want to know!" said Corah.

I'd barely acknowledged the girl stood in the doorway with her hands on her hips and a scowl across her face. I took a deep breath and found that I could. The tightness in my chest, the rocks in my stomach, the fear; they were gone. The energy surge must have undone whatever they did to us. Was that it? Was that what happened to Elodie the day I sat with her in the holding room at the labs? Even more questions without answers. Great. I hoped one day I'd be able to find someone who could answer them.

"They put you through Processing after the church, didn't they?" I asked Aiden. "Like they did with me."

He nodded, the blank expression gone. "I don't really remember being Processed or what they told me about it. I just know once it was over, I didn't care anymore. I didn't care about you anymore." My heart, the one that had lifted in hope once more, sank again. "You were just some girl who had found her way to me, and that was it," he continued. "But now…"

He let go of one of my hands and put it up to his chest where the pressure had built.

"Do you remember now? Do you remember what happened that night?"

"Every single moment," he said without taking his eyes off me. "But what *was* that?"

"It must have been an energy surge, what Hilroy told us about," I replied.

"I thought that was a myth."

"Me too. It's the biggest one I've felt so far. And now," I took another deep breath with my eyes shut, and opened them wide again, "It's gone."

"That's happened to you before?" he asked. "And what's gone?"

Before I could answer, Corah coughed loudly, and we both turned to look at her. She had been waiting with more patience than I had expected her to, way more patient than I would have been in her shoes, that's for sure! She seemed more baffled and inconvenienced rather than outraged.

The conversation between Aiden and Corah would be an awkward one. Perhaps I should have left them to talk it through alone, but I had already raised suspicion with the Regionnaires. They might still be looking for me. It also gave me the excuse to not leave them alone together, I wasn't sure I trusted her.

"So, that's it then? After like, one week, you want to be… uncoupled?" she asked.

"I'm sorry, I know I was helping you out of a difficult situation." Aiden ran his fingers through his hair awkwardly and then settled his hand on his chest again.

"How am I supposed to explain this to the Council, or to my parents? Now they will choose *for* me. Dammit Aiden, you told me you had no ties to anyone else!"

"They made me think I didn't! I think the energy surge, or whatever that was, undid the Processing. They'd made me forget."

"So now you're going to forget what you promised me?" she snapped back. Tears were forming in her eyes. I dug deep to find sympathy for her, but I struggled to find any. I'd made no claim over Aiden, but the whole Mirror Souls thing kind of made it a given.

"Alana is my Mirror Soul. I don't know what that means for us, but I won't walk away from it. I can't."

Corah's body tensed and her eyes widened, her whole demeanor shifting. "You're Mirror Souls?" she asked.

"That's what we've been told, yeah. Wait, you've heard of them?" he said.

She paused, sadness creeping in, her shoulders dropping. "My sister was one."

"Was?" I asked, my interruption of her conversation with Aiden changing her face into a slight frown.

"Yeah, *was*. My sister Tamsin and Drew were inseparable. But the more time they spent together, the more strange things happened. People around them were acting different, and the High Council took notice. They made Drew start a new Profession where he had to work at night, so they couldn't spend as much time together. They made the most of every second though."

Aiden and I glanced at each other. It was a familiar story.

"One day, he didn't come back from work. She never saw him again. Tamsin was beside herself; no one could comfort her. Then one night, she came into my room and told me she was leaving. She told me all about this place called 'the Underground' where she said they took Mirror Souls so they could be together without interference from the Avalon. I didn't understand what she was talking about. It was the first time she'd even mentioned Mirror Souls."

"The Underground?" Aiden asked. "Like, a hideout or something?"

"Something like that," Corah continued. "It's hidden well away from any Regions and from the Avalon. That's all Tamsin told me. Well, that and telling me how to get there myself in case... in case I ever found my Mirror Soul."

Corah shook her head, looking down at the ground.

"Why didn't you go with her?" Aiden asked.

"I couldn't. Not everyone has or is a Mirror Soul, and apparently I'm not one of the lucky ones." Now as well as looking sad, she sounded bitter on top of it all. "I wouldn't leave my parents behind. And I didn't want to leave Natalia behind either."

"Your other sister?" Aiden asked.

"No... she's a... close friend." I recognized the change in her expression when she said Natalia's name. That wasn't the look that came to you when you thought of a friend, even a close one. Suddenly, I felt better about who Aiden had been coupled with.

Aiden and I both froze at the same time.

"Do you hear that?" he asked me in alarm.

"Yeah, I do," I replied.

"Hear what?" Corah chimed in, confusion clouding her face yet again. Regionnaires were knocking on doors. They were looking for me.

Aiden looked left and right out of the window. "They're about six buildings down. We've got time."

"How did you hear them from so far away?" asked Corah.

I shrugged. The strange things that happened when Aiden and I were together were becoming less strange, just as they probably had for Corah's sister and her other half.

"You two should go," she blurted. "If they find you, you'll be back to where you started, and I'll get into even more trouble than I'm already in! Move away from the windows for god's sake!" Corah yanked Aiden's arm, pushing him to the other, more hidden side of the dome.

"If we stay together too long in one place, they'll find us. The two-hour time limit on the CTL, that was for a reason," I urged.

Aiden paced the room. Watching him in his anxiety reminded me of the same feeling I had got rid of with his help, and the tension began to build up in me again. I grabbed his hand to keep him steady.

"Where are we supposed to go?" he asked me.

"Go to the Underground," Corah answered instead. "They'll help you there, I'm sure of it." Footsteps were approaching the dome we were in. "Go to Region 12-0192. Find the Scavengers at the airfield. They'll take you there," she told us hurriedly as she scrambled around in one of the dresser drawers. She pulled out a scrunched-up piece of paper and shoved it into Aiden's hand.

"Come with us," I said to her. As much as I didn't want Corah to come with us—she'd taken more of Aiden's attention than I had ever wanted her to—she was so worried and so sad that it seemed wrong to leave her here alone to explain where her coupled partner had disappeared to.

"Like I said before, I'm not welcome there, no non-Mirrors are. There's no chance they'll let me in! I'll be okay, don't worry about me." She directed the second part towards Aiden as she placed a hand on each of his shoulders. I resisted the urge to stand in between them, despite realizing she didn't have the same feelings towards him as I did. "Thank you for trying to help me, even if it didn't work out. At least I could repay you in some way. If I'd have known you had a Mirror Soul — "

There was a loud knock at the door, and just as I hadn't, they also didn't wait for someone to answer before opening it and barging in. Aiden dragged me into the bedroom and shut the door behind us before the Regionnaires entered and questioned Corah on whether she had seen a female, about five foot four, dark curly hair, dressed in dark clothing...

"Quick, the CTL!" Aiden hissed.

With my heart beating out of my chest, I fumbled in my pockets, glad I at least had the sense to retrieve the small device from my coat before I had hidden it in the bushes. Lifting the lid and pressing the button yet again, we escaped just as the door to the bedroom opened, just in time.

# TWENTY THREE

ARRIVING BACK IN DRAY'S DOME, I was glad he wasn't there. There had already been enough awkwardness, and I wanted to talk to Aiden alone.

"Where are we?" Aiden asked, looking around. "This isn't your dome, is it?"

"Oh… no it's not. I've been staying with Dray."

Aiden glared at me. "Why? Who the hell is Dray?"

"Woah, calm down. I've just found you *coupled* to someone else. Who do you think should be the angry one right now?"

"That wasn't my fault." Aiden shoved his hands in his pockets and wandered the living room, looking out of the windows. It was getting dark in Rowhill. "Why aren't you at home?" he questioned with a gentler tone this time.

A lump rose in my throat. "Mom and Simeon are gone. The High Council took them somewhere. They're… gone." I slumped down onto Dray's couch, and Aiden was soon beside me.

"Gone? What do you mean? When did that happen?"

"They'd taken them and all their belongings by the time I

returned from the Processing labs." I could feel tears prickling in my eyes, but I held them back. Recalling the memory of walking into the home-dome to find everything gone brought back the anxiety, as my heart rate picked up and my breathing became uneven. Dammit, I thought I'd got rid of this completely. "Dray let me stay here because I couldn't bear to stay at home alone, especially after what they did to me at the lab."

"Well," Aiden sighed, "I'm glad you had someone to be with I guess."

"Dray is just a friend," I reassured him. "He helped me get to you."

"I see."

And he would see, considering Dray had walked through the door at that exact moment. Curfew was about to start and Dray, like me, knew the painful consequences of ignoring the rules. So much for having time alone.

Aiden jumped up from his seat, but Dray's eyes fell on me first. He stepped towards me and hugged me tight. "Thank god you're all right." He didn't hold on long; the daggers that Aiden's stare was giving him saw to that. "So, it all worked out then?" he asked me, eyeing Aiden warily.

I sighed and collapsed down onto the couch. "Just about."

Dray reached out a hand towards Aiden. "Name's Dray, I've heard a lot about you."

Aiden shook his hand briefly. "Wish I could say the same about you."

I rolled my eyes but neither of them noticed. We didn't have time for a macho standoff; we had to decide our next move and make it. Fast. Plus, this was awkward as hell.

"Aiden..." I reached one arm out, beckoning him to come and sit. He took my hand in his, electricity connecting them before they touched, and sat closer than ever to me.

He put his arm around my shoulders and kissed the top of my head. Dray turned away to take off his coat and hang it up.

"We can't stay here, we don't have long." Aiden sighed, pulling me closer. I wondered if there would ever be any rest for us, or a time where we didn't have to run or hide. Purely because of what we were when we were together.

"If you need to rest," Dray said, "Aiden could stay at your old dome while you stay here with me. Being apart will reduce the energy effect you two apparently create. They might not find you."

"Over my dead body!" Aiden retorted.

I put my hand on his knee as Dray threw his hands up in the air. "Whatever man, I'm just trying to help."

"Yeah, I'm sure that's exactly what you're trying to do."

"Right!" I said, standing up. "We're leaving."

They both looked at me in surprise.

"Where?" Dray asked.

"We're going to the Underground. Wherever and whatever that is. Somewhere that's 'safe' for Mirror Souls. It's got to be better than bouncing from Region to Region over and over." I stood up, and Aiden followed. "Will you program the CTL for us, Dray? Please."

I held out the crumpled piece of paper that Corah had given me along with the CTL and an awkward silence hung in the air. Dray reached out and took both the piece of paper and the silver device. He didn't say a word as he sat down at the table and pressed buttons, not taking his eyes off the screen.

As he worked, I went into the spare room, now my room, collected anything I thought of that might be useful and packed it into a small backpack. Aiden followed me into the room and sat down on the bed as I arranged the supplies.

He pulled the knitted blanket from his cabin onto his lap. "I didn't know you had this," he said, smiling.

"It was all I had to hold on to." I didn't want to think about all the nights I had cried myself to sleep, wrapped in the only thing I had to remind me of him.

"Listen, are you sure this is a good idea?" he asked. "We don't know anything about this 'Underground' place, or the people in it."

I looked up at him. "You don't trust your ex-wife, I mean... Corah?"

"That was unnecessary," he scolded. I couldn't quite shift the bitterness yet.

"They're like us, they're Mirror Souls. We might even get some answers! It's the only place I can think of where we can be safe from the Avalon." I lowered my voice so that Dray wouldn't overhear. "Or the Midorians for that matter."

"We can't guarantee that though..." His voice trailed off, and I carried on packing. I had made up my mind, and no one would change it. We had to leave.

"It's a risk we have to take Aiden," I urged. "Processing isn't the only thing we have to worry about now."

"What do you mean?"

"Keren. She's not like the rest of the Avalon, she's a thousand times worse! When I was at the High Council house getting a CTL to get back to you, I overheard her—"

"You stole a CTL from the Avalon council?" he interrupted. "Are you crazy?"

"That's beside the point! Listen, I overheard Keren *experimenting* on Mirror Souls."

"Experimenting? What kind of experiments?"

"They're trying to find out why we're different and how to get rid of us. Apart from that, I don't know what else they're doing, but I'm not sticking around to find out. Because whatever it is they're doing, it's probably worse than Processing, that's for sure. I won't stay here, being told where to go and what to be, letting the Avalon 'edit' us and making us puppets on a damn string."

"Okay, okay, calm down," Aiden soothed as he reached for my hand, calming my tension. "I just hope this 'Underground' is the answer. Because if it's not, I don't know where else we'll be able to hide."

I wished I could speak to Gen. She always had the best advice. I tried to imagine what she might say now. The old Gen would be hesitant like she had the first time but tell me to follow my gut. She was all about intuition and signs. The new Gen? Not so much. She'd be reporting me to her grandmother at the first opportunity no doubt.

Had it not been for the fact that she would likely alert the authorities, I would have found her to say goodbye before I left. I had no idea if we'd be coming back. It was only a few weeks ago that I had been so desperate to stay, mostly because of her, and now I couldn't wait to leave.

My stomach rolled as I remembered who I was leaving behind. Mom and Simeon were apparently still in Rowhill, but I didn't know where, and I couldn't trawl the Region looking for them. I was a fugitive now. I hoped to god the other Mirror Souls might help. Otherwise, what else would I do?

Dray called my name from the living room. He had finished the programming. He passed the CTL back without saying a word, and I knew there was at least one goodbye I had to make. I stepped up onto my tiptoes and put my arms around Dray's neck, hugging him tight. As much as Aiden wouldn't approve, considering he was standing in the doorway of my room, I couldn't deny Dray a decent goodbye. He put his arms around me, but he stood stiff. He wasn't okay.

"Thank you, for everything. I wouldn't have managed any of this without you," I whispered into his ear. His grip around my waist tightened into a gentle squeeze.

"I'll be here when you come back," he whispered back.

I moved to kiss him on the cheek but missed, catching my lips on his jaw instead. I stepped back. His eyes were filled with sadness, and I tried to keep the sadness out of mine and the blush rising to my cheeks.

I turned to Aiden, pushing down how torn I felt. "Let's go." I threw the backpack over my shoulder. He nodded, took the CTL out of my hand and flipped the lid. He took my hand into his and then glanced at Dray.

"Thank you. For helping her."

Dray opened his mouth to reply but thought better of it, so gave a quick dip of his head and then turned around and left the dome. He didn't say goodbye.

# TWENTY FOUR

SINCE I'D FOUND THE CTL IN MY POCKET the night before the Shift, I'd been jumping from Region to Region across Gaia over the past month. From the subtle calmness of Rowhill, to Nordlys' aurora-dazzled woodland, to the desert city Aiden shared with Corah. I thought nothing would surprise me, but I was wrong.

The coordinates Corah had given us had dropped us onto the most stunningly beautiful island I'd ever seen. The sun was high in the azure sky despite it having been close to setting back at home. We were stood on a beach of the whitest sand, with crystal clear waves rolling across it. It was picture perfect. I breathed in deeply, the salty air clearing my lungs and the sun warming my entire body.

"That's it," I said, "we're staying right here and not going anywhere else!"

"Let's do it!" Aiden laughed as he looked around. "Saying that, this place looks deserted. We'd have to fend for ourselves, and I'm not sure we'd make it with your lack of survival skills." He nudged me with his elbow, making me smile.

"*My* lack of survival skills? How are you going to keep us alive with your extensive knowledge of 'science stuff?'" We both laughed again.

This island did, in fact, seem deserted unless the line of trees behind us were hiding the domes and buildings that should have been there.

I closed my eyes, lifted my face up to the sun, and prayed to whoever that if I had to be moved on the next Shift Day, somewhere like this would do just fine. As long as I could bring everyone I loved with me.

The thought of Shift Day brought me crashing down to reality as I remembered sitting in the living room with Mom and Simeon, the waiting and the cookies. My heart sank. I may never see another Shift Day with them.

"Corah said there would be an airfield here. This is a strange place for planes, don't you think?" Aiden asked. He walked towards the trees to search out what we were here for.

Hesitant to leave the beauty of the beach, I followed him. I'd never seen a plane before. I hadn't known anyone still used them at all. Since the Avalon brought CTL tech to Gaia, they were unnecessary.

"Alana! Here!" Aiden's voice called from the thicket up ahead, where he'd entered a clearing. The trees had been hiding something, and the sand and waves were in stark contrast to what this island was actually used for.

The airfield.

This was no Region. The surrounding island was a myriad of colors; bright green palm trees, tropical flowers of orange and red, the sparkling blue of the ocean. The clearing was monochrome; a huge steel warehouse on the far side, a small gray communications tower, the black tarmac runway. And on the runway, the plane.

I'd only ever seen planes in class. We didn't learn much about how they worked or what they were like, just what they had been used for before the Reclaim and that they'd become redundant. Except this plane *was* being used. The huge gaping door at the rear of it was open, with the ramp extended out onto the ground.

A petite, bronze-skinned woman appeared out of the back of the plane, carrying a piece of metal that was twice her size. Aiden grabbed me by my arms and jumped into the cover of the trees before she could spot us. Ducking down behind a bush, we watched her as she hauled the metal bar across her shoulders and took it into the warehouse. After a few minutes, she returned to the mouth of the plane. I thought she'd continue unloading her cargo when she stopped half way up the ramp. She put her hands on her hips and turned towards us.

"I can see you, ya know," she shouted out in the direction of the undergrowth we were crouched down in. She waited, and we stayed silent, looking at each other in alarm.

"Seriously, though, I know you're there. I ain't stupid. Come on, I could do with some help."

As she disappeared into the belly of the aircraft, Aiden stood.

"Do you think it's safe?" I asked him.

"She's not a Regionnaire," he replied, "but yet again, we don't really have a choice. Corah told us to come to the airfield, so it's either that or go back."

"To the beach?" I said hopefully.

"Back to Rowhill. Or Nordlys. Or anywhere for that matter," he said.

There was no going back, that was clear to both of us. If Keren got her hands on us, it wasn't just Processing we would have to face. We were wasting precious time we didn't have.

As we reached the opening in the plane, the woman peered

out from around the edge of the opening. "Well finally, look who crawled out them bushes! No one told me you'd be coming. I 'spose you're here to get to the mainland, are ya?" she said with a huff.

"Yes ma'am, we're trying to get to… to the Underground," I replied cautiously.

She strode down the ramp and stood facing us, arms folded, and head held high. Her tank top was dotted with sweat and her cargo pants were lined with grease and dirt.

"Let's get one thing straight, little miss," Who was she calling little? I was half a foot taller than her! "Don't you be calling me ma'am. I ain't no ma'am. Y'all can call me Deena. Or Dee if you like. Who are you?"

"I'm Aiden, this is Alana. We're —"

"I know what you are. You're those Mirror Soul types."

I was sure Aiden hadn't been planning on telling her that, but our surprised expressions made her wave a hand in dismissal.

"Meh, don't worry, I won't tell no one," Deena said. "I've had a load of your type come through this way. No new ones for a few cycles though come to think of it. How did y'all get here?"

I pulled the CTL out of my pocket. Before I could do anything, she snatched it out of my hand, flipped it open, threw it on the ground, and stomped down hard. She lifted her foot, peered down at it, and stomped again for good measure.

"Lordy! Those things are tracked, ya know, unless it's been hacked. You'd have to know a highly skilled techy to have been able to do that."

I looked up from the smashed screen of the CTL. *Well, there goes Plan B.*

"What are you doing out here on this island?" I asked her. We didn't have time for small talk.

"I'm a Scavenger, little miss," she said. "I fly to the mainland, find what I'm 'sposed to find, and then fly on back."

I'd heard of Scavengers before but only in the list of Professions we were given in class. The Avalon had forced everyone out of the sprawling cities and into the Regions placed in more rural areas on Gaia. Fragments of our culture were left as a reminder of where we had come from, but the rest of it was being dismantled and reused or recycled. Scavengers were the ones who traveled to the crumbling cities of Gaia, outside of the Regions, to find things that could be useful.

"Why not just translocate to the mainland?" Whatever the mainland was. "Why the plane?" I asked.

Deena snorted. "What do they teach you in them edu-domes these days? No one can translocate to the mainland of the Americas. It don't work!"

*America!*

"This is America?" I asked, excited. My heart jumped up at the thought of getting to see the ancestral land that Dad had told me so much about.

"Does it *look* like America?" she replied, rolling her eyes. "No, these islands are on the brink of it though. We've gotta fly on in."

Deena stuck her hand out, hovering palm outwards in the air in front of Aiden and me.

"Hmmm. You two are stronger than what I've seen before. We need to get you out of here before y'all energy spike and get us all into trouble. Get in." She pointed into the back of the plane, then she strode off to the warehouse.

I led the way up the ramp, treading carefully as though it might break at any second. I'd never seen any vehicle in person before, not even a car. This would be quite a leap for first timers like us. In the Regions you had two options: walk or translocate.

Since most of us weren't allowed to translocate except for emergencies, there was a lot of walking, which I was getting used to now that I was working with Lefroy. I should have been working right now. Perhaps he'd already reported me missing.

The back of the plane was empty except for two long benches built into either side. There was a door at the far end which Deena was now opening, shoving a huge backpack inside. It was obviously the place where she'd fly this thing from. She smacked her hand hard onto a large button on the metallic wall, and the ramp reeled itself in as the door whirred shut. I was holding my breath when Aiden put his hand around my waist and closed the gap between us.

"There's no space for all three of us up in here," Deena said. "You two stay back in the hold. It won't take too long to get to the mainland, oh about three hours or so to where we're headin'. You might wanna rest while you get the chance." Giving a quick wave of her hand and a wink, she slammed the door hard.

To me, rest looked like a warm bed with thick blankets and soft cushions. Or like the white sands of that beach, the sound of crashing waves and the sunshine warming my skin. Rest did not look like the metallic stomach of a plane while it catapulted us thousands of miles into the air.

The aircraft shuddered as Deena kicked it into life, and we found what looked like straps that would keep us in our seats on the benches. I closed my eyes tight as the plane lifted from the ground, and my hand found Aiden's and squeezed it.

I glanced out of the window only to see the ground falling away fast, so I looked away again. Aiden seemed far more comfortable with this than me. As the aircraft leveled out and the roaring of the engines became background noise, he unbuckled the straps and laid himself across the bench. He dropped his head into my lap and looked up at me.

"What are you doing?" I asked. How could he be so relaxed while we're hurtling through the air at stupid speeds?

"Resting. That's what Deena told us to do." He gave me a cheeky smile.

I rolled my eyes and laid my head back onto the vibrating body of the plane, wondering when I'd ever find a place to rest. My hand naturally found its way to Aiden's hair as I brushed my fingers through it.

"Hey," he said, breaking the silence, "this is the longest time we've ever had together." He closed his eyes and smiled as my fingers massaged his scalp.

"Maybe it's the longest we'll ever get to be together," I said sadly.

"Try to think a little more positive. We're here now, let's focus on that."

I nodded and tried to forget that we were in a metal box, zooming through clouds with the ocean ready to catch us if we fell.

"I have a question I've been meaning to ask you," he said.

"Anything."

"Why did you come and find me? I mean, I understand why you wanted to, but it was taking a huge risk and... well, I wondered why you came to get me instead of trying to find your mom and brother."

"Instinct." It was the simplest answer I could give.

"Instinct?"

"I had to find you. I was following my gut, my intuition. Gen told me where to find you, and I found a way."

"Didn't you consider that it might not have made a difference? That I had been coupled because I didn't want you anymore?"

A pain rose in my chest, taking me back to the walk from the bush I had hidden my coat in to the walled city where I tried to find Aiden. Those were the exact questions I had asked myself, full of the anxiety that Keren had edited into me. But apparently anxiety isn't that easy to get rid of, even if you do have magical energy surge powers to fix what's been changed in you. My hands trembled slightly, and my heart wouldn't stay steady. Would it be too much to ask for things to go back to exactly the way they were before? Apparently so.

"I... I guess I hoped that you still wanted me."

He took my jittery hand which had been resting on his chest and lifted it to his face, kissing my palm. "I do still want you."

The tightness in my chest released and the same electricity as before replaced it, building as my heart rate increased to match it.

"I would never have coupled with Corah if they hadn't put me through Processing, you know that, don't you?" He looked deep into my eyes with a sincerity that couldn't be mistaken for anything else.

"I do now."

If it hadn't had been invisible, the sparks between us would have lit up the cabin of the plane with all the colors of the aurora. He sat up and twisted his whole body to face me.

"You saved me," Aiden said, his warm eyes bright.

"That's a bit dramatic," I replied with a laugh.

"It's true though. If you hadn't come to find me, I would have been stuck in that life forever."

"We saved each other."

He took my face in his hands, less gently this time, and kissed me for the first time since we had been taken away for Processing. He didn't hold back, and nor did I. Unbuckling the straps holding me onto the bench, I twisted my body towards his and pressed myself against him. As his fingers wound through my hair, slid down my back and found their way to the skin on my waist, the energy in our chests merged into one huge ball, swirling fast and waiting to expand outwards.

The plane lurched, my stomach dropping with it. Loud beeping sounds were coming from behind the door where Deena was, and we broke apart. The door flung open, all we could see was a waving arm and a pointing finger.

"Oi! Whatever you two are doing, stop it! You're wreckin' my equipment with your damn energy thingies. Sit apart ya fools!" Deena shouted from the driver's seat. She pulled the door shut again, cursing loudly.

Giving me one last quick kiss, which wasn't nearly enough, Aiden moved from his spot next to me and sat on the bench on the opposite side of the plane.

"See, even when we're together, we can't be *together*," I groaned, the longing plain and clear in my voice and the electric feeling of his touch still moving across my skin.

"We'll find a way," he said as he gripped the bench he was now sat on, his cheeks flushed. "One day. I promise."

# TWENTY FIVE

I HAD TRIED TO SLEEP and had managed a small amount. Moving across time zones was always disorientating. The constant drone of the plane was giving me a headache and having Aiden in front of me but still out of reach was a huge distraction. There was a subtle tilt downwards as Deena shouted to us again from the door.

"Almost there kids, buckle ya belts!"

I turned to look out of the window in excitement. The only images I had seen of America were the ones in the Holodome, and that had been so long ago. I'd only seen them once, I must have been about ten or eleven. After seeing the burning destruction of the cities and the thick heavy poisonous vapors that hung in the air, I had nightmares for weeks. I vowed never to view them again and instead held onto the more positive stories that Dad told us every Shift Day.

I didn't know what I'd expected to see, but it wasn't this.

We were flying over a city in ruins. Islands of crumbling buildings all pushed together as far as the eye could see. The raised sea levels had claimed some of it, and streets were full of water where once they had been streaming with people instead.

Deena had obviously done this before as she expertly pulled the plane around in a semi-circle and landed it at a disused airport in the city. The engines switched off, but my ears were still ringing from the noise.

"Welcome home!" Deena said as she bounced out of the driving cabin.

Home? I doubted it. Lifting sections of the benches to access storage compartments beneath them, she produced three breathing masks, passing one to each of us.

"Welcome to what us folk call 'The Poisoned Apple.' Or what they used to call New York City."

"Poisoned?" I asked, alarmed and wishing we'd stayed on the island. I ducked my head to stare out of the window at the gray world outside.

"You learned 'bout the Americas in class, right?" she asked.

Aiden and I nodded together, although I distinctly remembered not paying attention in that class on purpose. Dad's stories were better, but at this point I was wondering if any of them had been true.

"Then you'll remember that this country was at the center of it all, and it was destroyed by the wars first and the Cataclysm second. The air here ain't all that fun to breathe in, so I recommend puttin' that there breathing mask on so we can get underground as soon as possible."

I hadn't even considered that the 'Underground' was literally that, underground.

Turning to Aiden, he saw I was unsure, and he reached out a hand to hold. Before we closed the gap between us, Deena slapped our hands apart.

"None of that! You'll get me into trouble with Bronson!"

"Who?" I asked.

"You'll see, he'll want to meet you two…" She raised one eyebrow at us. "Come on, get movin'. We've hung about long enough."

Each of us slid the breathing mask over our faces, elastic wrapping around the back to hold it in place. There were no tanks of clean air, so I assumed that the masks filtered the air from outside somehow. Even though I didn't know how they worked, I hoped they did. We hadn't come all this way just to die from poisoned air.

The back of the plane yawned open with the same loud whirring, and we followed Deena down the ramp out onto the runway. My mouth dropped open as much as the plexiglass mask around my jaw would allow as we stepped out onto the dimly lit tarmac. Ahead of us, adorning the horizon, was The Poisoned Apple. The towering buildings reached into the sky, tinged in pink and orange from the setting sun, and even from this distance I could see their crumbled edges and smashed glass.

"This place is a gold mine for us Scavengers," Deena yelled through her mask. "We've been here for decades and still not scraped the surface of how much stuff we can find!" Her eyes lit up. It was clear the Avalon had given her the right Profession.

She led the way away from the city skyline and towards the long, curved building on the other side of the plane. I guessed this was where people would have waited for their ride to arrive back when this city was home to millions.

Deena walked fast for a 'person of limited height'—she was shorter than me—but I had trouble keeping up with her. Aiden kept up, but I had to break into a jog now and then to close the space between us. Deena reminded me of Gen, or at least the way Gen used to be. She looked nothing like Gen, of course; Deena was all Gaian, nothing Avalon about her. But her tenacious attitude and long stride at least reminded me of my friend. I pictured Gen now, sitting at the windowsill in her bedroom looking out across the Village. She'd be dreaming of working in the fields and being out in the sunshine, enjoying peace and laughter with the locals. It saddened me to think of how far she was now from that dream. I still wasn't sure if it was my fault or hers.

The doors to the building were jammed open just only wide enough to squeeze through. Pieces of ceiling lay broken across the floor, grime lining the tiles on the walls.

We kept walking. Or in my case, half walking, half jogging.

Posters were ripped from their holders, and we passed a bank of seats, broken and hanging with torn fabric. Some were missing, perhaps scavenged by Deena and others like her. Long mechanical walkways, long past working, were scattered with leaves and debris.

Aiden kept looking over his shoulder to make sure I was still all right. I shuddered as we walked along. Ghosts filled these huge rooms; it felt like I'd been here before and been part of it. I'd never seen anything like this place, but it was familiar all at the same time. I could so easily imagine the throngs of people that would be crowded in the waiting areas, the sound of voices filling the air. It was the weirdest case of déjà vu. But the people were long gone, and the only sounds now were our footsteps echoing down the wide corridors.

The deeper we got into the building, the bigger the spaces became. The steel-beamed ceilings rose high above us, with most of the glass panes they used to hold now smashed into pieces on the ground. Huge screens covered one wall, rooms that must have been shops and places to eat and drink, I'd seen nothing like it before.

"You need to hurry," Deena shouted back at me. I couldn't

help but slow down to take it all in. "I mean it, you two can't be together long. Even here."

My heart pounded hard, partly from having to run but mostly from the thought of being parted from Aiden yet again.

As I caught up with Deena and Aiden, we reached a staircase in the middle of a hall, that delved down into the floor. Deena skipped down them as though she had done it a thousand times. Aiden and I had to tread more carefully, avoiding pieces of glass and rubble.

At the foot of the stairwell, there were huge steel doors that didn't seem like they belonged to the original setup, with a lit-up keypad to the left. Deena pressed four buttons in quick succession and a speaker buzzed into life.

"It's Dee. Y'all got visitors from the island. More Mirrors."

There was a brief pause of silence, then the doors clunked and opened inwards. Deena pushed us inside before the doors swung shut again.

We were underground.

# TWENTY SIX

**A**S THE DOORS SLAMMED SHUT, the hairs on my arms stood on end. The claustrophobia of being trapped welled up, and I grabbed Aiden's hand to ground me. I'd never been a fan of enclosed spaces nor enclosed Regions. We followed Deena deeper in.

We were in a long tunnel, the left half of which had been blocked off. On the right-hand side was a half-width of a long platform, with a track running parallel to it. I leaned outwards across the track to see how far down it I could see when Deena grabbed me by the arm and yanked me back in.

"Ya wanna lose your head, little miss?" she said, "The train'll knock your head clean off!"

Trains? Yet more vehicles we didn't have in the Regions.

"So, this was an old underground travel system?" I asked.

"Definitely didn't listen in class, did ya!" Deena rolled her eyes at me. "This is the New York City subway, loads of people hid out down here through the wars after the Cataclysm. They built these rooms all along one side and kept the other for the trains. There're miles of 'em. The Mirror's use 'em now."

Just as I was thinking it strange that we hadn't met anyone yet, a man took a side step out of a room. Through the huge glass pane that made up most of the wall of that room, I could see screens lining the back wall and computers sitting together. It was a security center, or something like it.

"Deena," the man said, giving a curt nod.

"All right, Billy!" Deena gave him a hefty smack on the arm as a greeting, which he didn't seem too impressed about. "These here are more of you Mirror Souls type. They appeared on my island, wanting to get to the Underground. Figured I'd bring 'em to Bronson."

"They can't stay together, you know that, right?"

Aiden coughed loudly; apparently he liked being talked about as though we weren't here as much as I did. "We won't be separated," Aiden said, "not until we've got the answers we came for."

The man, Billy, frowned. I'd have bet anything to say he had been a Regionnaire in a past life. "You better hurry. You've already been together too long, and your energies are already way stronger than we usually allow. Walk two meters apart, that should help even a little. Dee, you okay to take them up to Bronson? I'm busy here."

Deena's eyes brightened and her back straightened. She gave an exaggerated roll of her eyes and shrugged. "Sure, it's not like I've got any scavenging to do or anything!"

Billy waved a hand to shoo her away, and we kept walking to the end of the platform where Deena hit a large green button recessed into the tiled wall. She turned, facing towards the track and sat down on the floor cross-legged.

Aiden and I stood on either side of her, two meters apart. We looked at each other in bewilderment and back down at the wild woman acting like all of this was perfectly natural. A gust of wind blew from down the tunnel, and the residual fear still inside me told me that someone was translocating there. But even if that were the case, we wouldn't feel the wind at all, not at this distance. A rumbling sound soon followed, and bright lights came into view. A train was hurtling along the tracks towards us, and both Aiden and I took a large step back.

The train slowed and came to a stop in front of us, filling up most of the platform we had just walked along. As the doors opened, a small group of men were standing, waiting in the carriage. A tall, broad man with a crop of blonde wavy hair headed the group, and he was smiling.

"Bronson!" Deena exclaimed. She stood up, looking embarrassed.

"Deena, my dear. How lovely to see you again." The smile the blond man's mouth made didn't translate to the rest of his face. He stepped out of the doors onto the platform and took one of Deena's hands into both of his. His deep voice echoed down the platform. "It's so kind of you to bring these people here." He glanced at the both of us. "But you're aware of the rules, I've told you before. Time to go!"

Deena's cheeks flushed, and her brow furrowed. This was obviously not the way she hoped things would go. "You should have told your security team then! When're you gonna to let me see her, Bronson? It's not right! You should let me see her!" Deena raised her voice so loud that it bounced down the platform and back again. Two men who were still standing in the train took a few steps forward.

Bronson waved one arm behind him, keeping hold of Deena with the other, to tell them to stand down.

"Deena, you can't keep coming here. I can't let you through, no matter how many Mirror Souls you bring here."

"But she's my mother!" Deena's eyes shone with tears, and

my heart broke for her. She was missing what I was. At least she knew where her mother was.

Bronson looked to one side, and gave a quick, authoritative nod. Billy had followed us down the platform since the train arrived, and now he stepped behind Deena and gripped both her arms, holding them down by her side. She didn't bother to fight him. I got the feeling she'd been here, just like this, many times before. Bronson gestured into the train with one graceful sweep of his arm.

"Please, come with us," he said. As we entered the train, he followed behind, and then turned back to Deena. "I will let your mother know you were here," he said brightly just before the doors shut and the train pulled away in the direction it had come from.

As the train lurched into motion, I grabbed onto Aiden to stop myself falling flat on my face. He'd thought to hold on to one of the poles that ran from roof to floor. Deena's angry, sad face disappeared, and I realized I hadn't thanked her for everything. Maybe Bronson could pass on that message, too.

"Please, take a seat," Bronson said, pointing to the empty row of seats down the side of the train that was now picking up speed. "I rarely do things this way," he said. Standing in front of us, legs wide apart for stability, he put one hand on his chin in thought. "I often wondered when something like this might happen. There's not a precedent for what to do when it did."

"What are you talking about?" Aiden demanded. "Who are you, what is this place, and what are we?"

The lights in the train flickered. I'd never seen this side of Aiden before. There were plenty of sides to him I hadn't seen, considering we'd spent such a small amount of time together. He stood up facing Bronson, demanding answers.

"Calm yourself, Aiden Merrick. Yes, I know who you are,"

he said, as Aiden gave the man a hard stare. "And you, Alana Cain. You've both marched into *my* domain, so I should be the one asking questions." Bronson looked at me. "You've had quite a challenging few weeks, so I've been told? Your eyes tell quite the story…"

My eyes had been burning on and off since we arrived at Deena's island. If only I'd had a mirror so I could see how violet my eyes were becoming.

"Let me start from the beginning. Sit down and I'll tell you everything I can." Bronson clasped his hands in front of him as Aiden took a deep breath and sat back down next to me.

"You are both Mirror Souls, just like the rest of us who live here. No one yet knows what we are. We are an anomaly. We are evolution, whether natural or manufactured. Being a Mirror Soul is both a blessing and a curse."

Aiden found my hand and held it in his. The lights in the train carriage flickered again, and it shuddered violently. Bronson reached out a hand towards us.

"That… that right there! That is what I mean."

Aiden and I looked at each other. We could feel the electricity building up within yet again, and we had no way of stopping it.

"When you find the mirror side to yourself, it's the most exhilarating, heart-wrenching, and intolerable thing that will ever happen to you. The longer you are together, the bigger these energy surges will get. And the harder it will be to stay apart."

In response, the lights flashed again, and the train slowed down.

"If you wouldn't mind…" Bronson gestured for me to swap seats with the man who sat opposite me. "A small distance helps, but not for long." His eyes narrowed. "You two have a stronger connection than most, especially considering you haven't known each other for long."

"You seem to know so much about us, and we know nothing about you." I said, and he smiled.

"It's my job to know, Alana. My name is Rhys Bronson. I started the Underground many cycles ago when people's other halves went missing. We needed somewhere to hide. Somewhere safe."

"And a city full of poison was your best bet?"

He chuckled. "Oh yes! No one can reach us by translocation; it doesn't work here on the mainland. And they had already set these tunnels up for hiding people long before we got here, after the Cataclysm. It was a perfect match."

"What do you mean about people's other halves going missing?" I questioned. I thought back to Corah and her sister. Her Mirror Soul disappeared without a trace, and she'd come here alone, leaving Corah instructions of how to follow.

"Ah yes, it's unfortunate. The non-Gaian races amongst us don't appreciate the Mirror Souls and what we can do. The Avalon especially don't like it. Those energy surges you experience have an interesting effect on people. They consider you to be rather… inconvenient."

So that must have been what happened to Elodie when they had us locked up in the lab holding room together. Perhaps I had some residual energy from when I was with Aiden that had made her act so different all of a sudden.

"Someone is taking the male half of the Mirror Souls. We're not sure why or where they are taking them." Bronson's eyes sparkled, subtly enough to be barely noticeable. But I noticed. I couldn't put my finger on it, I didn't trust him. "You'll find that being together creates many experiences for you. For example, Alana. Your eyes have changed color."

I blinked more than usual at the mention of my eyes again. "Yes, it started the second time I met Aiden."

"The energy between you has been reverting your DNA. I can only assume someone has tampered with yours. Your data-files at the Info Center list you as Gaian…" His eyes narrowed again.

"Well, I guess they're wrong then, aren't they," I said, sitting back in my seat and crossing my arms. I refused to admit it out loud, especially to a stranger. It would make it even more real. *I am Midorian, and no one has told me.*

Bronson raised one heavy, blonde eyebrow at me. "The Avalon are never wrong."

Through the window of the train, another platform sped past. It was the same as the last one, steel columns holding up a curved tiled ceiling, rooms taking up half of the tunnel. Although from what I could tell, this one was much more populated than the last ones we'd already passed.

The man I had swapped seats with sat up in his seat. "We're almost there," he announced.

"Almost where?" asked Aiden. "Where are you taking us?"

Bronson grabbed a nearby pole as the train curved around a tight corner.

"As much as I'd love to invite you both to stay here, I cannot. Your energies are too strong. The strongest we've seen in fact. Even if we separate you, as we do with all the Mirror Souls here, I'm not sure we can contain you when you *are* given the opportunity to be together." He rubbed one hand across the light stubble on his cheek. "It's unfortunate."

"So, that's it then? We've come all this way for nothing?" Aiden's hands fisted into knuckles, and he looked tired. Tired and stressed out. This had been the longest day for both of us, considering we'd only found each other again this afternoon.

"If we can't stay here, then where the hell are we supposed to go?" I demanded, panicked. This wasn't the plan at all. Not my plan at least! "If we go back to our Regions, they'll find us. We've already been together too long! We came to the Underground for a safe place to be. So we could be together."

Bronson shook his head. "No matter where you are on Gaia, if you're together and cannot control the energies... they'll find you. There's no fooling me Alana Cain, you didn't come here for sanctuary. You came here for answers and for help. You want to find your mother, Caliza Cain and your brother, Simeon. You already know they didn't leave your Region."

Aiden's eyes shot to mine. I'd been so focused on escaping the clutches of the Avalon, I hadn't told him I knew where Mom and Simeon were. Surely he'd assumed that I wouldn't stay here until I'd found my family? I shifted in my seat, uncomfortable at the level of information this stranger had about me.

"What do you know of it?" I hissed, causing him to raise one eyebrow again.

"I am aware of where they both are. And I have means to get you to them, and a way to get them out."

My heart raced. Was Mom here in the Underground? Did she bring Simeon with her? Maybe the Info Center was wrong about them still being in Rowhill; it had been wrong about Aiden after all.

"Where are they?"

"As I said before, they're where you left them, in Region 82-1056. Rowhill. Your half-Avalon friend already told you that, did she not?"

"But they're not there, the Regionnaires took them away!"

"Then your friend didn't tell you the whole story, did she? How interesting. I can tell you where they are, and how to get them out."

"And then what?"

Bronson's face lit up. "And then, you must bring them back

here. To me."

"But you just told us we can't stay here," Aiden interjected.

"I'll find a way, Aiden. If you can bring them here, we'll find a way to contain you both."

# TWENTY SEVEN

**T**HE TRAIN SLOWED as we approached a large station, different from the rest. This one was full of people. The doors slid open and Bronson stepped out first.

"We'll take you away from the city on a boat, just off the coast. Once we get some distance between you and the mainland, we'll be able to translocate you back home. One of my men will go with you."

Bronson beckoned the dark-haired man who had sat next to me after I'd swapped seats. He stepped forward and stuck out a hand. "Name's Killian." I shook his hand without saying a word. His handshake was just as awkward and weak as he looked.

"Perfect, well I'll be going then. I have business to deal with on the other side of the city," Bronson said. "Killian will show you the way to the ship, and he'll direct you to where you need to be once you're home."

I opened my mouth to ask a thousand questions, but Bronson was already back on the train, alone this time, and the doors were closing. He gave a half-hearted wave as the train pulled back out of the station.

My ears were ringing again after being in the rattling train, and the noise of the crowds here wasn't helping. The hubbub of voices was deep and manly.

Killian walked ahead, and Aiden and I followed, with little other choice. My head was spinning. Were Mom and Simeon really still at home? How could that be possible? Gen had said it still listed them in Rowhill on the Info Center database, but I thought it had been a mistake. I'd bounced from Region to Region all in one day, jumping time zones. Now I was having to go back to where I started.

"Alana," Aiden whispered loud enough so I could hear him over the crowd, "did you notice that the only people here are men?"

Before I could respond, Killian whipped his head round. "They keep the Mirror Souls separated. For both our own safety, and to keep the energy levels down."

"Keep the energy levels down?" I asked.

"Every Mirror Soul pair creates energy, like you two do. Although not as strong as you in most cases. They're kept apart, given scheduled time to be together. This side of the city houses mostly men. On the other side are the women. It's not an exact science, not all pairs are male to female just as they're not all romantic. And some of us don't have their other half here at all," he said, bitterness dripping from his voice.

"What happens if the energy levels can't be kept down?"

Killian snorted a laugh. "We all get found and killed. Or, worst-case scenario, the world ends."

The train station that Bronson had brought us to was next to the port where we were shuffled onto a small power boat. Donning breathing masks for the second time today, Killian made us stand as far away from each other as possible. Aiden's eyes were on me, and I wished that telepathy had been a Mirror

Soul talent instead of this crazy 'energy surge' thing. I wanted to talk to him. No, I wanted to disappear with him, away from all these strangers. Away from the Avalon and the Midorians. Away from it all.

The crumbling skyline disappeared into the distance, the poisoned air blowing through my hair as we left the mainland and headed into the darkness.

"Safe zone!" Killian shouted as he tore the breathing mask off his face.

Aiden and I did the same, both of us taking in deep breaths of the salty sea air. It was so good to be away from the city. The air was stale and dead there. Now I could see his face clearer under the lights on the boat; Aiden was wearing a deep frown and staring out to sea. I willed him to look at me, to tell me what was wrong. To talk to me. But it made no difference.

The boat slowed down, and Killian clapped the driver on the shoulder and whispered something into his ear which I never would have heard over the roar of the engines and the sound of the water rushing past us.

"Ready?" Killian asked us, producing a CTL from a bag sat next to the driver.

Was I ready? Not really. Aiden reached for me and I took his hand, its electric warmth rushing up my arm and filling my whole body with heat. His frown had gone, and he smiled at me. He was trying to make me feel better. Killian took hold of Aiden's wrist and pressed the button.

*Here we go again.*

The wind died down and my vision cleared. We were standing next to the bridge by the hydro-station where I'd first met Dray. It was dark in Rowhill; the sun had long set. Jumping from one zone to the next and being underground for so long had killed my perception of time.

"Right," Killian said, "we need to hurry and be invisible. Where are we headed?"

Aiden and I both stared at him.

"Bronson told us *you* would know what to do once we got here," said Aiden.

Killian laughed, too loud for 'invisible.' "Bronson will tell you a lot of things," he said. "I don't have a clue. All he said to me is that Alana would have to ask the people she knows."

They both looked at me and my body tensed. My family had been in the same Region as me for weeks and I didn't even realize. Now I had to come up with a solution? All I knew was I had to come up with a plan in the shortest time possible. We couldn't be here long.

There were only three people here who I trusted to ask for help. Or at least, mostly trusted.

Dray. He would be at his home-dome, alone. Asleep by now, no doubt. I wondered if he was thinking about me. For a second, I was thankful that mind-reading wasn't a talent that Mirror Souls had. The thought of Aiden knowing some of the thoughts I had turned my stomach. Dray knew how to access parts of the Info Center database that we didn't. Perhaps that would help us.

Or there was Lefroy. He would be working, though, so he could be anywhere at this point. Lefroy was everywhere and anywhere in Rowhill, like a ghost. He knew how to see and be unseen. Maybe he knew where Mom and Simeon were.

And Gen. My heart jumped and ached all at the same time. A month ago, Gen would have moved mountains to help me. But now? I didn't recognize her anymore. And unfortunately, she'd be our best bet for finding Mom and Simeon. Being part of the High Council, even at a low rank, meant that she had access to everything we would need to search Rowhill. But would she help us? I doubted it.

"Alana?" Aiden put a hand on my arm, and I raised my head up from where I'd been staring down at the ground. "Can you think of anyone who might know where your family are?"

I straightened my back and held my head high. Aiden didn't need to treat me like a frightened creature anymore. The determination rose within me. I hadn't traveled from one side of Gaia to the other in one damn day to give up now.

"Genevieve. She'll be able to find them, I know she will," I answered.

Killian swept an arm sideways, just like Bronson had. "Perfect, lead the way."

We moved quickly, crossing the river on the narrow, metal bridge. Walking in a line, I lead the way with Killian following and Aiden not far behind him. Aiden and I had to keep our distance even though it was the last thing we wanted right now.

We skirted the edge of the Village. Lefroy had taught me well how to stay hidden and which routes to take that would be least likely to come across another person. I silently thanked Lefroy for his unwitting help in a task I had no idea I'd ever have to undertake.

We reached Gen's house just as it started to rain. I went to the back of the house, climbed over the crumbling wall and knocked on the back door. The lights were on inside, which surprised me since it was so late. I hoped Gen was here and not still working.

Audelia opened the door and stared at me in surprise.

"Alana?" she asked, squinting into the darkness, the bright light of the kitchen illuminating her from behind.

"Yes Mrs. Portbury, it's me. Can we come in?" She ushered

us in quickly and just in time too as the skies opened and the rain poured down.

"What are you doing here?" she asked in a hushed tone. "It's not safe here! You should be far away."

"What's that supposed to mean? I'm here to find my mom and brother. I need Gen's help."

Audelia sighed sadly. "Please don't involve Genevieve, she's in deep enough as it is. She's just not the same since… since Keren."

I recognized the look in her eyes as one I knew all too well. Fear.

"Where is she? I need to see her. Now," I demanded. Audelia took a step back and gasped as I stepped forward into the light.

"What happened to you, Alana? Your eyes… they're… you're…"

I put both my hands on her shoulders. "I wish I had time to explain all of this to you, but we don't have any to spare. If Aiden and I are here together too long, they'll find us. I need Gen's help. Please. Where is she?"

She glanced behind me at Aiden and Killian, who still stood awkwardly by the door, and then looked back at me. "Gen's still at the High Council house," she replied. "She works a lot, I… I barely see her."

I put my arms around her neck and hugged her tight. I knew exactly how she felt. She had lost her daughter as much as I had lost my friend.

Tears spilled down her pale cheeks. "Alana, help her if you can. I don't know what else to do. It's like Keren has put a spell on her."

Of course she had. Except it wasn't a spell, it was something far more obvious. Why hadn't I seen it before?

"I'll do what I can," I said, taking her hands in mine. If

Audelia Portbury was like a second mother to me, then Genevieve was my sister. And I wouldn't give up on her now. "Don't tell anyone I was here."

Audelia nodded, and we left quickly, the rain pouring down upon us.

# TWENTY EIGHT

**T**HE SKY WAS DARKER THAN USUAL, the thick, heavy clouds throwing out rain. The last time I had been in rain this heavy it had been with Aiden, who had held an umbrella over my head as he held onto my waist. I sighed. Tonight wasn't so cozy. We all lowered our heads to stop the raindrops pelting our faces in the wind as we wound through cobbled streets towards the High Council house. We had to be quick.

My heart pounded, either from having to move so quickly as we were running out of time, or from not knowing what kind of greeting I would get from my once closest friend.

We stepped up to the huge front doors that were thankfully under a large overhanging porch so we could at least escape the rain.

"Now what?" Killian whispered.

I held my palm up. This had two chances. "Now, we hope and pray that Lefroy hasn't got my access rights revoked. In theory, I should be able to get into any building in Rowhill…"

Before either of them could say anything, I held my breath and slammed my hand down onto the scanner. As soon as I did,

I realized that my data was probably flagged, and I imagined Regionnaires translocating to this very spot in seconds. Thankfully, nothing dramatic happened except for the scanner beeping and the door latch clunking open. I breathed again. They would know I had been here, but hopefully by the time they figured it out, we'd be long gone.

Pushing the door open, we slid inside as quietly as we could. Killian shut it behind us. The lights were off in the lobby. No one else had stayed to work this late, except for Gen it would seem.

The three of us stood in the darkness with our backs against the door. Aiden had found himself not separated from me by Killian this time, so he took my hand in his.

"Alana," he whispered, turning his face to look at me.

"Yes?" I whispered back. I'd already noticed the electricity building before he'd even touched me. But this time I didn't mind; he just needed to wait a minute or two.

"I haven't had the chance to say before now, I'm... I'm glad we found each other."

"We didn't find each other, Aiden, they forced us to find each other." I smiled at him, though I wasn't sure he could see in this light.

"That doesn't matter to me, they gave us a helping hand, that's all. An early start. I wanted you to know, regardless of what happens here, I'm glad we found each other."

Stifling a nervous laugh, I wanted to tell him that now wasn't the time to be pouring his heart out to me, but I also didn't want him to stop.

"You've already said that," I whispered.

He turned his whole body to face me now, and he put both hands on the side of my neck, sending warmth through me in waves. Killian's hand appeared over Aiden's shoulder, frantically gesturing for us to break apart. But there was no stopping this.

"I need you to know," he said, his voice louder than before, "that even if we weren't Mirror Souls, I'm certain I still would have fallen for you."

He needed no light for his lips to find mine. Nor for my hands to slide from his collar bones to settle onto his chest. Our bodies pressed together, and the electricity expanded. I'd stopped caring. If an energy surge happened right here and now, then so be it. I never wanted this moment to end.

Killian fought to pull us apart, as best he could at least, with one hand on each of our shoulders. "For God's sake, will you focus?" he hissed. "We're here for a damn reason, and this is not it!"

I laughed quietly and took Aiden's hand. "Hold that thought," I whispered into his ear and his hand tightened in mine.

We slipped up the curved staircase and down the corridor, and as we reached Gen's office, I placed my hand on the scanner next to the doorway. There was no chance they would have given me access to these rooms, but it was worth a shot. The scanner turned a deep shade of red and the beep echoed down the hallway. Killian stared at me wide-eyed, and I wondered what was in it for him to even be here with us.

As my hand hovered over the door, ready to knock on it, the scanner beeped again and turned green. The door swung open.

Gen was sitting at her desk, but she wasn't alone.

"Dray! What are you doing here?" I sputtered much louder than I should have. Dray jumped out of his seat.

"Alana!" He looked both uncomfortable and surprised to see me, then glanced at the two men standing on either side of me. "What are you doing back here?"

"I came back for my family. What are you doing here?"

"I'm looking for your family too." *What?* "I hoped you'd come back, and that when you did, I'd be able to help you get to Cal and Simeon." He glanced across at Aiden, who stayed quiet. "Gen said she'd help me."

"Oh…" I replied.

Gen looked far less surprised than Dray to see me. "I wondered when you might bother to come see me," she said with a bitter edge, sitting back in her chair and folding her arms. "Need my help again? Is that all I'm good for these days?" She didn't even acknowledge Killian and Aiden, who stood next me.

I stepped forward, the desk between us. She still didn't stand up.

"Why would I bother to come see you Gen? You're not the same person anymore. It's not like I can come hang out with you in this place! It's awful here. Plus, I'm a fugitive now. But of course, you knew that."

Her eyes narrowed, and her upper body tensed. "So you *do* need my help," she stated.

"I need to find Mom and Simeon. Where are they?"

"I've already told you all I know. The system says they're still here in Rowhill, and I can't tell you any more than that."

I slammed my hand down on the edge of her desk, making everyone jump except Gen. "You're the granddaughter of a High Council elder!" I yelled. "You know more than you're telling me. When was it we started keeping secrets? Was it when you got Processed?"

Her face flushed red, and skin radiated with light, her Avalon side more dominant than it used to be. "I have no idea what you're talking about. I have no more information for you. You've wasted your time," she said through clenched teeth.

Aiden stepped forward to stand next to me.

"Gen, please, we need to find them and get out of here.

There's not much time. If we stay here too long…"

Gen held up a hand and cut Aiden off. "I'm aware what happens when you stay too long. I've learned a lot in the past few weeks about the Mirror Souls." She spat the words out at us. "You're in high demand from what I've heard. What are you going to do, Alana? Forever be on the run? Or turn yourself in?" she snarled at me.

Anger flared within me, except it wasn't directed at her. This wasn't the Genevieve I knew. The Gen I knew would have greeted me with a huge hug. She would have been ridiculously excited to meet Aiden. She would have been complaining about this stupid damn Profession and craving being out in the fields in the sunshine and fresh air. She would have *cared* and helped me!

"Was it Keren? Did *she* do this to you? You know they're experimenting on the Mirror Souls, don't you? Don't you care?" I seethed.

She stood up now, making me feel small. "My life is none of your business, and nor are the workings of the Avalon High Council. I have important work to do here."

"None of my business? You're my best friend, Gen!"

"Not anymore. I must fulfill my Avalon duty. It was you who suggested it in the first place, remember?"

"And I'm regretting it!" I shouted. Her glow intensified, and the electricity uncoiled inside of me. It started in the pit of my stomach and rose into my chest. Aiden felt it too, turning to face me and taking my hand.

"Alana, don't," he pleaded, "they'll find us."

"I don't care," was my only response. And I didn't. I would do anything now to undo what Keren had done to Gen. It wasn't right, changing someone like that. I turned to face him back, and I softened. "Help me."

"We don't know how to control it," he said.

"You don't control it," Killian piped up from behind us. "You only need to let it happen."

"What are you talking about?" Gen said.

I leaned forward over the desk, closing the gap between us. "I refuse to let this be how you end up, Genevieve. If this is my fault, then I will fix it." Before she could reply, I turned to Aiden. "Are you ready?"

He nodded, taking my hand and placing it onto his chest with his laying on top. He laid his other hand on my chest, reaching from one collarbone to the other. We each took a synchronized deep breath, and I closed my eyes.

My heart rate quickened, and with every beat, the energies increased.

"I don't have time for this crap," Gen said, "Dray, walk me home."

The pressure intensified, and now every beat of my heart brought a pulse that felt like it was radiating outwards from the center of my chest.

I opened my eyes and turned to look at her without letting go of Aiden. Gen had one hand on the side of her head, and her glow had dimmed.

"Dray, we need to leave, now!" Both of Gen's palms were pressing hard into her temples. "What the hell are you two doing?"

Dray was looking down at the ground and shaking his head as though he had something loose inside. He was holding his stomach.

The pulses continued, faster now.

"Stop it, it hurts. STOP!"

Aiden turned my face towards his with one hand under my chin and rested his forehead onto mine. "Focus. We can do this."

We both closed our eyes. It could no longer be contained.

The energy surge invisibly burst in every direction away from us, and Gen screamed.

# TWENTY NINE

I PULLED AWAY FROM AIDEN and rushed around the back of the desk to Gen. She had stopped screaming, but she had crumpled back down into her chair and was sucking in huge gasps of air. Her face was in her hands and she was shaking.

"God, Gen, what did they do to you?"

She looked up at me, her eyes bloodshot but shining. "Alana?"

Putting my arms around her, desperation filled me as I hoped the surge had done what I needed it to do. I held her upright with my hands on her shoulders. "Are you okay?" I asked her.

"Not really! What was that?" She took a deep breath and turned to Dray. "Are you all right?" she asked him.

Dray was massaging his temples now too. I hadn't even considered how the surge would affect everyone else in the room. "I'm fine. Don't worry about me," he replied.

Gen's long eyelashes blinked away tears as she turned back to me. "Alana, I'm so sorry. I didn't realize... I mean, I wasn't in my right mind. My grandmother, she's... she's not a good person, Alana. You *have* to forgive me."

"What?"

She stood up from the chair, shaking her arms down at her sides and taking another big breath of air. "Keren. She put me in Processing just before I started my Profession, soon after Shift Day. She told me it was just to give me the strength to do the work of the High Council. I had no reason to not trust her, so I went along with it. She's had me in Processing pretty much every other day since then, telling me it's all part of the job." She rubbed her hands on her temples just as Dray had. "God, my head hurts so bad. What the hell did you do?"

"Aiden and I created an energy surge. Mirror Soul stuff. It must have undone the Processing. It's happened before," I answered hastily. "Listen, we have to get out of here as soon as possible. They can track our energy when we're together."

Killian looked down at his watch. "I'd say it's already too late, love. You've been together too long already, and they will *definitely* have picked that surge up."

"So you are Mirror Souls after all." Gen swallowed and looked nervous, for good reason.

"Where are they?" I asked her, my hands back on her shoulders. "Where's my mom? Where is Simeon?"

"I should have told you before," she replied, her voice as shaky as her body had been just a few moments ago. "They're here."

"Here here? In this building?" Aiden asked.

My sympathy for her evaporated in an instant.

"Yeah, here." She looked down at the desk, avoiding my gaping stare. "I'm sorry, she took Simeon from the Medical Center while you were in Processing at the lab. Your mom was already here. My grandmother has been... experimenting on them." She sucked in another short breath and then dared to glance up at me. "I didn't like it, Alana, but there wasn't anything I could do! And she insisted it was necessary for the survival of the Avalon!"

The words rushed out of her as though saying it fast would make it less of a knife in the back. I felt sick to my stomach. My cheeks flushed with rage, and I clenched my fists into tight balls. My intense stare threw daggers at Dray next. He must have known about this too.

Dray threw his hands up in the air. "I swear I didn't know a thing about it! I would have told you if I had known!"

"We're leaving. There's no time for this," said Aiden, sensing my rage. "Show us the way, Gen."

She motioned to move to the door, but I held up one hand to stop her. "I already know the way. I know where Keren carries out her dirty work," I said, storming out of the room, with Aiden following close behind me. Gen, Killian, and Dray weren't far behind, although Gen held back further than the other two did.

As I half ran down the corridor of doors, the whimpering of the man we heard when Lefroy and I were last here echoed through my whole being. Whatever the technician had been doing to him, they'd also been doing to Mom. And maybe Simeon. So much for the Avalon trying to help him! My heart was pounding, but I had to keep it together, especially with Aiden here. If we caused a second energy surge, we had no chance.

Rushing down the stairs, I tried not to trip over my own feet. I could hear my heartbeat throbbing in my ears. I went straight to the door that Keren's voice had boomed from when I had been here with Lefroy. It was closed this time, and I stood in front, not knowing what I'd find behind it.

Gen had caught up. She swept behind me, with her head still looking down at the floor. Good. She should be more than ashamed of herself. I hoped she hated herself for this, forever.

"She's not in there," she said hurriedly. "They've been keeping her in the holding rooms. Follow me."

Gen made her way down the corridor and around the corner, with the rest of us trailing behind. It was though it was just another day at work for her. I had hated the Processed version of her, and I wasn't sure how I'd ever let go of that.

Without hesitation, Gen placed a hand on the scanner in front of yet another identical door, which clicked open. She stepped back from it as I tore into the room without a second thought.

This room was identical to the one they had kept me in when they Processed me at the lab. Cold, white, stark. Two 'beds' if you could call them that. A shuttered window.

And there she was. Mom was huddled in a corner on one of the thin mattresses on the floor, much like Elodie had been. It'd only been a few weeks since they'd brought her here; why was she so thin and worn?

"Mom!" I rushed to her and kneeled at her side.

She could barely lift her head to look up at me. "Alana? What are you doing here? You… shouldn't be here."

Taking her face carefully in my hands, I lifted her face upwards. "I'm here to get you out, Mom. My god, what have they done to you?"

Her eyes were circled with darkness, she was exhausted. She reached out a hand to touch my face. "Don't worry about me, what did they do to you? Your eyes…"

"Yes, we'll have to talk about that."

Mom's squint turned into a frown, and she dropped both her hand and her face at once. "There's so much I haven't been able to explain to you. I wouldn't know where to begin… You were supposed to stay with Hilroy. He should have got you out, got you somewhere safe."

"They found us in Nordlys, Mom, I don't think there is anywhere safe for us anymore."

Only just noticing that Aiden had also crouched down in front of Mom at my side, he put one hand on my elbow. "We need to get her out now. Right now."

"Help me get her up."

"I don't need help." Mom shook her head as she heaved herself up from the mattress bit by bit. "Keren hasn't Processed the fight out of me yet! We need to get to Simeon, too," she said, shakily leading the way back out into the corridor, coming face-to-face with Gen.

"Come to your senses now, have you?" she said to her, her voice seething with anger.

Gen held her head high this time. "I've only been doing my Avalonian duty," she replied, with an air of arrogance. Maybe we hadn't fully cleared her Processing. Or perhaps this was what had always been bubbling underneath Gen's surface.

"Get out of my way, I'm going to get my son."

"You can't." Gen's eyes gleamed with fear, but only I saw it.

"And why's that? Are you going to stop me?"

"He's with Councilor Keren."

Mom's eyes widened. "No!"

An adrenaline rush kicked in, and Mom's weakness turned into strength as she ran off down the corridor, the rest of us trailing behind and trying to keep up. She stopped at the same door I had moments before.

"Open the door!" she demanded. Gen stepped in front of the door, facing Mom with both her hands up.

"Don't do this. I'll get Simeon out when she's not around," Gen hissed urgently. "You don't know what she's capable of, Mrs. Cain. She's got more power than you realize."

"I'm not leaving without my son!" Mom screamed out, pushing Gen aside and hammering her fists on the door.

The door slid open, disappearing into the wall. Keren was standing facing us all, glowing with ferocity.

"Ah perfect, just in time. I was just finishing up here," she said, as though she had fully expected the group of us to have arrived at that very moment. She turned and glided back into the room.

I pushed past Mom who was rooted to the spot in shock. They had strapped Simeon into a chair like the ones in the lab, with wires protruding from him down into the floor. My stomach tightened, and the rage stirred deep within me.

"You witch! What gives you the right to do this to us? Let my brother go!"

Keren smiled. "Feel free to take him yourself."

I marched into the room to the side of my brother, who looked as gaunt and worn as Mom. I shook his shoulders, but it didn't wake him. He was unconscious.

Aiden, Dray, Mom, and Gen all followed me into the room, and the door slammed shut. My head span round. Killian stood next to Keren, handing her the CTL.

"Thank you for bringing them here, Killian. You will be rewarded accordingly." Keren held the CTL that had brought us here, the CTL that was to get us *out* of here, in her palm. Her eyes met mine, and she slowly closed her hand on top of it, crushing it flat as though it were made of paper and not metal.

"Killian?" Aiden exclaimed. "Why?"

Killian shrugged and didn't utter a word. He'd made a deal with the devil to save his own skin. Why should he care about a few strangers?

Keren was looking at Gen now.

"How interesting that you reversed Genevieve's

Processing..." she mused. "I must add that to the records. I had tried to stop you getting to your Mirror Soul, Alana. But I'm glad I failed. Now that you're here together, I'll be able to learn even more. I hadn't thought of it that way."

"We're just one big science experiment to you, aren't we?" Mom shouted. "You don't care about the pain you put people through, the loss we have to suffer!" She had made her way to my side and was holding Simeon's hand.

"Come now, Caliza, it's for the benefit of everyone. We need to learn the power that the Mirror Souls hold to make sure you hurt no one else. And what a happy accident to stumble across the Cain family in Rowhill of all places, to find that you and your children carry the DNA of the Original Midorian."

Mom's face flushed red and her eyes brightened to violet briefly before returning to their normal brown color.

"Oh, I see," Keren continued, noting the confusion on my face. "You haven't told Alana and Simeon that revelation just yet. Interesting. When were you planning on telling them that their DNA holds the key to destroying everything we have built here on Gaia?"

My heart skipped a beat, and the energies building up inside me floated away on an invisible breeze as I turned to frown at my mother.

More lies? More deception?

Keren chuckled and walked to the other side of the room towards a screen mounted on the wall. She tapped it, entering information in the coded language I would never understand. We had to get out of here. Our CTL was on the floor crushed to a quarter of its size. Killian was standing in front of the door, blocking the only exit to the room.

Out of the corner of my eye, I saw Dray whisper something into Aiden's ear. Aiden had tried to keep a blank expression, but

I saw a sparkle in his eye I recognized. He turned to me and his face spoke a thousand words. He didn't need to say anything, I knew what I must do.

I took Mom's hand from Simeon's, holding it down by our sides, and kept my other hand on top of my brothers. Aiden, who was standing on the opposite side of her took Mom's other hand and she looked up at him in surprise. He nodded ever so slightly.

"Hold on," he whispered as loud as he dared.

In one deft movement, Dray produced a CTL from his pocket and flipped it open. He grabbed Aiden's free hand and pressed the button down hard. We'd been warned against translocating this many people at once, and I had a feeling we were about to find out why.

Everything went into slow motion.

The wind blew into the fiercest gale and the pressure built. Keren swung her body around once she realized what was happening and lunged towards us, leaving a trail of light in her wake. Gen leaped into her path, smashing her entire body weight directly into her grandmother's chest, both crashing onto the floor.

Killian jumped forward at the same time and made contact with Dray's exposed forearm, and then we all disappeared with the wind.

# THIRTY

**M**Y EYES WERE OPEN but there was only darkness. I could hear so many voices all talking or shouting at once, all blurring together. People were moving around, and I was being jostled from side to side. It was mayhem out there. But until I could see what was going on, I couldn't put together the pieces. I rubbed my eyes again; they should have cleared by now. Translocating often had this effect on me, but this was something different.

Pressing my hands against my face, I willed my ears to pick up on any clues that would tell me what was going on.

"You didn't tell me that would be such a damn risk!" Dray's deep voice boomed through the confusion. I couldn't pick out the response to him.

Someone pulled my hands away from my face.

"Alana, what happened? What's wrong?"

Aiden.

"I can't see anything, it's all dark. My vision isn't coming back. Where are we?"

"We… we're not on Gaia anymore."

*What?*

Aiden pulled me close, and whispered in my ear. "We can't trust him, he's not on our side. We need to get out of here."

Before I could ask who he was talking about, Aiden was being dragged away from me, shouting and cursing, and someone else had taken me by the shoulders and was directing me in the opposite direction. My feet had no choice but to follow.

"Aiden!" I screamed.

"Calm down, it'll be all right." Dray's voice was even clearer now. He was the one guiding me. All the other voices faded away.

"Where are we, Dray? What's going on? Where did you get that CTL from?"

"I wanna answer your questions, I really do. But I've got to take you to someone who wants to talk to you first."

I shook my head and blinked my eyes furiously as he pushed me forward. Light was filtering through, but no shape yet. "Where's Aiden? Where are Mom and Simeon? What happened to Gen?"

Dray stayed quiet, and he reached forward to open a door which he guided me through. The light shone brighter in here, but I couldn't pick out where the source of the light was coming from.

"Thank you Dray." It was a male voice, lighter than Dray's. "Sit her down over there until her vision recovers."

He let go of my arms now and took my hand, leading me to a chair. I had to feel around with my hands to get my bearings. It was a metallic chair, cold to the touch. Not comfortable but I sat down anyway, exhausted.

The man with the light voice was standing in front of me, my vision was clearing enough to identify the blurry shape of his figure. "That will be all, Dray. Return to Rowhill," he said.

"Keren will be looking for me now; it's not safe for me to go back there. And if it's all the same to you, I'd rather stay here." Dray still stood next to me, one hand still on my shoulder.

"You want to make sure she's all right. I see. She will be."

"I need her to understand that what I did…"

Why was he talking about me as though I wasn't here?

"I'll explain it all. You'll be debriefed soon, and we'll assign your next task. Go back to your quarters. That's an order." It didn't sound much like an order when it came with such a gentle tone, but Dray listened regardless. He squeezed my shoulder once, let go of it and left.

"Where am I? What's going on? Where are my family?" I demanded.

"Calm yourself, child. Let's sort out your little problem first."

Through the blur, I watched him crouch down in front of my seat and he carefully placed the heels of his palms into my eye sockets. I shivered. The same energy I experienced with Aiden emerged again now. But how? Instead of starting in my chest or my stomach they were starting in my head, and they *hurt*. My face flushed with heat and my eyes were on fire.

I pushed the man's hands away from my face and rubbed my eyes yet again. As soon as I opened them again, my vision had been restored. Looking back at me with an almost amused expression stood an old man wearing thin metallic rimmed glasses, with gray hair and a closely cropped gray beard.

And his eyes were the brightest violet.

"There you are." He stood up, opened his arms wide and smiled. "Welcome to Nimbus, Alana Cain."

We were at the edge of a vast metallic room with high ceilings and no windows. Behind the man stood rows and rows of trees and plants, growing under artificial lights. So that was why this room had been so much brighter. We were in an arboretum, except these trees and plants were not from Gaia.

"Are you able to walk and talk?" he asked cheerfully.

"Sure."

Still in shock, the only way I'd get answers was to go along with whatever he wanted me to do. Within reason. I stood up and followed the gray man down the path that had formed between the carefully planted flora.

"Do you know who I am?" the man asked.

"No, sir. And I'm wondering how you know who I am," I replied.

He chuckled. "Most of the important people on and off Gaia know who you are now, Alana. I'm afraid there's no reversing that. The secrets you weren't even aware you had have been revealed, and you're now a sought-after commodity."

"Commodity? What is *that* supposed to mean?" Why did everyone talk so goddamn cryptic all the time?

"My name is Maloret, or Mal if you prefer. I'm the leader of the Midorian Intervention."

The man my mother had been working with. "You don't look like much like a leader." Maybe if I provoked him, he'd send me back to the others.

Mal straightened his back, standing as tall as possible. Which to be honest, didn't amount to much. "Looks can be deceiving, child," he said with a grin. "That is one lesson you must learn, and soon."

"What is this place?" I brushed my hand down the trunk of a tree as I passed it. Its bright green leaves glowed with a blue aura. I was sure I'd seen it somewhere before.

"If you mean this room, this is my propagation room. These plants are all from Midoria." He lovingly held a huge flower bud hanging from a bright yellow shrub in both his hands. "But if you mean this whole place? We are on Nimbus, the largest of the Midorian ships that orbit Gaia."

Ships? Orbit? My knees felt weak.

"Wait… you mean… we're in *space*?" My eyes widened and Mal laughed again, louder this time.

"Yes, dear. That's why your translocation experience was a little… fraught. Well, that and the fact that so many of you translocated at once. That wasn't the plan. I only asked Dray to bring you, your Mirror, and your mother."

I stopped walking.

"Dray. He's been working for the Midorian Intervention this whole time?"

"For many cycles, yes. We placed him in Rowhill so he could bring you back to us. We even got him placed in the edu-dome so that he'd be able to befriend you. That backfired on us a little when the High Council gave you your Profession early. We weren't the only ones playing a move, I suppose."

A knot formed in my stomach. Dray hadn't wanted to be a friend. He didn't have feelings for me; he was just playing me to get a job done. The revelation upset me more than it should have.

"Why did you bring us here?" I asked.

Mal waved his hands in the air casually as though I'd just asked him what the weather was like outside today. "Oh, we'll get to that. Why not ask me the *less* obvious questions?"

Aiden's face appeared in my mind's eye. I hoped he was safe. But even if he wasn't, even if none of them were, I had zero control over it.

"What do you know of the Mirror Souls?"

"Aaaaahhhh," he said, in one long, drawn out tuneful note. "That is a perfect question. I've made it my business to learn everything I can about the Mirror Souls, but there are still unknown factors that have passed me by. Like where you come from, for example."

"You don't know where we come from?"

"No one does. You're a glitch in the system." He chuckled to himself as he picked up a watering can and filled it from a nearby tap attached to a tall narrow metallic tower that spanned from the floor to the ceiling. "Look around you. Every plant in here is different. You see that?" he asked. I nodded, confused by his change in subject. "This one here, for example. Breathtaking isn't it?" He stopped watering and crouched down at the base of the shrub we had stopped in front of. The stalks were a deep red, with long green feathery leaves sprouting out of them and cascading down.

"This species grows from seedling to maturity in only seven days. It's rather impressive to watch. Like a Phoenix being born from the ashes. No one makes it grow that quick, it simply does. It's part of its make-up, part of what makes it unique. Just like you and Aiden. Your connection together grew just as quick, did it not?"

How did he know that? I nodded again, I didn't want to give him any more information than he already had but he was staring at me expectantly, bright-eyed. He walked ahead and stopped at a different shrub, this one much more like the ones we had on Gaia.

"This one has been growing in my garden for thirty-eight cycles. Thirty-eight! Can you believe that?" He looked at me again as though he supposed me to understand what he was trying to get at.

I gave a half-hearted shrug, which seemed to satisfy him enough for him to carry on.

"Now, if I stop watering and caring for either of these plants, what happens to them?"

"They… die?" I replied.

"Precisely. It doesn't matter the speed at which something amazing forms or how powerful it is, if you don't tend to it then it will die."

Mal emphasized the word 'die' a little too strongly for my liking.

"Mirror Souls are the embodiment of the most powerful energy there is. Love." His eyes lit up. "Love is a choice. Whether it is chosen with ease subconsciously, or consciously chosen day by day, it's always a choice. It's the most empowering choice you can ever make, and its effect has no bounds. The Mirror Souls will show the world the power that love and acceptance can have."

Mal continued to walk forward down the path through the towering trees, but I stood still again, trying to decipher what he was saying.

He turned to me. "Come, let's continue our lesson."

"Our lesson? That's what I'm here for? A lecture about... about what? Biology? Relationships?" I balled my hands into fists. "I don't know who you are. You've brought me here, taken me off Gaia against my will, and taken me from my family against my will. I don't want or *need* your lessons!"

He turned back to face me and tilted his head as he contemplated me. He didn't seem even the slightest bit upset at my outburst, which made me all the angrier.

"Feisty. That'll be the Midorian in you, young one. I've taken you away from Aiden for both your safety and ours. If you create energy surges all over the place, especially at the strength you and he seem to manage, you may very well bring Nimbus crashing down onto the surface of Gaia herself. Let's try to avoid that, shall we? As for your mother, she has other things to do here. And your brother... well, he's a whole other story."

"I want to see them. All of them. Now!"

Mal laughed gently. "So, my warning about bringing a spaceship to her knees with the aid of your Mirror Soul didn't change your mind eh?" He shook his head lightly. "You'll see them soon. Oh, except for Dray. He'll be going back to the surface soon."

"He's best off avoiding me anyhow," I said, folding my arms across my chest.

"Now, now, Alana. He was only doing his duty, just like your mother was."

"So, everyone was in on this 'Midorian Intervention' except me and Aiden, is that it?"

"Oh, not quite," he replied happily. "Your brother was also none the wiser. He isn't even aware that he's half Midorian." Mal winked and the anger rose again, flushing across my face. He noticed it and took a step forward. "Have it your way, Alana. You may ask me one more question and then I will take you to your mother."

I took a deep breath and closed my eyes, willing time to go backwards. Back to when Gen and I were waiting for Shift Day. Or to just wake up and this be all a dream. I opened my eyes. Mal was waiting patiently, and I was still stood in a forest on a spaceship with more questions than answers. As always. But I could only ask one.

"How did you fix my sight before? When you put your hands on my eyes. How did you do that?"

"Interesting choice of question," Mal said, raising one eyebrow. "It's simple. I'm a Mirror Soul, just like you. Except I have spent many cycles learning how to control my energy unlike the rest of you. And if you are willing, I will train you to do the same."

I stared at him. No, I didn't want to learn how to control the strange energy rolling around inside me that I hadn't even asked for. I wanted to be in my living room, with Mom and Simeon, playing cards and waiting for the sun to rise on a new day. I wanted the High Council to announce my Profession at age eighteen like *everyone else* and go with the flow, let them move me to wherever they want to move me. Meet someone nice, someone without an agenda, and settle down. Maybe get chosen to be a child-bearer. Anything but this.

The guilt hit me like a knife in the stomach. In those few seconds of dreaming up an alternate life in my head, I'd left Aiden out of it. I didn't have time to analyze what that meant as Mal beckoned me to follow him after I hadn't responded to the answer he gave to my question. We walked down winding paths through the dense faux-woodland and I wondered how he knew where he was going. Where were we going?

We reached the edge of the garden, at a small door in the huge metal wall. Mal opened it and let me walk through it first.

The space I entered was nothing like the one I had just left. This one had windows, one huge long window in fact, that spanned the entire width of the room. The view was full of stars and swirling shapes in the blackness. The reminder that we weren't on Gaia anymore made my head spin, so I took my eyes off the window to examine the rest of the room.

It was so dark in here compared to the propagation room, my eyes took a while to adjust. Once they had, I saw Mom standing across the other side. She had her back facing me and it took a second for me to realize what she was standing in front of. A long and narrow metallic box raised up on a dais, surrounded by others identical to it. I assumed it had a glass top to it because a blue light was glowing upwards from it.

A casket.

My head swam again, and my feet and legs turned to stone. The faces of the people I loved cycled through my mind over and over and over.

Aiden. Simeon. Gen.

Aiden. Simeon. Gen.

Aiden. Simeon. Gen.

Aiden. Simeon...

The spinning wheel stopped on my brother. He had been unconscious when we translocated out of Keren's lab of horrors. Didn't he make it? I had assumed he would be okay, I thought they were just doing tests on him! Fighting back the urge to throw up, I ran up beside Mom and threw my hands on top of the glowing glass and leaned over it.

My heart and breath stopped in unison.

The peaceful, sleeping face inside was one I hadn't seen for over nine cycles, except in my thoughts and dreams. One I never thought I'd see again.

Dad.

# THIRTY ONE

**A**LL I COULD DO WAS STARE at the figure laying in the glowing box and force myself to breathe. He looked exactly how I remembered him. Or did he? Was his hair always that gray? The only sound in the room came from the humming of the coffin-shaped boxes that filled the room and the beeps coming from them. Heart monitors. He was alive? My dad was alive!

Mom put her hand on my shoulder, making me jump. So much so that I shifted away from her, out of her reach. "I'm so sorry, Alana, I wish it had been possible to tell you," she started.

"You knew Dad was still alive?" The words unintentionally came out as a whisper. I fought panic, yet again. Most parents keep things from their children to protect them. But these were not small things.

My father was still alive.

I was part Midorian.

I was a Mirror Soul.

I was a commodity and a threat.

"Yes, I knew. But trust me when I say there was no way I

could have told you. It was too dangerous! You must understand, we went to great lengths to hide this from the Avalon. The Midorian Council instructed him to be kept here on Nimbus for his own safety. For the safety of all of us."

I pulled myself away from the glass and stood tall.

"You lied to me and you lied to Simeon. I thought my father was dead! That I'd never see him again. How could you?" I breathed, the emotions raging within competing for prominence.

"You were so young, you wouldn't have understood! It's for a bigger reason than you could possibly understand. Please don't hate me. I'm only trying to do the best I can." Tears formed in her eyes, which I assumed were naturally violet, like mine. She must have seen a liar and a fake every time she looked in the mirror.

Mal stepped forward. I still had one hand pressed against the glass top, hovering above Dad. He had been laying here sleeping for so long, he wouldn't even recognize me anymore.

"Perhaps it's best for me to answer your questions, considering it was I who instructed your father to be put into cryostasis."

I whipped my head around to look at him.

"More lessons?" I spat the words out at him. "I didn't ask for any of this. I bet Dad didn't either! Why have you brought us here?"

"The Avalon want to destroy you, Alana! They want all the Mirror Souls dead and gone. They only needed to destroy one half of the couple, and they left the other to grieve and feel empty for the rest of their days," he replied.

I imagined Aiden being taken. Gone. Dead. My heart shattered into a thousand pieces at the thought and rebuilt itself again. He was still alive. For now.

"Why do they want us dead?"

"The energy surges undo their dirty work. They undo the Processing."

"So?"

Mal chuckled lightly as though this were small talk held around a dinner table. "Dear girl, do you not know what the Avalon are doing when they're Processing Gaians?" He stepped forward a little more, lowering his head to stare at me over the top of his glasses. "They're not just editing their character and behavior, they're changing their DNA. They are slowly converting all of the Gaians into Avalons."

I stared at him in disbelief, the bombshell Mal had just dropped trying to sink in. I wasn't sure it ever would. That would mean that the Avalon were trying to take over the planet. In secret. And the Gaians were letting them.

"That's why the Midorians are intervening," he continued. "We created the Gaian race alongside the Avalon. We don't want to see them become extinct."

"And my father agreed to being locked up in a glass box for cycles on end, just for your world peace shit?" I shouted, turning my whole body to face Mal, enraged. "He had a wife and children. He had a life!"

"Well he wouldn't have had a life for much longer!" Mal shouted back. I stepped backwards in surprise at the sudden change in him. "The Avalon had found out about him and your mother and they were planning on murdering him. So, we faked his death and brought him here. We had to put him in cryostasis, to keep him from trying to get back to your mother. If someone had separated you from Aiden, wouldn't you do anything to get back to him?"

"You make it sound like Mirror Souls have no will power at all," I answered, and he guffawed, tipping his head back.

"You don't! It's built within us, to always need to be at the side of our other half. You can't help it. Fascinating really. Inconvenient at times."

"So, what, he stays here forever?" I snapped. "Glass prison and all?"

"No. Ortis stays here until we're ready to fight back. And now we have you and Aiden that time is approaching at great speed." He smiled and leaned back to prop himself up on one of the other glass coffins. I hoped it was an empty one.

"Me and Aiden? Why us?"

Mom lifted her gaze away from Dad's face and looked at me. "Because you're different. You can do things the others can't."

Mal gazed at me with both interest and awe. "Yes indeed," he said. "Alana Cain and Aiden Merrick. The Mirror Souls that will change the fate of the rest of us. Whether you like it or not."

I didn't care. "I want to see him. Where is he? Where is Aiden?" My eyes jumped from glowing box to glowing box. There were about twelve of them in this room, had they already shoved him in one and closed the lid?

"Don't worry, he's not in cryostasis. Yet…" Mal smirked. "Not unless he misbehaves. He's on the other side of Nimbus. We need to keep you two far away from each other until we've taught you how to control yourselves. I'll be teaching you and Lefroy will teach Aiden."

"Lefroy?" What the hell was he doing here? Was everyone except me living a double life?

"I pulled strings at work," Mom jumped in, "to make sure you were working with someone who would protect you."

I didn't turn to her when she spoke or even respond to her, I didn't know how I'd ever be able to look her in the eye again. Gen's betrayal was one thing; Keren had Processed her which had caused the change. My mom had been lying to me my entire life.

My heart felt heavy. In fact, every cell in my body felt heavy.
I was done. So done.

I pressed the heels of my hands to my eyes and then dropped
them down to my sides, shoulders drooping. "I need to rest. It's
been… a long day."

"Of course." Mal stood up again. "Your mother will take you
to the guest quarters."

Glancing at Mom who was looking down at her feet, I sucked
in a sharp breath. "I'd prefer for someone else to take me."

There was silence for a long and awkward moment until Mal
broke it.

"Oh, I see. Well yes all right. I suppose I can take you. Follow
me."

I placed a hand on top of Dad's glowing cell once more and
silently vowed that one way or another, I would get him out of
there. Following Mal out of the door on the opposite side of the
room to where we had entered, I left my parents behind without
a backwards glance.

Mal didn't stop talking, but I had stopped listening. We
walked down corridors, around corners that held more
corridors. Identical door after identical door. Yet another maze.
It reminded me of the High Council house. Gen must still be
there. Who knows what Keren was doing to her now? Re-
Processing her maybe? A twinge of guilt tugged at my heart.
She'd helped us get away, and we'd left her there to suffer even
more. Though I wasn't sure if she would have been any better
off here. What would they have thought of someone like Gen
showing up here?

Mal stopped in front of a door which he opened with no
scanner or key required. Security clearly wasn't so much of a big
deal to the Midorians as it was to the Avalon. The door led to a
room, which was a similar size to the holding rooms in the

Processing lab, though I was thankful that it was much homelier with a real bed instead of a mattress on the floor. The whole back wall contained a window, but it was shuttered so I couldn't see out.

"Make yourself comfortable," he said. "There are spare clothes in the cupboard, hopefully you can find something to fit. You should have all you need here." He ushered me in but stayed out of the room. "Someone will fetch you in the morning to show you around. It's wise for us to begin our lessons straight away. The Avalon High Council will be searching for you."

"How will I know when it's morning?" I asked.

Mal laughed yet again. "The lights will come on," he replied, as though it was the most obvious thing in the world. Surely he realized I'd never been on a damn spaceship before. I was too tired to make a point, so I nodded and sat on the edge of the bed.

After he had said goodbye and closed the door with a small click, I laid back on the mattress and tried to let my body relax. Every muscle had been tensed for so long, ready to run at any moment. I tried to tell myself that I was safe here, but I didn't believe it for a second.

I stared at the metal ceiling of the small room that I guessed was my new home for now. I was used to starting over in new places, but this was something else! This was Dad's home. I still couldn't believe that he was alive, and I suddenly felt the urge to go back to him. I shouldn't have left in the first place.

I stood and headed to the door. If I couldn't remember the way back there, maybe someone could show me the way. *Dray would know the way*, I thought bitterly to myself. He was part of Mal's Midorian club, part of the 'intervention.' This was his home too. I shook the image of him out of my mind and turned the door handle. It didn't move an inch; the door was locked. *Are you kidding me? So much for lax security! Of course they wouldn't let me roam the ship alone. Because us Mirror Souls are so desperate for our other halves that we just can't help ourselves.* I rolled my eyes and slapped one hand on the door in frustration, as though that would do any good. So now I was a pawn in the Midorians' game, just like Dad.

Looking around the room, the claustrophobia reared its ugly head. I'd have to stay in this small space until someone decided otherwise. My heart raced, the walls of the room closing in on me. I desperately searched the back wall, finding a control panel for the window and pressing buttons until I found what I wanted. The shutters slid up, along the inside of the wall, disappearing into the ceiling.

The sight that appeared took my breath away. Nimbus practically filled the view from the window; the ship I was on was bigger than I realized. She was in the shape of a ring and I sat in the inner circle of her, which meant I could see the opposite curve of the ship. Aiden was over there somewhere. So close, yet so far. As always. An ache stirred in the depth of my chest and as much as I felt drawn to go back to Dad, the desire to get to Aiden was magnified by thousands. Maybe Mal was right, we just couldn't help ourselves.

I leaned against the cold glass, my forehead pressing against it and sending a chill through me. The blackness of the space around the ship was daunting and beautiful all at once. Beneath us lay Gaia, clouds swirling over her surface. She was a patchwork quilt of beautiful blues, greens and yellows amongst the vast, gray abandoned cities. Flanked on every side by glittering stars as she spun gracefully in place, I understood why the Avalon wanted to claim her. There was more to gain than just her beauty, except I didn't know what it was yet.

One of those desolate cities was The Poisoned Apple, New York City. The toxic hideout where my other family, the Mirror

Souls, sat waiting for a day to arrive where they could live free. Where they could live together without fear.

I thought of Mal and Keren. The Midorians and the Avalon. All violet eyes and glowing skin. In that moment, I knew that this was a war. Not for the Mirror Souls. Not for Gaia. This was a war for humanity. The Gaians were on the brink of losing themselves and apparently, we were the only ones who could stop it.

And if it meant that Aiden and I were finally allowed to just be, then we would.

The Mirror Souls would stop it.

*To be continued…*

# ABOUT THE AUTHOR

JULIA SCOTT IS A BRITISH AUTHOR, whose goal is to take you out of 'regular life' and teleport you to new worlds and alternate futures through her writing. *The Mirror Souls* is her debut novel, and like many sci-fi and fantasy books, it started off as a dream.

In her 'other' life, Julia lives in Essex, England with her husband and two children. She spends her time writing, prettifying books (via Evenstar Books), graphic designing, singing, and digging or planting stuff up in the garden without really knowing what she's doing.

To find out more, and to sign up for the newsletter that will let you know when Julia writes even *more* books, head over to juliascottwrites.com and find her on Instagram @juliascottwrites and @evenstarbooks.juliascott.

She'd also absolutely love to know what you thought of *The Mirror Souls,* so please consider leaving a review on Amazon or Goodreads, or anywhere else you'd like to.

# ACKNOWLEDGEMENTS

WHEN YOU FIRST START WRITING A BOOK, you think to yourself, *how hard can it really be?* Well let me tell you, it's been quite the learning curve and I wouldn't have been able to do it without all the fantastic people I have in my life. I consider myself truly blessed and so here are the shout-outs!

First and foremost, to my husband Daniel, who fought for me, with me and was the constant voice of encouragement and positivity in my ear. Who endured my evenings spent writing and rewriting and who held my hand when everything got too much.

To my most beautiful creations, Ethan and Olivia, who put up with grouchy mummy when she stayed up too late writing. Who encouraged me and gave me the biggest 'why' to keep me going. I hope one day, when you're both old enough to read my novels, you'll be proud of your mama and be inspired to follow your own dreams and smash your own goals.

To Hannah Bauman of Between the Lines Editorial; editor extraordinaire, who was so nice to me even when I was freaking out and who never once mocked me for my overuse of interrobangs!?! This book would not have been what it is without you. I'm so glad I found you!

To my 'Dream Team', who have been a constant source of encouragement, learning and joy. You guys are ridiculously awesome!

To my parents and my sister Hayley (and her fam), for always backing me up, encouraging me and being on hand to support me whenever I needed it. I'm truly thankful for all of you.

To my Twinny, Rhona, for taking the time to critique my very early work and setting me on a much better path. I can't wait to read your work someday too. Soul sistahs for life!

To all the amazing, beautiful people who I have met on the Smule Sing app and who have encouraged me through this whole process. But especially to; Jess, the very first person to listen to my crazy ideas and tell me she loved them; Nikki, who inspired me and lifted me up even when she was down; Angie, who diligently read everything I threw at her; The Chus, who never stopped cheering me on and playfully mocking my 'author pose'; and The Guild, who loved me through the bad days.

To all my friends and family who consistently asked how it was going and who wanted me to let them know when it was ready to be published. Here it is! I hope you love it. And to the friends, old and new, who kept me motivated and accountable through the initial writing of *The Mirror Souls*.

And saving the best for last; to you, the wonderful person who has purchased and read my book. Thank you for taking the time to read *The Mirror Souls*. I hope you loved reading it as much as I loved writing it. And never forget; love is always the answer.